The Little Things

a Small Town Age Gap romance

Second Hope Series

Jessica Prince

For those of you who love your heroes a little dusty, a little rough, and a lot dirty.
Zach is for you.

Let's Connect

By signing up for my newsletter, you're guaranteeing you'll stay up to date on all new releases, cover reveals, giveaways, sales, and all the other exciting book news I have coming!

I pinky-promise to use my emails for good only, not to spam you, and make sure each one is enjoyable for everybody.

Sign up on my website at
www.authorjessicaprince.com

A Note from the Author

Thank you so much for coming back to Hope Valley with me. I knew from the moment I started the Hope Valley series that I wanted to one day to revisit and see what the next generation was up to, and that time has finally come.

If you're curious about where Rae and Zach got their starts, I've attached a little graphic below to make that easier for you.

Zach
PAULSON ♥ _Rae_
BLACKWELL

son of
Cord & Rory Paulson
STAY WITH ME

daughter of
Roan & Alma Blackwell
VAMP

I hope you enjoy this story as much as I enjoyed writing it!

Happy reading, and all the love,

~ Jess

Discover Other Books by Jessica

SECOND HOPE SERIES
The Little Things

ASHLAND SERIES
Dead to Rights

WHITECAP SERIES
Crossing the Line
My Perfect Enemy
Turn of the Tides

THE PEMBROOKE SERIES:
Sweet Sunshine
Coming Full Circle
A Broken Soul

Should Have Been Me

WHISKEY DOLLS SERIES
Bombshell

Knockout

Stunner

Seductress

Temptress

Vamp

HOPE VALLEY SERIES:
Out of My League

Come Back Home Again

The Best of Me

Wrong Side of the Tracks

Stay With Me

Out of the Darkness

The Second Time Around

Waiting for Forever

Love to Hate You

Playing for Keeps

When You Least Expect It

Never for Him

REDEMPTION SERIES
Bad Alibi

Crazy Beautiful
Bittersweet
Guilty Pleasure
Wallflower
Blurred Line
Slow Burn
Favorite Mistake
Sweet Spot

THE CLOVERLEAF SERIES
Picking up the Pieces
Rising from the Ashes
Pushing the Boundaries
Worth the Wait

THE COLORS NOVELS
Scattered Colors
Shrinking Violet
Love Hate Relationship
Wildflower

THE LOCKLAINE BOYS
Fire & Ice
Opposites Attract
Almost Perfect

CIVIL CORRUPTION SERIES

Corrupt

Defile

Consume

Ravage

GIRL TALK SERIES:

Seducing Lola

Tempting Sophia

Enticing Daphne

Charming Fiona

STANDALONE TITLES:

One Knight Stand

Chance Encounters

Nightmares from Within

DEADLY LOVE SERIES:

Destructive

Addictive

Chapter One

Rae

Well, I had really done it this time. I'd finally gone too far.

As the heavy metal door slid closed with a resounding clang, the iron bars breaking up the view from the other side of the jail cell I was standing in, I knew without a shadow of a doubt I'd screwed up *big time.*

"Oh my God," I whispered, slapping my hands over my face as the enormity of my situation finally crashed down on me. "My parents are going to *kill me!*" I cried, the words muffled by my palms.

"First time in lockup, sweetie?"

I turned to the only other person in the cell with me. When I was first escorted in—my hands cuffed behind my back after having the world's most unflattering mugshot taken of me—she'd been stretched out along the bench on the left side of the concrete and cinderblock room. At the time, I thought she'd been asleep and couldn't fathom how that was even possible. I had so much adrenaline pumping through my system that I wasn't sure I'd be able to sleep for a week. Even if I had my king-sized pillow-top mattress and expensive-as-hell luxury bamboo sheets beneath me.

"Um." I pulled my lips between my teeth and bit down hard, hoping to stop the quiver in my chin. It was bad enough I'd been arrested. I was not going to be that socialite who bawled like a freaking baby in the middle of her jail cell. I was made of tougher stuff than that, damn it.

Okay, I wasn't. But fake it 'til you make it and all that jazz, right?

"Is it that obvious?" I asked once I managed to fight the tears back.

The woman sat up and spun around, resting her back against the cold gray wall and crossing one leg over the other. If I had to guess, I would have put her some-where in her late thirties, maybe older, but it was hard to tell with all the makeup she had caked on her face and the thick black eyeliner and mascara. She'd obviously been in here for a while and looked content to stay until, well, I wasn't sure how the hell we got out of a place like this. I'd never been arrested before!

"Oh yeah," she said with the raspy laugh of someone who smoked at least two packs a day. "Obvious as hell you just got your cherry busted tonight, girly." *Eww.* "If I were you, I'd wipe that deer in the headlights look off your pretty face real damn quick. It's bad enough you're in here sporting a dress that probably cost more than my rent, you don't want to draw more attention to the fact that you're a spoiled princess. Once this place starts filling up, they'll eat your ass alive."

I worked hard to do as she suggested, despite the fact that being called a spoiled princess caused that burn in the backs of my eyes to start up all over again. I wanted to argue, to tell this woman she didn't know the first thing about me. But the truth was, she'd hit the nail on the head with painful accuracy.

I *was* a spoiled princess. The dress I was wearing was one I'd purchased straight from the designer after I saw it on the runway model during Paris Fashion Week. I hadn't even bothered to ask the price before passing over my credit card. Well . . . my dad's credit card. However, I did know how much the red-bottom heels on my feet cost, and my new cellie wasn't too far off the mark. Rent in L.A. was astronomical, and so was the cost of these shoes.

Honestly, I felt like an asshole standing in the middle of the holding cell in designer duds, the hair I'd paid an ungodly amount of money to have professionally blown out earlier in the day now lying flat against my head, and the makeup that had been artfully applied by the makeup artist I used every morning smudged from crying. I was a fraud and the chick on the bench across from me knew that with just one look.

My expensive heels click-clacked against the hard concrete floor as I moved to the metal bench along the back wall and sat down, tugging at the hem of my minidress and crossing my legs tightly so I didn't accidentally flash anyone that might walk by. This dress wasn't exactly made to be sat in. It was more for showing off than anything. It had been designed to *be seen* in. Comfort and modesty hadn't come into consideration at all.

I gripped the edge of the bench tight enough that the metal dug into my skin, trying to ignore the fact that there was a toilet . . . out in the open . . . less than five feet from where I was sitting. I made the mistake of looking at it and gagged before quickly facing forward once again.

"You look familiar." My spine went stiff at my new roommate's declaration. I had been hoping to get through this whole ordeal without being recognized, but it looked like that hope was in vain. "Do I know you from somewhere?"

I lowered my face and stared at my lap, trying to hide behind the curtain of my hair. "I don't think so," I mumbled.

"No, I do. I totally know you from somewhere. Where do I—?" I knew she'd placed me when she sucked in a gasp and snapped her fingers. "You're one of those people who's famous for no reason, right? Because you got a rich mommy and daddy. You were on that reality show where all those spoiled-ass rich kids had to live a week in the jungle or something."

God, I hated that I'd agreed to do that show. It made us look like fools. I was just thankful the viewers didn't know it was all bullshit, and that we spent each night in a private villa belonging to the tropical resort we were filming around while trying to trick the world into believing that we were roughing it the whole seven days.

"So what did you do to get yourself thrown in here, sweet cheeks?"

Shame flooded me, staining my cheeks an angry red I couldn't possibly hide. "It's, um, kind of a long story."

She lifted her arms at her side and looked around sarcastically. "I think we both have time."

"What are *you* in for?" I threw back, trying to take the attention off me.

She waved a hand down the front of herself like the answer was obvious. "What's it look like? You think I'd wear something like this because it suits my complexion?"

Well, I hadn't wanted to assume. Fashion was ever-changing, evolving. The torn fishnet stockings, pleather miniskirt, and neon pink tube top could have been her way of making a statement.

"I'm in for solicitation. I got busted hookin'." She lifted her shoulders in a shrug like it was nothing. "Wasn't the first time, probably won't be the last."

"Hey, you have to make a living somehow, right?"

She didn't hide her surprise at my response. If she expected me to judge her, she was going to be waiting a long time. I had a lot of opinions on prostitution, and most of them centered around the fact that our laws in regards to the oldest profession known to man were in serious need of an overhaul. Instead of punishing these women for doing what they felt they needed to do, whatever their reasons may be, it would have been better if laws were set in place to ensure their safety as they did it.

"What about you, princess? I shared, now it's your turn."

"Well, I guess I'm in for breaking and entering. And . . . maybe a little bit of arson."

My cellmate's eyes flared as she leaned forward, the picture of curiosity. "How does someone get popped for a *little bit* of arson, exactly?"

"It was a small fire," I defended. "A baby fire, really. It didn't even burn half the room down, and I got it mostly put out before the police arrived."

Her mouth dropped open on a laugh of bewilderment. "You're kidding me. You're telling me you broke into a place and set it on fire? *You?* The little princess?" Her ridiculing bark of laughter bounced off the walls and rattled around my skull, making the headache that had been pulsing in my brain and behind my eyeballs that much worse. "No way. I don't believe it."

I folded my arms over my chest, holding myself protectively. "It wasn't like that. It was an accident."

A huge, incredibly stupid accident that could have been prevented if I could just start making better decisions. But that wasn't exactly something I was known for doing, and it had finally come back to bite me in the ass. Big time.

If I made smarter choices I would have told my best friend Kendall no when she suggested I throw a party to cheer myself up after not getting picked for that new reality TV dating show I'd auditioned for. I wouldn't have trusted her when she assured me she had the perfect place to host a rager or that I should post about it all across social media.

I should have listened to my gut when it started screaming at me that something wasn't right. That Kendall had been lying when she insisted the only reason she had to pick the lock on the front door of the mansion in the hills was because she'd lost the key the homeowner had given her, and that they were totally okay with us inviting over a hundred of our closest friends to swim in their luxurious pool and grotto and help ourselves to the expensive wines in their wine cellar.

But I didn't do that. I'd shut off that voice of reason and went with the flow just like I always did. Because that was how you stayed on top in the social circles I ran in. Not rocking the boat and being known as the girl who was always up for a good time was the only way to keep from being a social outcast. It was all about who could throw the best party. Who had the most expensive car or penthouse apartment or wardrobe. Who was dating the hottest actor or athlete at any given moment.

Tonight had been one hell of a wakeup call. There wasn't a single thing of substance to me or any of the people I'd considered my friends. All those so-called friendships had shriveled up and died as soon as we heard the sirens and they all bailed, leaving me holding the bag—and the fire extinguisher—as I tried to snuff out the flames one of those geniuses had started in the kitchen when they wanted to prove they could pull off a fire breathing trick with a mouthful of vodka and a culinary butane torch.

As it turned out, the house belonged to the parents of the guy Kendall had been hooking up with until very recently, when he traded her in for a Brazilian swimsuit model. The B&E and the party that trashed their house was her way of getting revenge. On him for dumping her, and on his folks for convincing their son he could do so much better than a twenty-two-year-old Instagram influencer whose singing career ended before it could begin when someone leaked a version of her single without the autotune.

I'd tried my best to be supportive in her endeavor, lying through my teeth when I assured her the song was going to be a banger in all the clubs across Los Angeles. Not that it would have mattered if I told her the truth. Her gift for fooling herself into believing she excelled at all things was her only real talent.

My cellmate whistled. "Girly, when you do something, you do it big, don't you?"

She wasn't wrong about that. But it wasn't something I was particularly proud of. The truth was, I didn't really have a reason for all the stupid shit I tended to get myself into. My parents hadn't mistreated me growing up. They didn't throw money at me to keep me out of their hair like so many people I knew. They weren't mean or neglectful or abusive. My parents loved me like crazy, and I had grown up feeling that love every single day.

The problem occurred when I was old enough to realize I had two parents with incredible gifts that the world adored them for. My father was a famous country singer who had managed to cross over into mainstream and become a world-wide icon in the music industry. My mother had started her career as a crazy-talented burlesque dancer at a club in Virginia. She'd grown so popular that she traveled to places like New York and Chicago, Paris and Rome, where she headlined these huge reviews that sold out every single night.

Because Roan and Alma Blackwell were who they were, the world just assumed I would be some sort of a wunderkind, that the talents of my parents would pass down to me, and I'd be the next big thing. The expectations from as far back as I could remember had always rested heavily on my shoulders. My parents never made me feel like they expected greatness—unachievable or otherwise. They never seemed disappointed I hadn't followed in either of their footsteps, but that didn't mean I hadn't felt the pressure from everyone else. I didn't have my father's vocal talents. Far from it, in fact. My singing voice sounded like a thousand cats being thrown into a woodchipper. And unlike my mother, I had two left feet. Any time I tried to dance, I would end up tripping over my own feet and seriously hurting myself.

As I grew older, I eventually let that pressure get to me. The bitterness at not being as amazing as they were ate at me until I finally decided to do what a lot of kids and young adults in my situation did. I leaned hard into that whole nepo-baby stigma, surrounding myself with other people who would never live up to the fame or success of their parents.

Take Kendall, for example. Her hotelier father had always hoped she'd go into the family business, but she had been more set on partying and posting all over Instagram and TikTok. Problem was, Daddy tended to have to use his money and connections to dig her out of the holes she dug for herself constantly when she said something insensitive or offensive—which was *way* more often than should have been acceptable. There was one political rant in particular that was so bad, it nearly got her cancelled. But her family's money was able to hire the best spin team around and get her out of it. However, it was only a matter of time before she pulled another stunt that set the internet ablaze. It was as if she got off on pushing to see just how much she could get away with without burning her whole world to the ground.

If I'd really stopped to think about it, I would have realized I didn't even *like* my best friend. In fact, I couldn't stand her, but that was the thing, I didn't stop to think. Because in the groups I ran in, liking the people I called friends didn't matter just as long as I was photographed with them regularly. Jealousy ran rampant through our circle, constant rumors of this person talking behind that person's back. So-and-so sleeping with what's-her-name's boyfriend to get back at her for some petty slight. There was always some sort of drama, and most days it was exhausting. But it was the life I had chosen, and I had been determined to stick it out.

Thus began the long line of shitty choices that kept getting me into all kinds of trouble. And this was where I ended up: behind bars, a slew of paparazzi outside the police station waiting for a chance to snap a photo of me looking like a hot mess, while I waited for my parents to swoop in and save the day.

Chapter Two

Rae

Shame coated my throat like thick, rancid syrup, leaving an awful taste behind and threatening to choke me. The silence that had enveloped the room pressed down on my shoulders so hard I felt as if it might flatten me right into the plush, four thousand dollar area rug beneath my feet.

My parents had lapsed into silence more than five minutes ago, after I'd finished explaining, in great detail, the events that had taken place the night before, and honestly, I would have preferred they yell. It would have been so much better if they'd screamed and cursed and raged at my stupidity. Anything other than their silent disappointment that was slowly suffocating me.

I could see the exhaustion on their faces, the jetlag hunching their tired frames from the hours they'd spent awake. All because of me. My father had been on the European leg of his tour, performing in sold-out stadiums for eager fans who were dying to see him live for the first time in fifteen years. I'd been eight when he made the decision to stop touring. He hadn't wanted to disrupt my life more than necessary by dragging me along for months at a time, and he couldn't stand being away from my mom and me for more than a day or two at a time. When he announced earlier that year that he'd be hitting the road again to promote his latest album, they couldn't put the tickets up fast enough. Shows across the globe sold out in record time.

With me being grown and out on my own, my mother decided it was the perfect time to go with him, working her schedule out so that they could use the trip as a second honeymoon of sorts. She had retired from performing a while back, claiming no one wanted to see a middle-aged burlesque dancer. However instead of taking it easy, she started choreographing for hit Broadway musicals and other productions that took her all over. The good thing was she could make her own schedule, accept whatever jobs she wanted and pass on others.

At that very moment, my father was to be enjoying the one night he had off before having to hit the stage in Liverpool and performing for a crowd of thousands of excited fans, not here with me, having used what little free time he and my mother had to contact his lawyer to get his only daughter out of lockup and clean up the mess I'd created.

Never in my entire life had either of them told me I let them down, but I knew I'd disappointed them more times than I could keep count. Especially in the past four years since I'd decided to pack up and move to L.A., insisting I was ready to make it on my own. When it turned out that being a grownup entailed a hell of a lot more than I had been prepared to handle, they hadn't blinked at helping me out.

Not once did they throw in my face that they were still taking care of me, even from an opposite coast. From my luxury condo, to the cherry red Beamer down in the parking garage, to my utilities and groceries. They basically covered the cost of everything I needed in order to survive. I may have moved out, but I wasn't doing a damn thing on my own. That was for sure. They bankrolled my entire life, all while hoping I'd eventually get my shit together. But I had a feeling all of that was about to change.

"Will one of you say something? Please? I can't take the silence. I know you're pissed."

My father stood at the huge glass windows that overlooked the city below. His shoulders sagged on a massive sigh as he hung his head in disappointment. He wouldn't even look at me, and that probably hurt worse than anything else. I'd always been a daddy's girl. From the moment I came into this world, I had a bond with my father that had never wavered. My mom loved telling me stories of how he used to walk around the house for hours, holding me against his chest because he couldn't bring himself to put me down. It got so bad he bought one of those kiddie backpack things so he could strap me to his chest when he needed the use of his hands.

I was his girl. I lost count of the number of songs he'd written just for me, no one else, using them to sing me to sleep at night. Knowing I'd messed up so bad he couldn't bring himself to look me in the eye was like a knife straight to the heart.

"What do you expect us to say?" my mom asked, drawing my attention to her. The disappointment reflected back at me in her gaze was like taking a punch from a professional MMA fighter. My stomach twisted painfully, everything I'd put in it over the past twenty-four hours threatening to come up.

I hadn't only let them down, I'd failed at becoming a functioning member of society, something every human being on the planet did. They were finally seeing that now, and it crushed them, which, in turn, devastated me.

I shook my head, lowering my gaze to my lap where I

was clutching my fingers. "I-I don't know," I said on a low whisper. "I'm so sorry. I know I screwed up—"

"You *screwed up?*" My dad finally turned around to face me, but what I saw in his gaze made me wish he hadn't. It took everything in me to keep from bursting into tears and becoming a sobbing, snotty mess. "What were you thinking?" he asked, holding up his hand to cut me off before I could get a word out. "You know what? Don't bother answering that. I already know you weren't thinking."

"I—" The defense I had geared up, ready to throw out, died on my tongue. There was nothing I could say to fix this, no defense that wasn't at least partially bullshit. There were a million things I could have done to stop what happened the night before, starting even before Kendall pulled out those bobby pins and started on that lock. Yet I did nothing. "I'm sorry."

"I don't want to hear that you're sorry," my father clipped. The harsh tone was one he'd never used on me before. It caught me so off guard I flinched, causing the tears that had been welling in my eyes to break free and slip down my cheeks.

His expression went from enraged to ravaged at the sight of my tears. He'd always hated to see me cry, but as I watched, I could actually see him shoring up his defenses.

"This is over," he announced waving a finger above his head in a circle. "This lifestyle you've been living, this apartment, those worthless friends of yours— it's done. Finished."

"I-I don't understand. What are you saying?"

My mom took up explaining when he looked back out at the view, his hands planted firmly on his hips. "It means the gravy train has officially dried up. We've spoken to the family whose house you destroyed and offered to pay for all the repairs. In return, they've agreed not to press charges."

My shoulders sank in relief that turned out to be short-lived, because she wasn't even close to being done. "You'll be paying us back every single penny of what it costs to fix the damage you made."

I nodded in agreement. After all, it was only fair. "Okay. I'll find a job. I heard about this designer looking for models—"

"That won't be necessary. I've already found you work."

My gut started to sink, a voice in the back of my head telling me this wasn't going to be good. "Y-you did?"

She nodded resolutely. "Sure did. You're going back to Hope Valley. I have a friend whose son runs the family ranch, and they're always in need of help."

I shot to my feet, my hands clenched into tight fists at my sides. "But, Mom, my life is here! You can't expect me to pick up and travel to some Podunk town in the middle of nowhere for a few months while I work off my debt. What about my home?" I threw my arms out at my sides, indicating the condo I was standing in the middle of.

My father turned back to me, his arms crossed over his chest, his posture rigid. "Technically, this place belongs to me and your mother, and as of this moment, we're done paying for it."

Everything in my body locked up tight, including my lungs. I couldn't seem to pull in a full breath. "What?" I croaked as stars started dancing across my vision. "You— you can't do that."

"You moved out here because you were determined to make it on your own, remember? As far as your mom and I can tell, that has yet to happen, so we've decided it's time you get the chance to do just that. Make it on your own. We're putting this place on the market and using the money from the sale to go toward the cost of the damages. We've already been in contact with a realtor who's assured us this place will move fast. While you're working at the ranch, they'll provide housing, and your meals will be covered, but that's it. You'll be responsible for everything else. You'll be allowed to keep a portion of each paycheck to cover the rest of your expenses, but the remainder of it will go to paying us back."

"I don't even know the first thing about working on a ranch!" I cried, every fiber of my being rebelling against everything they'd set out in front of me.

I hadn't been back to Hope Valley in *years*. My parents always talked about how badly they'd wanted to raise me there, how it was such a wonderful place for a family. However, with both their jobs, staying in a small town for the long run simply wasn't feasible. I was little when we finally moved away, and though I remembered bits and pieces of the trips we'd taken back there over the years, I didn't have much memory of the place my parents were so fond of that they still kept a house there all these years later. They visited as much as their schedules allowed, but when I started turning my nose up at the small-town lifestyle, preferring the hustle and bustle of the city to the boring and quiet, they stopped making me tag along.

Going back now would be a nightmare.

"You'll receive on-the-job training," my mom said, her tone leaving no room for argument. "And hopefully they'll be able to teach you a few life lessons your father and I obviously failed to teach you ourselves."

I hated that they blamed themselves for the trouble

I'd caused, but the guilt of that was overshadowed by the panic coursing through me at the idea that my entire world was being turned upside down and shaken like one of those magic eight balls.

I held my middle tight, trying to hide the fact that my whole body was starting to tremble. "What if I say no?"

My mother lifted a single shoulder in a shrug, but I could see the pain etched into her face. "You're an adult, Rae, despite all the evidence to the contrary. Your father and I can't *make* you do anything. But if you choose to stay here, you'll be doing it with no apartment, no car, no phone, and no credit cards, since I've already removed them from your wallet. Anything and everything we paid for is officially gone."

"So you expect me to give up everything and everyone I know to go live in Rednecksville with a bunch of hillbillies who couldn't do anything better with their lives?"

My dad slammed his hand down on the table beside him so hard the objects on top rattled before falling to the floor and shattering. The slap cracked through the apartment like a gunshot, making me jolt. I had never seen my father so angry before, and it was all directed at me.

"That is the *last* time you'll speak about that town

and those people with that kind of disrespect. You understand me?" He jabbed his finger in my direction, his face growing red. "That place means more to your mom and me than you can possibly understand, and those are some of the best people you'll ever have the privilege of meeting. Moving away from there was one of the hardest decisions we ever had to make, and there isn't a day that goes by that we don't miss it and the friendships we built, the loved ones we left behind. Don't you *dare* speak ill of them ever again. Do you hear me?"

I blinked, causing more tears to break free as I nodded, unable to speak as I fought back the sob building in my throat.

"If I were you, I'd use this time to pack your things," my mom said, her tone flat as she stood from the sofa and started out of the living room. "We've already booked your flight out for tomorrow morning. And Rae?" She stopped at the mouth of the hallway that lead toward the bedrooms, turning to look at me over her shoulder, and when she did, I flinched at what I saw. "Don't let me hear that you went there and disrespected the people I love. It's bad enough you surrounded yourself with shallow, self-centered leaches during your time here, letting that poison rub off on you. I won't allow you to treat them the way all your so-called friends treated you when they left you to take all the blame."

With that perfectly placed shot, she turned and disappeared.

"I suggest you get to work," my father grumbled as he followed behind her. "Your flight is at seven in the morning."

Then I was alone, with nothing but my self-loathing to keep me company.

Chapter Three

Zach

Closing my eyes, I inhaled deeply, pulling in the smells of the trees and the water, the grass beneath me, the faint scent of sweat on my skin from a hard day's work and the dust of the animals. I filled my lungs with the scents of the land and the work I loved so much. I concentrated on the sound of the river rushing a couple yards away while the jagged bark of the tree I was resting against pressed into my back as I tried to block out the thoughts swirling around in my head, hoping to find the calm I always found whenever I sat in this spot.

It was a place I'd discovered years ago. My favorite place on the ranch I had called home since I was twelve years old. This place offered me peace when my turbulent mind got in the way, letting the memories of the past loose. But I struggled to find that peace today. It was buried deeper below the surface than usual, beneath the weight of the news I received earlier.

Giving up on trying to quiet the thoughts that were raging harder than the river before me, I opened my eyes and stared out at the endless beauty my family's land provided. It was easy to get lost in the what-ifs of my life if I allowed it. Usually I was better at blocking them out.

What if I hadn't thrown that rock?

What if Cord hadn't caught me?

What if Rory hadn't turned out to be the guardian angel I hadn't even realized I needed?"

What if, what if, what if.

Today those questions rattled around in my skull and scratched at my skin, refusing to be ignored. It wasn't hard to get lost in the work as a rancher, especially on a ranch the size of ours, but that blessed quiet just wouldn't come today. My past had come screaming back to the forefront of my mind with one unexpected visit, and I'd been distracted ever since. To the point I was making careless mistakes.

I managed to snag my hand on the barbwire fence I was repairing earlier and sliced my palm open. I wasn't paying attention like I should have been and nearly got a chunk of my ass bitten clean off by Gretel, a particularly ornery goat that had taken issue with me since the day she came to the ranch. I knew better than to turn my back on her and the tear in the ass of my jeans where she'd ripped the pocket clean off was proof of that. Thank Christ I'd worn underwear today instead of going commando like I sometimes did, or there would have been no end to the shit I got from my ranch hands.

After nearly getting kicked in the head by one of the young horses we were trying to break, I decided it was for the best that I got my ass out of the way before I got myself or someone else seriously injured and let my crew handle the rest of the work for the day.

I knew if I went home I'd get lost in my own head and most likely find myself at the bottom of a bottle of whiskey, so I climbed on Roam, the horse I'd gotten when I graduated from high school at eighteen, and rode him out to this spot.

It might not have worked its usual magic in helping ease the storm raging inside of me, but at least I had a clear view of the sun lowering over the jagged peaks and ridges of the mountains that surrounded Hope Valley.

The cloudless sky put on a show for me, the colors slowly bleeding into each other and shifting from light to dark as the sun tucked itself away.

The snapping of twigs alerted me to incoming company, and I knew who it was without having to look.

"Thought I'd find you out here."

I turned in time to watch my grandfather dismount, leading his mild-mannered thoroughbred toward Roam and looping the reins around the branch of a nearby tree before starting toward me. My chest tightened at the way he tried to hide his limp, at the hunch in his shoulders and the slight curve in his back that was becoming more prominent with each passing year.

I could still remember the Bill Hightower I met when I was twelve years old. The giant of a man who'd been so intimidating at first sight I nearly pissed myself. Then he'd spoken, and all that fear disappeared because I realized he was nothing like the countless people who'd come in and out of my life up until that point. There was nothing mean or evil about the man. He was good, through and through. Back then, he'd seemed invincible, larger than life. But seeing the way he favored his left knee thanks to the arthritis or how he constantly reached around to massage at the ever-present aches and pains in his back was a reminder he wasn't immune to time. He'd been old when I first came into his life, and in the twenty-three years I'd lived here, he certainly hadn't stopped aging.

He and my grandmother, Becky, were in their eighties now. Time was passing faster than I would have liked, and it was only a matter of time before I wouldn't be able to seek him out for his guidance or stop by their house to con my grandma into sneaking me some of whatever she'd baked that day.

I pushed that unhappy thought from my mind. There wasn't enough room for it among all the other unpleasantness already swimming around in there. "Figured it would be you who found me."

His body creaked and he let out a handful of grunts as he joined me on the ground, stretching his long legs out beside mine. I would have argued that he didn't need to sit on the hard, unforgiving ground if I thought for a second it would have done any damn good, but the man was almost as stubborn as his daughter, the very woman who'd fought tooth and nail for me, going head-to-head with anyone who attempted to stand in her way. I learned a long time ago not to bother arguing with the people who'd chosen me to be a part of their family. There was no winning. Not that I minded one damn bit.

"Mom send you out here to bring me back?"

He took the dusty, worn cowboy hat off his head and set it on his lap, letting out a sigh as he looked out across the land. "Nah. Believe it or not, she's resigned to lettin' you have your time. Knows you need to get your head on straight on your own. But you know your mama. She only has so much patience, so if I were you, I wouldn't take too long."

I let out a short, hollow chuckle as the screws in my chest twisted tighter. "So I'm guessin' everyone knows."

I felt my grandpa's gaze on me but couldn't bring myself to turn and meet it. "It's a small town, son. You know that. Would've found out sooner or later, was only a matter of time."

He wasn't wrong about that. I'd lived in Hope Valley most of my life, but until Rory pulled me from the nightmare of a foster home I'd been living in when I met her, I'd only been an outsider looking in. She had brought me into the fabric of this town, making me a part of something bigger than the small, closed-off world I'd been forced to live in. When she and Cord officially adopted me after they'd married, she'd stitched me in even tighter. I was officially a part of this place, so I knew exactly how it worked, and how thorough the grapevine was.

"I guess I should count myself lucky it took a whole day for word to spread."

Pop snorted, giving his head a shake. "Cord got the phone call not ten minutes after Captain Walker's truck pulled away from the barn. We've just been lettin' you process in your own way." He jerked his chin in the direction of my hand. "Which it would appear was a little more hazardous than any of us was expectin'."

I heaved out a weary sigh removing my own cowboy

hat and resting it on the ground beside my cocked knee as I raked my uninjured hand through my hair. "I don't know why this is getting to me the way it is. I should be over it."

His hand came down on my shoulder, my grandpa's grip still firm and strong as he gave me a jostle. "There's no gettin' over a nightmare like that, Zach. You learn to deal. Learn to heal. Learn to appreciate the good that comes along. But you don't get over it. Best you can do is keep pushin' forward. That's what you did."

I shook my head. My grandfather was the wisest man I'd ever known, but in that moment, I couldn't help but wonder if he was seeing something in me that wasn't actually there. "I don't know, Pop. I think maybe I just buried my head in the sand and chose to forget. It explains why hearin' that they got out would hit me so damn hard."

As long as they were locked up, it was easy to forget they existed, but that was what today's visit had been about.

I'd spent a good portion of my childhood in the foster care system, being bounced from one place to another. Foster houses, group homes, you name it. None of them were five-star luxury, that was for damn sure, but the last house I'd been in had been the worst. When Pop had referred to it as a nightmare, he'd been putting it mildly.

The Caswell home was a literal hell on earth, and I and the other kids who had been stuck there with me had spent each and every day in torment. Twenty-three years later and I could still remember the state of the house I'd lived in, could still smell the stench of filth and rot and decay. I could still remember the abuse. Being locked in a dark room for days on end, forced to sit in our own mess because we weren't allowed a toilet. Being beaten and starved to the point of desperation. It was the fear of starving to death that led me to my mom, Rory.

I used to dig through the dumpster behind her family's bar, the Tap Room, searching for food. There had been one time I was so frail, so weak with hunger and dehydration, that after I managed to climb into the dumpster, it had taken hours for me to find the strength to pull myself back out. I'd eat what I could, only enough to hold me over, and take the rest of it back to the other kids trapped in that hell hole with me.

When I snuck out of the Caswell's house one night to go dumpster diving for another meal, I found that Rory had installed a padlock, thinking raccoons were getting in and making a mess. The panic that had gripped my chest at the sight of that lock nearly took me to my knees. I didn't know what the hell to do if I couldn't get in there to get food. The Caswells had locked up the fridge and pantry, refusing to feed us as punishment for our sins. I'd only been twelve at the time, one of the oldest kids in the house, so finding a job so I could make money was impossible.

I'd molded that panic into rage as I grabbed up the biggest rock I could find and threw it right through the window of her bar. When I took off running, I remember being scared half to death of what would happen if the big man she'd been inside with caught me. And once he did, I remember thinking that my life was over. I never could have imagined that instead, it would officially start that night.

One look at me and Rory knew something was wrong. Cord, the man who'd raced after me and brought me back to face the consequences of my destructive actions, saw it too. He'd been a foster kid himself and knew all the signs.

That night had changed the entire course of my life. Rory took me home with her, and I never left. From that moment forward, I was hers. It had taken a while for her and Cord to bust through the thick granite walls I'd built around myself, but they never gave up trying.

They loved me and weren't afraid to show it, pouring that love on me until I had no choice but to fall in love right back. They married, adopted me as their own, then went about giving me a little sister.

For me, life started at twelve, and, Christ, it had been

a good life. I had the best parents. The best grandparents. Lennix, my little sister, could be a pain in my ass most days, but I wouldn't trade her in for all the world. I loved my job, my home. My town.

So when Hayes Walker, one of the detectives who had worked my case all those years ago and was now the captain of the department, showed up on the ranch today to tell me that Doreen and Charles Caswell had been paroled and were getting out of prison, it had been a blow I still hadn't quite recovered from.

"You truly believe that, you've let them win," my grandfather said in the hard, no-nonsense tone he had used throughout the years when the message he was trying to get across was an important one. "You let them poison everything that's been given to you since you came into our lives and everything you built for yourself. Don't let them have that power over you, Zach. Your head hasn't been buried in the sand. You chose to *live* instead of giving them more than they'd already stolen from you."

Those screws that had been steadily wrenching tighter and tighter since the visit from Hayes began to twist in the opposite direction at his declaration, loosening their hold enough for me to pull in the first full breath I'd managed in hours.

"You're right."

He leaned over, bumping his shoulder into mine. "Damn straight. Always am. Despite what your grandma and mom might say."

I let out a laugh, that peace I'd been struggling to latch onto finally filling me up and causing my chest to expand. As I looked at everything before me, I was able to see it all with the appreciation I usually felt.

This ranch had been my safe haven from the moment Rory brought me here twenty-three years ago. Hence the name, Safe Haven Ranch. For generations it had simply been Hightower Ranch, but when my grandparents officially handed it over to me, they'd told me to rename it. I was family, blood or not, but I wasn't a Hightower. I was a Paulson, having taken Cord's last name after he and Rory married and the adoption was finalized. My grandparents wanted me to carry on the family legacy, but they'd also wanted me to give it a name that meant something. I'd wracked my brain for weeks, trying to find something that fit this place perfectly, each name I came up with sorely lacking. Until I landed on Safe Haven. Because that's what this place was.

And as much as I hated knowing those monsters were out there somewhere, free to walk the streets and breath fresh air, Pop was right. I'd be damned if I let them take more from me than they already had.

"Ah, I see you finally managed to work it out and get

yourself back to center. Knew you'd get there. You always do." The pride in his tone eased my heart that had been aching all damn day.

"Mom'll be relieved it didn't take me too long."

Pop chuckled. "She sure will. Because I was lyin'. She did send me out here. Told me I had until she got back to town in the mornin' to screw her boy's head back on straight or she'd be doin' it her damn self."

I smiled, because that sounded more like Rory than her giving me time and space. "Wait. Where'd she go?"

"Stayin' in the city tonight so she can be at the airport on time."

My head fell back against the rough bark of the tree I always sat against whenever I came out here. "Ah, fuck."

When my mom came to me a couple days ago, asking for a favor, I hadn't blinked before telling her yes. It was something I instantly regretted as soon as she told me what the favor was.

An old friend of hers would be shipping her trouble-maker daughter here from California in the hopes that roughing it out here with us might scare her straight or some shit. I didn't have the time or inclination to deal with some spoiled brat traipsing around my ranch, but despite my mother asking first, I really hadn't had much choice in the matter.

"Yep." Pop clapped me on my shoulder, then used

his grip on me to shove himself back to his feet with a long groan and a ton of crackling, like his knees were full of marbles. "Figured I'd take your mind off one shitty situation by replacin' it with another." He chuckled and shot me a teasing wink over his shoulder, knowing I wasn't on board with what was happening. "You'll be fine, son. Just remember, this place is magic when it comes to giving second chances."

Damn it. With a parting line like that, how could I argue?

Chapter Four

Rae

My stomach sank as the cityscape gave way to long empty country roads surrounded by a whole lot of nothing. For a while it seemed like we were the only car on the road, and with the cell signal dropping in and out, my dread slowly built. It felt like I had been tossed into a horror movie where the victim was driving along in the middle of nowhere, on some desolate backroad where a killer was waiting for a chance to disable the truck she was in so he could drag her back to his lair and use her skin to fashion some kind of coat.

I suddenly regretted making it a habit to exfoliate and moisturize regularly. I was a skin-wearing serial killer's wet dream, damn it!

"The signal will pick back up as soon as we get into town. It's not that much farther."

I looked over at the woman who had picked me up from the airport—an old friend of my mother's named Rory—and offered her a smile I was sure looked grim as hell. She must have sensed my rising panic and was trying her best to ease my fears. I didn't bother telling her it wouldn't work.

She'd been really nice so far, talking about her family, the ranch, and the town I was going to call home for the foreseeable future, but every word out of her mouth was like nails being driven into my skull, a reminder of how far I'd fallen. I didn't want to be here. I didn't want to work on a *ranch*. I kept praying this was a nightmare and I had fallen asleep while watching an episode of *Schitt's Creek* that had somehow carried over into my dreams, so I'd wake up any minute now and find myself curled up in bed in my apartment. I actually had bruises on my arm from pinching myself, hoping none of this was real.

When we hit the town limits of Hope Valley, she started pointing out different things she thought I might have interest in: a salon, the local diner, the bar her family owned. I had to admit, it wasn't quite as bad as I'd been expecting. It was . . . quaint. The view was impressive, what with the mountains and trees and stuff, and it was nice not seeing a layer of smog painting the horizon in a dingy gray. But I was a city girl. I wasn't exactly big on nature. The small shops lining the streets were a far cry from Rodeo Drive, and there wasn't a Sephora or Starbucks in sight. I appreciated what Rory was trying to do, but I seriously doubted a place called *Muffin Top* was capable of making a half-decent cup of coffee.

I blinked, and just like that, we were through the small downtown area and heading toward the foothills. She made a turn a few minutes later, the faded black asphalt road giving way to gravel as we left civilization behind in the rearview mirror.

The road we were on could barely be called that. It was more of a rocky, bumpy path than an actual road, and the farther we traveled, the tighter the pressure in my chest grew until I worried the only way to release it was screaming bloody murder at the top of my lungs.

"This is it," Rory said as we drove through a wooden arch with the words *Safe Haven Ranch* carved into the sign hanging from the top. It was a catchy name, I'd give her that at least.

On my right, cows grazed in a field of emerald green grass, separated from the road by a barbwire fence. "This is all yours?" I asked as I leaned closer to the window, lifting my hand and placing my palm against the glass. As much as I hated to admit it, it was beautiful out here.

Flat pastures gave way to forest that rose up into foothills and mountains beyond. It wasn't anything like the city I'd called home the past few years. When I looked out my window in L.A., all I saw were more buildings, some new, some rundown. The streets below were clogged with cars, and the brownish-gray pollution haze was constant.

There was none of that out here. The sky was a clear baby blue that looked like it went on endlessly, dotted with fat white cotton-candy clouds. The truck's tires crunching on the gravel was the only sound not from nature. I was sure if I rolled down my window, the air would be fresh and crisp, scented with pine instead of exhaust and the occasional whiff of urine.

"It's my family's," Rory answered. "This ranch has been in my family for generations. My son runs it now. My daughter manages the Tap Room in town. I'm sure you'll meet her soon enough. She's actually excited to have another woman her age on the ranch."

A large, rustic ranch house came into view, the sun catching off the black metal roof and drawing my attention. It was a charming house whose wooden exterior and stone accents made it fit perfectly with its surroundings. Thick wooden beams and stone pillars supported the wide porch that looked like it wrapped around the entirety of the first level, and brown wooden siding made up the rest.

"Is that your house?"

She smiled and shook her head. "No. My husband and I have a house about five miles from here. Still on the ranch, just a different section. But I did grow up there. That was my parents' place until they had something smaller built a few years back. We've been trying to convince Zach to move in since he's running things now, but he can be an obstinate pain in the ass when he sets his mind to it. Says it's too much house for just him." I had so many questions, the biggest being why someone wouldn't want to live in a house that looked so warm and inviting, but Rory wasn't finished pointing out different landmarks.

She pointed through the windshield. "That's the main barn there," she indicated, drawing my attention to the massive barn about two hundred yards back from the ranch house before moving her arm and tapping the glass on her driver's side window. "And if you turn left here and follow it to the end, you'll end up at Second Hope Lodge. My folks also live down that road."

I turned to face her. "A lodge?" I asked curiously. "My mom didn't say anything about a lodge." If this place was some kind of resort, that meant it had to have amenities, right? Maybe this wasn't going to be such a disaster after all.

"Yeah, we opened the lodge about four years ago." She gave me a sideways look, like she knew what was running through my head. "It's a lovely building, but I don't think it's going to be what you're expecting. You won't find any massages or facials here."

I faced forward in my seat, my hopes dashed. So much for booking spa treatments.

"You'll help around the ranch when Zach needs an extra pair of hands, but you'll also work at the lodge. My mom is in charge of everything, and we have a staff to handle all the rest. You'll float between the different departments like housekeeping and the waitstaff. Everyone is on rotation to cook dinner for the ranch hands and lodge staff every night, so you'll be added to that as well."

My heart shot up into my throat. The extent of my time in a kitchen had started and ended with that fire I'd been trying to put out the night I'd been arrested. I didn't know the first thing about cooking, but I kept that bit of information to myself. I'd already started off on the wrong foot before I even got here, no sense in tarnishing my poor reputation even further. This might not have been what I wanted, but I was still determined to do my best with what I was handed. My heart still ached at the disappointment I had seen on my parents' faces. I wanted so badly to prove to them I wasn't the screwup I'd led them to believe I was. I would suck it up and put on my bravest face, using my time here to show them I could do better. I was sure I could figure out what to do when it came time to cook. I'd watched the chef at home enough times that I had to have picked up a few skills. It couldn't be that hard, right?

"So I'll be staying there?" I asked, wondering why we were driving *away* from the lodge instead of toward it.

"Oh, no." Rory laughed, tiny, fine lines from a life full of humor and smiles creasing the skin around her eyes. "No, Second Hope is fully booked. But we have a few cabins around the ranch that are empty."

I'd have my own cabin. That didn't sound so bad. I could definitely work with that.

At least that was what I thought until Rory pulled her truck up in front of the building I would be living in indefinitely.

From the outside, the entire thing looked like it could fit into the living room of my old condo, and the inside wasn't any better.

I stopped just inside the door, my heart racing and my throat tightening as I took in the single room that seemed to be the living, dining, and kitchen area all in one. The kitchen consisted of four cabinets, an old-school fridge that was shorter than I was, a stovetop that was built into one side of the L-shaped countertop, and a small sink in the other. There was a tiny dining table to the right of the kitchen, sitting beneath a dingy window against the back wall. It was only big enough for two chairs and was a gross, dated yellow pine that matched the small coffee table and end table surrounding the single two-person sofa in the living area—because that was all there was room for.

The loveseat looked like it was from the eighties, with a blanket folded across the back that someone's grandmother had to have knitted by hand. There was a painting of horses hanging on the wall across from the sofa—in the spot where you'd expect to see a television.

My gaze darted around frantically, in search of the TV, but I didn't see one anywhere.

"Uh . . ."

Rory stepped up beside me, dropping, "Bedroom and bathroom are just down the hall. No one's been in here for a while, so it's a little dusty, but nothing a bit of elbow grease and a few open windows won't fix right up. There should be some cleaning supplies under the sink in the kitchen. I stocked the linen closet in the hall with towels, and the sheets on the bed are fresh. I also had one of the waitresses from the lodge stock a few staples to hold you over until you have a chance to get to town and do some shopping for yourself. You know, coffee, milk, bread, stuff like that."

Well at least there was coffee. There was zero chance I would make it through this whole ordeal without that.

There was just one problem. "I—um, I don't have a car." I would gladly take myself to town if I had the means to get there, but like my apartment, my shiny, candy apple red BMW had been sold, the cost going toward the embarrassingly large sum I still owed my parents.

Rory waved off my concern. "That's no problem. The ranch has plenty of work trucks you can borrow. We keep the keys tucked in the passenger side visor." She laughed when I looked at her like she lost her mind. "This isn't like the city. No one's coming up on the ranch to steal old, beat-up ranch trucks, trust me."

If she said so. I was just relieved I had a way to get the hell out of this place from time to time.

"I'll leave you to get settled. Work starts tomorrow," Rory stated before turning and heading the two feet to the front door of the cabin. I was finally going to be alone for the first time since this whole nightmare started. I'd been keeping a tight grip on my emotions for the past few days, not wanting to crack in front of other people, but it would be a relief to finally get it all out. Hopefully over a bottle of wine and a hot bath. I just prayed alcohol was something Rory considered a staple.

But before she left, she stopped and looked back at me, her features awash with sympathy. "And Rae, I know this may seem like you've been dropped into your worst nightmare, but if you give it a chance, I swear you'll come around. I know your parents really well, and they love you like crazy. They wouldn't toss you in the middle of some kind of unrelenting torture. Keep an open mind, yeah?"

I gave her a nod, unable to speak past the tightness in my throat, and waited until the door closed behind her to let out a wobbly breath.

With no other choice but to embrace this new world I'd been thrust into, I grabbed the handles of two of the four large suitcases in the middle of the living room and wheeled them down the hall toward the one and only bedroom in the cabin. I stopped at the first door on the right, peeking inside at the bathroom. While the space was small and there was only a single pedestal sink beneath an oval mirror, the clawfoot tub was a welcome surprise. It needed to be scrubbed like most of the surfaces in the place, but it was long, with a perfectly curved back for optimum relaxation during bubble baths. The curtain hanging from an oval rod that came down from the ceiling looked as old as the furniture in the living area, but it would do.

To the right and a little farther down was the bedroom. The queen-sized bed took up most of the tiny space, leaving room for a single bedside table and a chest of drawers that didn't look like it would hold even a third of my clothes, all in that same dated pine.

I opened the only other door in the room that led to the smallest closet I'd ever seen. It was so damn tiny you couldn't even step inside the thing. There was a wooden bar stretched from end to end for hangers, and a single shelf above where I was supposed to fit all of my shoes.

I rubbed at my temples and moved toward the bed, shocked when I sat down that the mattress felt like sinking into a pile of downy feathers. The bedding wasn't luxurious, but at least the cotton had been washed enough that it felt soft to the touch. I could sleep here. It was better than the cold metal bench of that holding cell, for damn sure.

My cellphone pinged with an incoming text, and when I pulled it out of my back pocket my stomach sank.

Kendall: *Bitch, where are you? Desi's throwing a party at her parents' house in Calabasas tonight. EVERY-BODY's gonna be there. Get off your ass and hit me back.*

It was the first time I'd heard from my supposed best friend since she bailed on me and left me to deal with the police all by myself, and instead of checking to make sure I was alright, she was texting about *another* party?

How the hell had I been friends with her for so long? She didn't give a damn about me. She didn't even care enough to reach out. That text was the first time I'd heard from her in three days.

On a weary sigh, I took in my surroundings. It was no mansion in Calabasas, but it wasn't so bad. At least it had a cozy bed and a great tub. Everything else was just details.

Pulling in a fortifying breath, I squared my shoulders and lifted my chin. I could do this. I could make this work. I could toughen up and make the best of this like Rory suggested, and who knows? Maybe she was right and I'd end up falling in love with this ranch and this town like my parents had.

Everything was going to be just fine.

Chapter Five

Rae

O h, God. This was not going to be fine. *Nothing* about this would ever be fine.

The screech of something being brutally murdered outside the cabin ripped me from my sleep. I shot up in bed, shoving my sleep mask up to my forehead as the sound came again, loud and shrill, like someone's soul being physically ripped from their body and dragged to hell.

In my disorientation, I forgot where I was, expecting there to be more mattress when I flung myself across the bed for my phone and ended up stumbling over the edge onto the floor. The sound came again as I pushed to my feet and rushed across the room, crashing straight into a wall I hadn't expected to be there.

"What the hell is that?" I cried out to no one as my

heart threatened to beat right out of my chest. I pushed myself up onto my hands and knees, crawling around the pitch-black room and feeling blindly for the end table. I finally found it and managed to get my phone, flip on the flashlight, and drag the white beam across the unfamiliar space as the person being butchered to death outside continued to scream.

"Oh my God," I panted, my breaths coming so fast I thought I was hyperventilating. "Oh my God, oh my God, oh my God. I'm going to die out here!"

I crab-walked away from the single window in my new bedroom, trying to escape the noise, until my back hit the wall. Pressing deeper into the corner, I curled into a tight ball as I panned the lights over every inch of the room. Finally, the fog of sleep let go completely and I remembered where I was.

I was in hell.

All the reassurance Rory had offered me, the words that had worked to calm my nerves before I crawled into bed hours ago, was gone in the wake of that terrifying racket coming from outside the cabin. I didn't know what I was supposed to do. Should I call the police? Would they even come all the way out here in the middle of the night?

I checked the time on my phone, seeing it was barely after midnight. After unpacking what I could fit in my

new home, I'd taken Rory's suggestion and cleaned—
something I had never done before—in the hopes that it
would help to make the cabin feel more homey. The
cleaning supplies had been right where Rory said, and I
had spent the next three hours scouring every inch of the
tiny space, scrubbing away what felt like years of dust
and cobwebs. I might have lost my mind a little bit when
I found a dead rat in one of the lower cabinets, but I
sucked it up and managed to get the tiny carcass outside
before I threw up everywhere.

I had to admit, I'd been pretty damn proud of myself
after putting in the hard work. I even worked up a sweat,
something that only happened during my sessions with
Zelda, my personal trainer back in L.A.

There hadn't been any wine like I'd hoped, but I
found a bottle of bourbon stuffed in the back of one of
the cabinets that I decided to celebrate with—until the
first sip I took nearly melted a hole right through my
throat.

I threw together a peanut butter sandwich from the
meager findings that had been stocked for me, then
soaked my sore muscles in a hot bath. All that scrubbing
and dusting, the sweeping and mopping, had worn me
out, so after a bit of self-pampering with a calming sheet
mask and a bit of guided meditation from an app on my
phone, I went through my nighttime skincare routine

and crawled into bed. It was barely after nine, but the weight of everything over the past few days had finally taken its toll, and I was out before my head had a chance to hit the pillow.

Now I was wide awake, adrenaline coursing through my bloodstream, and I knew there wasn't a chance in hell I would be getting back to sleep tonight. Not with the grisly murder happening right outside my window.

The sound came again, and I clamped my hands over my ears, squeezing my eyes shut tight as I prayed that whatever was dying out there would get on with it already. I didn't want to wake Rory and have her think of me as some worthless, helpless socialite who couldn't make it a single night without the silver-spoon lifestyle I'd been living up to this point. It was how most people looked at me, if I were being honest, and it was a reputation I'd earned all on my own. Not that I was happy about it.

I wasn't exactly roughing it out here. I had air-conditioning and electricity. There was clean, running water. I had food and a roof over my head. Hell, there was even Wi-Fi, so I'd been able to stream my favorite shows on my laptop. It wasn't like I was living in a van down by the river or something, but the longer I stayed in this cabin, the more my privilege showed. The more I realized I had taken everything my parents had given me for granted. I'd taken *them* for granted.

Resolve steeled my spine. I was a grown woman, for Christ's sake. I could take care of myself. I didn't need to run to someone else every time things got hard.

The screeching came again, but instead of continuing to cower like a big baby, I pushed myself to my feet. My knees wobbled a bit, but I held steady, inching my way toward the door. I ran the instant I cleared the threshold, rushing to the kitchen in search of a weapon. There were no large, sharp knives, no ice pick. As I slammed cupboards and drawers in search of something to defend myself, my heart pounded against my ribs so hard I was afraid it was going to bust right out of my chest.

Whatever was outside didn't seem disturbed by the racket I was making inside the cabin, because it was still screaming. Finally, my hand wrapped around the handle of a big skillet in one of the lower cabinets, and I yanked it out, letting out a yelp when I lurched toward the floor against its weight, nearly smashing my toes with the damn thing.

"Jeez," I grunted as I used both hands to pick it up. "This freaking thing's heavy." I heaved it upward, using all my upper body strength to wield it like a baseball bat as I started toward the front door. "You can do this, Rae,"

I assured myself, my voice sounding muffled against the blood rushing in my ears. "You got this. You are a strong, independent woman." I inched toward the door. "You once made it through an entire hot yoga class with a hangover after a weekend at Coachella and didn't puke until it was over."

I pulled in a fortifying breath, then slowly counted to three in my head. Just as the screeching started again, I yanked the door open and, with a battle cry that was so loud it made my throat hurt, I ran out into the night, brandishing my weapon like a sword.

I made it to the gravel driveway, stopping as the jagged edges of the small pebbles jabbed the soles of my feet, and looked around for the culprit. The noise started again, drawing my attention upward toward the tops of the trees that surrounded my cabin. "What the hell is happening?" I shouted into the darkness.

The sound came again, and I finally spotted where it was coming from. My arms dropped, the cast iron skillet bumping hard against my thigh. Sucking in a massive lungful of air, I closed my eyes, dropped my head back, and bellowed out my frustration at the weird looking bird up in the tree that had just taken about seven years off my life. Seven good years that I had planned to enjoy. "You've got to be shitting me!"

The screaming bird replied with another shriek before blinking its big round eyes.

I heaved out a sigh and slumped forward, my shoulders sagging in defeat. "Yeah, you win this round, asshole. But you screw with me tomorrow night and, I don't know what kind of bird you are, but I'm eating you."

It squeaked, almost like it understood my threat. I turned on my heels, the adrenaline leaving my system in a rush as I started back toward the cabin. Only, before I reached the porch, I looked up, noticing the sky for the very first time in all the chaos.

"Whoa," I breathed out, my chest depressing as all the air whooshed from my lungs in a single gust of breath. I had never seen so many stars in my life. It looked like a midnight canvas that had been speckled with white paint.

It was one of the most beautiful things I'd ever seen. Almost worth the screaming bird scaring the life out of me.

I blinked, so overwhelmed by the beauty above me it made my eyes burn. The first tear that broke free and slid down my cheek was like a dam breaking. Everything that had happened over the past few days came crashing down all at once, tearing a ragged sob from deep inside my chest.

Once it started, I couldn't get it to stop. Standing outside the dinky little cabin I now lived in, I let it all out. I cried for the girl I had always wanted to be but failed to live up to. Then I cried for the girl I had become instead, a version of myself I didn't like. I cried for all the shitty choices I'd made, not just recently, but over the past several years. I cried for my mom and dad who I had hurt with my careless behavior. I cried because I felt so out of place and because I wasn't sure I could do this. I didn't know if I could make it out here on this ranch. I wanted to, so badly. I wanted to prove to my parents that I was better than the person I'd allowed myself to become. Hell, I wanted to prove that to *myself*.

I didn't want to be someone nobody in my life took seriously. I wanted to actually accomplish something.

My shoulders felt heavy as I moved inside, closing and locking the door behind me before padding through the dark house back to my room. Curled up beneath the covers, I flipped the lid to my laptop open and cued up the next episode of *New Girl*.

The last thing I remembered was Schmidt getting his penis broken on the show just as the sky outside the window starting to lighten with the rising sun. I must have passed out because the next thing I knew, I was rattled awake by someone beating on the front door of my cabin. I jolted out of the fitful sleep I'd managed to fall into, noticing the sun was spilling through the window and my laptop screen had gone black, most likely from a dead battery.

The banging started again, warring with the dull throb in my head. My eyes were swollen and tender from my earlier crying jag, and I was sure I looked an absolute mess as I untangled myself from my mass of blankets and moved through the sun-lit cabin. My mood was sour from lack of sleep, and whoever was banging on the damn door was about to get an earful. Only, as soon as I pulled it open, the words that had been on my tongue dried right up, along with all the saliva.

The rugged cowboy standing on the other side was so damn hot he short-circuited my brain. Every idea I had in my head about what my ideal man would look like went up in a puff of smoke. My tastes had always leaned toward clean-cut men who either dressed in suits or like they were about to spend the day on the golf course. It was how most of the men I associated with in Los Angeles dressed.

But the man standing in front of me just then, the one revving my engine in a way it had *never* revved before, couldn't have been more different from my typical type. From his dusty boots to his faded Wranglers to his chambray shirt that looked bleached around the collar from sweat, this dude screamed *I know how to use my hands better than all those city boys you used to know*. It was a look that had me clenching my thighs against the ache that had suddenly formed.

This man was built like a brick house from long, hard days of manual labor, not from some fancy gym. I was willing to bet he'd never set foot in a gym in his entire life. He didn't need to, he blew every gym rat I knew out of the damn water.

Dark blond whiskers coated his hard, square jawline and surrounded full lips that looked surprisingly soft. His nose looked like it might have been broken a time or two, but that only added to his overall ruggedness. His eyes were shaded from the cowboy hat on his head, but I was still able to make out the rich brown color—as well as the fact that he was staring me down with a look that was far from pleased.

"H-hi. Hello."

Then he spoke, and the fantasy that had been forming in my head as soon as I opened the door withered and died right there on the vine.

"Don't know how things work in your world, Hollywood, but we don't have the luxury of sleepin' 'til after ten around here."

"Um . . . sorry?"

"Get dressed and meet me at the barn. You have fifteen minutes."

With that order, he turned on his boots and stomped off, leaving me wondering what the hell was going on.

Chapter Six

Zach

I was being a dick. I knew it, but I couldn't seem to help myself. The moment the new girl had opened the door, wearing nothing but that skimpy negligee, my dick had twitched in response, making my already foul mood that much worse. It was bad enough I had to babysit some spoiled city girl, the last thing I needed was to be attracted to the woman who was already proving herself to be an epic pain in my ass. I didn't have time to take out of my busy day to chase her ass down because she couldn't be bothered to show up on time for work.

Resting my arms against the top railing of the corral where a few of my cowboys were working the young red roan mare that was proving to be full of piss and vinegar, I scrubbed at my face with one hand before lifting the tin mug of coffee to my lips and taking one last sip. My face pinched up in disgust as the cold, bitter contents hit my tongue. I'd let it sit too long as my mind drifted to places it had no business going and now it was no good. I dumped the cold coffee onto the dusty ground near my boot. It was my third cup so far this morning, and it wasn't doing a damn bit of good.

I'd been up since *she* ripped me from a deep, peaceful sleep when she came running out of the cabin closest to my house the night before, brandishing a cast iron skillet and yelling at the top of her lungs.

At any point as I watched her through my living room window, dressed in that goddamn nighty with that ridiculous sleep mask pushed up to her forehead, I could have stepped outside and explained it was just an owl and nothing to freak out over, but I would have been lying if I said I didn't get a bit of enjoyment out of watching the show. She really was a fish out of water, the performance she put on the night before more than proved that.

I should have known my mom would put her close to me. She asked that I keep an eye on the woman, give her the lay of the land, and make her feel welcome, none of which I'd taken the time to do yesterday. Admittedly, I'd ignored Rory's requests out of spite. After the upheaval that had been the first twelve years of my life, I wasn't necessarily big on change, and having some chick from California invade my sanctuary, *my* ranch, all so she could learn a lesson, left a bitter taste in my mouth. I doubted she wanted to be here, that she appreciated this place for all it was. She probably thought she was too good for us and this land, this simpler way of life, and that made my disdain for her that much worse.

However, when her shouts of confusion and agitation gave way to deep, body-wracking sobs, the humor I felt at watching her lose her shit immediately dried up. Guilt clawed at my insides as I witnessed her crumble. She wasn't crying like someone who was stuck somewhere she didn't want to be. She cried like her heart was breaking. I went from hating the woman I didn't even know to feeling sorry for her in less than five minutes. I spent the rest of the night replaying how her pretty face had twisted up with heartache and how her entire frame sank with sadness until I gave up on sleep all together and dragged my ass out of bed to get to work, even though there were still hours of darkness ahead of me.

Just as the sun had started to rise over the mountains, I told myself I was going to do as my mom asked and show her the ropes, only, as the hours ticked by and the valley flooded with sunlight, that ire I'd lost a bit of the night before came back with a vengeance. She'd had her little breakdown, and now she was blowing off her responsibilities.

I had shit to do that didn't include waiting around for her snobby ass to decide to wake up and grace us with her presence, so I'd stormed over to her cabin, ready to rip her a new one. Unfortunately, she was still in that fucking nightgown when she answered the door. A nightgown that left very little to the imagination. I had to bite my cheek so hard at the sight of her straining nipples through the silky fabric that I nearly took a chunk out of it.

That first up-close glimpse of her quickly revealed two things. First, she was fucking gorgeous, even with red, puffy eyes from crying all night long. Her pink bee-stung lips would tempt any man to taste them, and her warm caramel eyes had the power to pull you in against your will and never let go. They were the kind of eyes a person could easily get lost in for hours at a time. Second, she was young. Way too young for me to be thinking about kissing her or wondering how soft her skin was or what was beneath that nightie.

She was too fucking young to make my dick stiffen behind my jeans like some hormone-addled teenager, and the fact I hadn't been able to control my hard-on only pissed me off more.

I'd snapped, speaking to her in a way that would

have had Rory or my grandma smacking me upside my head. When those eyes went big, panic swimming in their warm depths at my harsh tone, I forced myself to turn on my heel and carry my ass back to the barn before I acted like an even bigger asshole. If that was possible. I'd been berating myself ever since as I waited for her to show up.

I pulled myself out of my own miserable thoughts just as my foreman, Hal, came walking over, taking up a spot on the fencing beside me. He had one of the ever-present toothpicks he chewed on tucked into his cheek. He rested his arms on the top rung of the corral and propped a booted foot on the bottom one. "Hey, boss. All good?"

"Yep. All good, Hal. How about you?" Hal had been working on the ranch since before I came to live here. My grandfather had hired him on as a hand years ago, and when I took the place over, I promoted him to foreman. There was no one I trusted more to help me run this place and keep the other hands in line than Hal. He was a hell of a cowboy, ran the bunk house in a way that kept the others in line while still earning their respect, and loved this land almost as much as my family did. This was home to him, and he treated it with the respect it deserved. He'd more than earned his position a thousand times over. He had helped turn me into the rancher

I was today, he and Pop. They'd bred in me a love for the land and the animals we were responsible for, and I didn't know what the hell I'd do without him.

"Can't complain. The sun's shinin' and I'm still kickin'." He jerked his chin in the direction of the horse currently throwing the rider on her back into the dirt. "Hell of a spirit in that one. She's gonna give you a run for your money, for sure."

A slow smile curled the corners of my mouth as I watched the horse give my cowboys hell, tossing her head back and forth, making them struggle to catch her reins. "Looks like it."

Hal chuckled. "Horse like that, she'll make you earn her loyalty, but once you got it, you probably won't find a better animal on this green earth."

I had a feeling he was right about that, but before I could voice my agreement, I noticed a few of the guys in the corral shift their attention from the young mare to something off in the distance. I turned to follow their gazes, curious about what had stolen their focus from their work, and the moment I spotted her, a coal in my gut began to burn hot.

"What the fuck?" I grunted under my breath, my vision narrowing as my eyelids pinched into vicious slits.

Hal let out a long whistle, making a show of taking the hat off his head and fanning his face with the brim.

"Christ almighty. That the new girl we been hearin' all about?"

She was. She was also about to be the fucking death of me.

Without giving Hal an answer, I pushed off the railing and stomped in her direction, noticing her rushed pace.

"Sorry. I'm so sorry!" Her eyes were frantic as she skip-walked toward me. "I know you said fifteen minutes, but I got a little turned around—"

I stopped in front of her, slamming my hands down on my hips, the pads of my fingers digging in deep to stomp out the itch tingling beneath my skin, an itch that had me wanting to reach out and grab hold of her. The frayed denim shorts she was wearing were so short every single inch of her legs, from mid-calf to the bottoms of her ass cheeks was on display. The white racerback tank was cropped, leaving a good two to three inches of her midriff exposed. And those boots. Jesus, the boots she was sporting were a fucking joke. They were the type of boots city folk wore when they wanted to play at country life. The stitching was neon pink, they were covered in something sparkly, and the stiff leather creaked with every step she took. And don't even get me started on the floppy wide-brimmed hat she was wearing or the oversize sunglasses she currently had tucked in the collar of her shirt.

"What the hell are you wearing?" I gritted out through a clamped jaw.

She looked down at herself, her brow furrowed in confusion. "I—clothes."

Christ, this woman was going to do my head in, no doubt about that. "Let's get one thing straight. When you're workin' on this ranch, you don't walk around in shorts, and you sure as shit don't wear boots that look like they'd fall apart if they got so much as a drop of water on them."

Her head came back up and I saw those warm brown eyes had cooled considerably, growing sharp. The trepidation that had been there a moment ago was gone, replaced with something much fiercer. And fuck if it didn't make my dick twitch. He and I would be having a talk later tonight. We needed to come to an understanding that this woman—the *barely legal* woman—was off limits.

"I know you aren't about to shame me for what I'm wearing," she started, her tone scolding. "Listen here, cowboy. I've had a *really* shitty week, and I'm not in the mood for whatever lecture you're dead-set on giving. If you're about to tell me I have no business walking around in front of all these guys in shorts and a tank top, I swear to God, I will lose my freaking mind. A woman should be allowed to show as much or as little of her body as she chooses without having to worry about a *man's* reaction. If they can't keep their dicks in line, that's *their* problem, not mine, and I'll be damned if I let you or anyone make me feel like I'm at fault or in any way responsible."

I squeezed my eyes closed and pinched the bridge of my nose to fight off the headache pulsing behind my eyeballs in time with my heartbeat. "Stop," I said, holding up my hand to silence her tirade. "Jesus Christ, please just stop." Her mouth snapped closed so fast her teeth clacked together. "I don't give a shit what you wear on your own damn time, Hollywood. But this is a goddamn ranch. *My* ranch. There's a reason everyone you see is dressed in jeans, sleeves that at least cover part of their arms, and practical boots. We dress for function here. For protection. I don't give a shit about some cowboy's boner. What I do give a shit about is you fryin' all that skin that's gonna be exposed to the sun all damn day, or being feasted on by bugs. It's inconvenient enough, havin' you here and havin' to stop and explain everything that the rest of us already know, I don't need to deal with you whinin' the next day because you dressed like you were ready to spend the day at the beach."

I caught a flash of uncertainty in her gaze just before she covered it up with a heavy dose of bravado. "First of all, my name is Rae, not Hollywood. And second, I'm not a child. I understand the importance of sunscreen, thank you very much. And you won't hear me whining about anything. I'm more than capable of taking care of myself."

I opened my mouth to argue, but quickly decided against it and snapped it shut. If this woman—*Rae*—didn't want to take my advice, that was on her. Throwing up my hands, I took a step back, officially done with this interaction. "You know what? Whatever happens is on you, but don't say I didn't warn you."

She crossed her arms over her chest and glowered up at me from beneath that ridiculous hat. "Fine. I won't."

"Hal," I barked out, calling my foreman over before Rae could say another word and possibly cause the vein that I could feel throbbing in my forehead to burst.

I didn't take my eyes off her as I heard Hal's *sensible* boots come to a stop beside me. "Yeah, boss?"

"This is Rae, the new girl. This is her first day, but she's already made it clear she can take care of herself, so don't pull any punches." I turned to my foreman, lifting a brow as I added, "Got me?"

Hal's Adam's apple bobbed on a swallow of discomfort. "Uh . . you sure about that?"

Rae cut in, answering for me. "I'm capable of doing anything the rest of these guys are. I don't need to be babied."

A smile that had to have looked as wicked as it felt pulled at my lips. "You heard the lady," I said, grinning at Hal like a cat who just caught the fattest canary. "She doesn't need to be babied. I expect you to treat her like you would any other hand."

My foreman let out a resigned sigh, knowing as well as I did that this was about to be a shitshow of epic proportions. "You're the boss."

Damn straight I was. And if today ended with sending Rae running for the hills and getting her out of my hair, I'd consider it a win.

Chapter Seven

Rae

The bathwater had grown tepid, but instead of getting out, I pulled the plug to drain the clawfoot tub so I could refill it. The scalding water was the only thing that eased all the different pains throughout my body.

I twisted the nozzle, making the water pouring from the spout a little hotter, then squeezed my eyes closed against the burn. I was *not* going to cry, damn it. Even though every muscle in my body throbbed. Even though every inch of my legs were covered in bruises and scratches. Even though the sunburn on my shoulders and arms left my skin feeling chilled and the blisters on my feet wouldn't stop bleeding. I would not cry, no matter how badly I wanted to, because I wasn't going to give that mean cowboy the pleasure of knowing he'd been right.

This had been one of the worst days of my life. I didn't know what the hell I was doing, and if the occasional snickers from the men I worked alongside were anything to go by, they all knew it too.

They weren't rude, exactly, more like they just watched, waiting for me to quit. But I wouldn't give them the satisfaction. No matter how badly I wanted to, I pushed myself until I thought I might break, then further when that didn't happen. If my entire body didn't feel like one gigantic pulsating bruise, I would have been pretty damn proud of myself. I accomplished more than I thought I could. It was all out of spite, sure, but I'd still done it.

The one bright spot in my day had been Hal. The ranch foreman, which I learned was the highest position a person who didn't actually own the ranch he worked at could have. He hadn't taken it easy on me, per say, but he had been kind, at least. When he saw me struggling, he helped. When it was obvious I didn't know what I was doing, he took his time to explain it to me, exuding patience until I finally got it. When I'd been attacked by a goat that looked too adorable to be as damn mean as it was, he had laughed good-naturedly and assured me Gretel, the asshole goat, treated most people that way so I shouldn't take offense.

He never once made me feel out of place or incompetent. I actually got the impression that he was silently rooting for me, which wasn't something I was used to. Other than my parents, I didn't have many people in my life cheering me on, so Hal's steady guidance and help had come as a pleasant surprise.

He'd taken the time to tell me about the ranch and the family who owned it. He talked about Rory and her parents, then explained that the mean cowboy was Zach, Rory's son. He assured me Zach was actually nice. A "good man and fair boss", but I wasn't buying that. So far, in our very limited interaction, I hadn't seen either.

When it was finally time to call it a day, it had taken everything I had not to weep tears of joy that it was over. Hal told me everyone usually headed over to the lodge for a home-cooked dinner—something I would eventually have to make—and invited me to ride with him, but despite the fact my stomach had been growling like a bear coming out of hibernation, I politely declined, claiming I wasn't all that hungry even though it felt like my stomach was about to start gnawing on my backbone at any moment. The truth was, I'd reached the limit on my ability to fake it, and I needed to break down in peace.

I barely made it back to my cabin without limping like a lame horse—an expression I learned today. Zach had been right about my boots. They were a joke. The only thing they had managed to do was rub the soles of my feet and the backs of my heels raw. My blisters were so damn big they had blisters of their own. The longer the day wore on, I started to feel like those devil shoes were filling with my blood. I wanted to rip them off my feet, set them on fire, and scatter the ashes to the wind.

As soon as I was behind closed doors, I ripped off everything I'd worn today, cursing every article for basically being worthless, and hobbled to the bathroom. I still hadn't made it to the grocery store, but I scribbled bubble bath and bath salts onto the mental shopping list I had running in my brain.

I didn't have my credit cards any longer, but I wasn't completely broke. I had money for some necessities, and hopefully a few pairs of jeans, a couple shirts, and boots that wouldn't scrape off the top two layers of skin on my feet.

Honestly, I didn't own a single article of clothing that would stand up to the work I'd be doing. They were all made for fashion, not function, and for the first time ever, I kind of hated all my clothes.

I soaked in the tub until my fingers turned pruney

and had actually started to doze off in the warm water when the sound of knocking brought me back into full consciousness. I waited, wondering if I had dreamed the noise, but heard it again a few seconds later. It was a much lighter knock than the one from the grumpy cowboy earlier that morning, so it couldn't have been him.

"Just a second," I called out, then pushed myself to my feet with a pained groan. My arms trembled under the strain of lifting myself up, and I couldn't help but worry how I was going to get through the following day.

Another knock sounded as I rushed the towel over my skin to dry off. I threw on the silk robe I had hanging on the back of the bathroom door, my wet hair soaking the material at my shoulders, and hobbled into the living area. "Coming," I called just before reaching for the knob and giving it a twist. I pulled it open to reveal a woman who looked to be roughly my age with long, glossy black hair and deep forest-green eyes that sparkled, thanks to the beaming smile she had stretched across her face.

"Thank God you're here!" the stunning beauty exclaimed, pulling me into a startling hug that made my entire body protest in pain. "It's so good to meet you! I can't tell you how happy I am to have you here. Don't know if you've noticed yet, but this place is a real sausage fest. Sure, that might seem like fun, but trust me, it's not."

"Ouch," I hissed, followed by a low whimper I couldn't help but let out when she squeezed, activating all the pain receptors in my sunburn and aching back.

"Oh my God!" The woman quickly released me, taking a step back. She looked me up and down, noting all the injuries on my legs, my blistered feet, and the sunburn stretched across my nose and cheekbones with a sympathetic wince. "Looks like you had a rough first day. I'm really sorry."

I blinked, my confusion at who this person was palpable. "Um, thanks . . .?"

"Oh, crap. Sorry! I just unloaded all over you and you probably don't have any clue who I am. I'm Lennix."

"Oh. Rory's daughter," I said, once recognition of the name dawned.

"That's me," she beamed brightly. "I wanted to stop by and introduce myself yesterday, but I was stuck at the bar. Speaking of, I thought you might be in need of a little booze after your first day." She snatched up a bag that had been setting on the wooden Adirondack chair on the cabin's small porch and reached inside, producing a six pack of beer. I wasn't much of a beer drinker, honestly, but after the day I had, I was willing to try anything, even more of that rot-gut bourbon that tasted like pure gasoline.

"You're a lifesaver," I declared, immediately deciding this woman was my new best friend. She giggled happily and extended the pack to me. I happily took it, holding it to my chest like my most prized possession. "Would you like to come in and have one with me?" I offered, taking a step to the side to make room for her to enter. I didn't know this girl at all, but suddenly the idea of being alone didn't hold the slightest appeal. To tell the truth, I was lonely, and it wasn't just from being in a new place where I didn't know anyone. I'd been lonely for a while now. Even when I was surrounded by people. The longer I was away from my life in L.A., the more I realized how empty it had been. None of my supposed friends really knew me. Hell, I barely knew myself. That wasn't really a recipe for true and lasting friendships. Not that any of the people I surrounded myself with were looking for such things in the first place. We were all a bunch of coattail riding, opportunistic fakes.

She smiled at my invitation. "Sure, I'd like that," she said, taking a step across the threshold. "I've got some other stuff in here as well." She lifted the bag in indication. "Hal said you didn't make it to dinner, so I fixed you a plate in case you were hungry. I also have some clothes. I'd guess we're about the same size, so they should fit. I took a chance we were the same shoe size as well and brought you a pair of my old boots. They aren't fancy or anything, but they're comfortable."

"Oh, wow. That's—" I had to clear my throat against the lump of emotion that had formed there. "That's really nice of you."

She shrugged like it was no big deal. "The food was my idea, but my brother is the one who asked me to swing by with the clothes."

Her admission caught me by surprise. Fortunately, even my eyelids hurt too much to go wide with shock. "Your brother?"

"Yeah. Zach? I'm sure you met him today."

Oh, I had, that was for damn sure, but I couldn't believe the guy who'd ripped me a new one earlier that morning would be thoughtful or nice enough to ask his little sister to spare me some clothes and boots that wouldn't murder my feet. "Yeah, I met him. But I've been referring to him as Grumpy Cowboy."

Lennix dropped her head back on a laugh. "I'm sure he'd love to hear that."

A sudden wave of panic crashed into me. "Please don't tell him I said that," I pleaded, unable to mask my desperation. I didn't know this Zach guy well, but I couldn't afford to lose this job. If I got kicked off this ranch on day one, my parents would be so disappointed. I wouldn't be able to bear it.

Lennix's expression shifted, the humor falling into a frown of concern. "Hey, I was just teasing." She reached out and wrapped her fingers around my forearm, giving it a comforting squeeze. "I won't tell him, I promise. But I assure you, even if I did, he wouldn't care. He's actually really sweet when you get to know him. He's just a little weird when it comes to change."

The tension that had knotted up my shoulders let go, and I let out a sigh of relief, needing one of those beers even more than I had a second ago.

She moved toward the small kitchen table with the kind of ease that indicated she'd been in this cabin before and knew her way around. She placed the bag on top and fished around inside, unearthing a dish covered with tinfoil. "How about I heat this up for you while you get dressed, then we can have a couple beers and get to know each other while you eat. Sound good?"

It sounded great, actually. A hell of a lot better than the night I had planned, which basically consisted of curling up in bed and watching more mindless TV on my laptop until I eventually fell asleep. Hopefully that stupid bird wouldn't be a problem again.

I made quick work of whipping off my robe and throwing on a pair of sleep shorts and a matching camisole—I was sorely lacking in the casual clothing department. I ran a brush through my damp hair, working out all the tangles, and twisted it up into a bun at the top of my head before heading back into the living area just as the microwave above the stovetop started dinging.

Lennix popped it open and pulled out the plate, immediately filling the small space with the most delicious smells. My stomach immediately made its hunger known with a growl that sounded like it belonged to a wild, ferocious animal, but I was too hungry to be embarrassed. I hadn't realized I was supposed to bring my own lunch with me, so all I had to eat the entire day was half a baloney and mustard sandwich that Hal had offered me when he realized I was empty-handed. I'd never had baloney before, and I could now say with certainty that I was not a fan. But it had gotten me through the day, which I appreciated. I was set to make myself another peanut butter and jelly for dinner, and could have wept with gratitude when Lennix waved me over to one of the chairs at the kitchen table and plopped the plate down in front of me.

I barely bothered looking to see what I was eating before snatching up the fork and stuffing the first bite into my mouth. I let out a loud moan as the flavors burst on my tongue.

"Good, right?" She pulled up the chair across from me and sat down. "It was Nicky's night to cook. He's part of the grounds crew for the lodge, and he's damn good in the kitchen. He woke up early to prep the pot roast and get it going in the slow cooker."

I wanted to find this Nicky guy and give him the biggest hug. I wasn't sure if it was simply because I was starving, but this had to be one of the best meals I'd eaten in a really long time. I bit off a chunk of cornbread muffin, the texture moist and fluffy but pleasantly dense at the same time. "Does your family eat with the staff every night?" I asked mainly out of curiosity, but also because I wanted to know if I would be breaking bread with my new boss night after night.

Lennix shrugged as she uncapped two of the beer bottles, sliding one my way before taking a sip of her own. "Not always. They're all great people, and we're all close, but we understand that sometimes they need a break from the bosses for a bit."

"Well, I appreciate you bringing me this," I said with a wave at the plate that was somehow half-empty already. "I haven't had a chance to get to the store yet, so I was going to have a peanut butter sandwich. This is much better." I lifted the beer bottle to my lips and took a drink, schooling my features to keep from wincing at the bitterness, but it was unnecessary. There was no bitterness at all. In fact, it was surprisingly good. "Oh wow." I took another sip, the refreshing, icy brew going down smooth and quenching my thirst. "I really like this."

Lennix smiled like I just paid her the highest compliment. "I'm glad. I don't know if my mom told you much about our bar."

I shook my head, drinking more beer. "We only drove past it."

"Well, we're basically a brewhouse. We have every kind of beer you could imagine, plus our seasonal brews. I thought long and hard about what a girl from Los Angeles might like when I was deciding which one to bring you. Glad I picked right."

Her thoughtfulness really got to me, causing my sinuses to tingle. I couldn't remember the last time someone other than my parents had taken my likes or dislikes into consideration. I bit into the muffin again, chewing slowly to give myself time to fight back my emotions. "That was really nice of you," I said through a full mouth. "Thank you very much."

"No biggie," she said easily. "It might not seem like it right now, but we look out for each other here. You'll see that. And you'll get to know the real Zach soon enough."

I kind of had the feeling that I already met the real him and that the problem was, the real Zach simply didn't like me. It sure as hell wouldn't be the first time someone had made a snap judgement of me, and I was doing my best not to let it bother me.

My attention caught on the bag once more, and I couldn't help but wonder about his motivation. Was Lennix right? Or was it that he didn't want his newest ranch hand out of commission before he got his money's worth.

I pushed those questions from my mind and turned back to the woman sitting in front of me, returning her smile. I really hoped she and I could be friends. "Thanks for the clothes and the boots too. I feel stupid saying this, but I was *not* prepared for what this was going to be like."

"It's nothing. I figured you wouldn't have the right wardrobe for this kind of work, and I'm happy to share." She waggled her eyebrows. "And I'll admit, I might have had ulterior motives."

I lifted my brows. "Oh?"

"Yeah. We might be a small town, but that doesn't mean there's nothing to do." She shrugged and took another drink. "Maybe you'll feel like returning the favor one night when we go out and let me wear something of yours. I'm thinking something small and sexy that'll turn a guy's head, if you know what I mean."

I loved the sound of all of that. Of sharing my clothes, of going out with her for a night on the town. I liked it so much I actually felt a niggling of excitement at the prospect. I smiled my first real, genuine smile for the first time in days. "That I can most definitely do."

She let out a little squeal and hopped in her seat. "Yes! I knew it was going to be great having you here."

Hearing that someone was actually happy—excited even—to have me around made me feel better than I had in a really long time. Even before the sound of police sirens led to my entire life being turned upside down. Maybe being here wouldn't be so bad after all.

Lennix hung around a little while longer, keeping me company until my yawns became more frequent and my eyes were growing visibly heavy. Having her here had been so nice I wanted to ask her to stay, but I wasn't sure we were at the sleepover level of friendship yet, and I didn't want to do anything to scare her off, so when she said it was time for her to go, I didn't argue. We said our goodbyes at the door, and I stood in the opened doorway as she climbed into an old-school truck that looked like it had been completely rebuilt. She gave me one last wave before climbing inside and starting it up. I returned the gesture and was about to head back inside, but as I turned, her headlights illuminated something resting on the arm of the Adirondack chair, catching my attention.

I reached out, picking up the small plastic baggy and holding it up to inspect what looked like a pair of foam earplugs inside. I grabbed up the folded piece of paper beneath them and opened it, reading the sharp, slanted handwriting scrawled across it.

In case the owl comes back, was all it said, and at the very bottom it was signed with a single letter: Z.

My head shot up and my eyes darted around. For the first time since I moved into this cabin, I noticed a small house not too far away, partially hidden by a grove of tall, thick trees it was tucked into. I couldn't make it out fully thanks to the trees and the fading light, but it almost looked like a bigger version of my cabin.

I only knew of one person on the ranch so far whose name started with a Z. Was that where he lived? And if he knew about the bird—apparently an owl—did that mean he'd seen the whole scene play out the night before? Including my breakdown?

Any other time, I would have been embarrassed at having someone witness me in such a weak, vulnerable moment, but instead, warmth bloomed in my chest, slowly branching outward and warding off the numbness that had filled the space for days now.

He wasn't making fun of me for my temporary loss of sanity the night before. He was *helping*.

I stepped back into the cabin and closed the door behind me on a single thought. Maybe Hal and Lennix were right. Maybe Zach wasn't so bad after all.

But I still wasn't ready to let my guard down completely.

Chapter Eight

Zach

I hated computers and paperwork. Unfortunately, both were necessary for any job, as it turned out, even owning and operating a ranch. If I had known the job of rancher was going to come with so much administrative work, I would have brought someone on at the very start, but now that I was in the thick of it, especially with calving season right around the corner, I didn't have the time to interview for the position. And Hal would rather have all his teeth ripped out with dull, rusty pliers than spend even a second behind a desk. That was a direct quote.

I preferred to be out with my crew, moving cattle or haying or fixing a fence, any of the other thousands of day-to-day tasks where I got to spend my time using my hands or on the back of Roam, but at least once a month

I was forced to hole up in the little office off the back of the barn working on the books, updating our records, and inputting data into spreadsheets. It was a full-time job that I crammed into less than a handful of days, and those were my least favorite days of every month.

Leaning back in the squeaky chair that probably needed to be replaced back when my grandpa sat here doing this very thing, I heaved out a weary sigh and pulled off my glasses, tossing them onto the desk on top of the stack of invoices I still hadn't gotten to and the account ledgers spread out on the scarred wooden surface. Another thing that I had been working on was slowly moving all the ranch's records over to digital files. Pop hadn't been big on digital, despite technology having lapped him several times over when he still ran the show. I had been at it since I took the reins *years* ago, and by my record, I was barely halfway done. It was the kind of work that took a backburner to all the other administrative tasks I had to complete monthly, and then fell even further behind my job of actual ranching. I did what I could when I could, but it felt like I was trying to climb a hill with the ground washing out from under my feet.

My eyes were starting to cross from sitting in front of the damn computer for too long, and if I had to look at one more spreadsheet, I was liable to lose my mind.

When Hal rapped his knuckles against the door frame and popped his head in, I welcomed the distraction. "Hey, boss. How's it goin' in here?"

I held my arms out at the disaster that was my office. "How's it look like it's going?" His weathered face scrunched as he chuckled, his skin creased and permanently tanned from years and years of working outdoors under the sun. "Anything you want, Hal. Any amount. I'll pay it. Just give me a number and it's done. All you have to do is take this shit off my hands."

He shifted the toothpick from one side of his mouth to the other. "Not gonna happen." The lines around his eyes and mouth deepened as he smiled unrepentantly. "I already told you. I'd rather take a hoof to the nuts than have to sit behind that desk."

My face fell into a half-hearted glare. "Then why'd you come in here if it wasn't to spare me the torture of clerical work? You just feel like buggin' the shit outta me?"

"Somethin' like that." He pushed off the doorframe and came into the office, taking the cracked leather chair across from me and kicking his dusty boots up on my desk, making himself right at home. "It's been a few days now, and I thought I'd fill you in on how the new girl's doin'."

I did my best to hide my interest on the subject of

Rae Blackwell. After pawning her off on Hal that first day, I'd kept myself busy on a different part of the ranch, helping some of the cowboys move cattle. After that, I'd been bogged down in this administrative nightmare and hadn't seen her since I walked away from her and Hal. That had been two days ago.

I wasn't going out of my way to avoid her. Well, that was a lie, I just wasn't willing to admit it to myself, but the paperwork couldn't have come at a better time. I'd needed a chance to get my head on straight after my body's unexpected and inconvenient-as-hell reaction to her. Unfortunately, when I was at home, my self-control was harder to hold on to, and I found myself standing at my living room window a whole lot longer than was healthy on the off chance I might catch a quick glimpse. If she had any clue I did that night after night, she'd probably be freaked the hell out. I felt like the dirty old man creeping on the young neighbor who probably didn't know he even existed.

I leaned back in the chair, resting my elbows on the arms and steepling my fingers together. "Oh? And how's she doing? She throw in the towel yet?" The question left a sour taste in my mouth, and I felt like a dick for even asking it. It was all an act, after all, and it felt like I was trying to wear a suit that didn't fit right. Uncomfortable as hell, and totally unnatural. I wasn't a jerk so I didn't fully understand my need to keep pushing this one woman away. It felt a hell of a lot like self-preservation.

Hal smirked like he had one up on me. "Nope. In fact, I think she's gettin' the hang of things."

My mask of indifference slipped before I could catch it. "Really?"

"Yep. Girl's tough, I'll give her that. Holdin' her own and hasn't made a single complaint, even though you can see it on her face when she's hurtin'."

My gut soured like I'd just swallowed down a slice of two-week-old pizza. "She got hurt?" My back went straight. "Why the hell didn't you tell me?"

Hal waved off my concern, pinning me in place with a knowing look. "She didn't get hurt. I said she's *hurting*. This is tough work. You know that. Some city girl who's only exercise is probably doin' yoga or Pilates or some shit is gonna feel it before she gets used to it. But she isn't lettin' that slow her down." His chest puffed out with pride as he spoke about her. "I like her, Zach. The other guys were a little slower to come around, but she's more than proved her worth, and now they've got her back. She's one of the crew."

That sinking sensation deep in my stomach got even worse. Hal wasn't one to shower praise, so to have him speak so highly of Rae meant she'd earned his respect, something he didn't hand out easily. That could only mean one thing. She wasn't going anywhere. My efforts to avoid her were in vain. I couldn't ignore parts of my ranch, my job, to keep from working alongside her.

"Well . . . that's good to hear. I guess." I slid my glasses back on and scooted forward, grabbing a random piece of paper and staring at it like it was the most interesting thing ever. "Thanks for the heads-up."

His quiet chuckle filled the room, but like so many other things recently, I chose to ignore it, pretending I didn't hear it. "Sure thing, boss. I'll let you get back to work. Will we be seein' you at dinner tonight?"

I exhaled deeply. "Can't tonight. Mom's ordered me to her and Dad's place for family dinner." Usually I didn't mind family dinners. I loved my folks, and I was close to my little sister, no matter how much she bugged me. But I knew the reason Mom had insisted on tonight was because I'd been avoiding the topic of the Caswells for days now, and she was worried about where my head was.

With the new distraction of Rae coming to the ranch, I'd been able to push that ugliness out of my mind, but once the work day was done and I was at home alone, it never failed to pop back up.

I finally called it quits on the paperwork just as the sun was starting to dip behind the mountains. Locking everything up, I headed out to my truck and pointed it in the direction of my parents' place. They still lived in the same house Rory had brought me to that very first night after I shattered the window of her bar. The same house that had become my home at twelve years old and stayed that way until I eventually moved out.

It was still a place of comfort for me, the walls inside filled with happy memories, comfort, and love. Every time I stepped inside, it was like being wrapped in Rory's embrace all over again. No matter where I lived or for how long, this house would always be home. It was the first place I ever felt like I actually belonged. It was also part of the reason I hadn't been able to bring myself to move into the main ranch house my grandparents had moved out of a few years back. There was a part of me that was scared of the idea of moving in there and . . . clicking. Like the last piece of a jigsaw puzzle snapping into place. I wasn't ready to shed the feelings my parents' house offered and actually build a *home* for myself.

If I were to ask a therapist, I was sure they'd say that fear stemmed from my dislike of change. That was why I stopped seeing the one Rory forced me to go to years ago when I was a kid, after the whole debacle with the Caswells. I knew I was fucked up, I didn't need anyone to confirm that. I just needed time to sort my shit out myself, which I did, eventually. That nightmare was never supposed to make a reappearance.

Pushing all those thoughts out of my head, I twisted the knob of the front door, knowing from experience that it would be unlocked, and stepped inside. "I'm here," I called out over the sounds of laughter and my family talking over each other.

"Shoes off!" Mom returned, even though I was already toeing my boots off right inside the door.

I padded on socked feet deeper into the house, finding everyone gathered in the kitchen, like always. Mom was chopping something while Grandma stirred the contents of a sauce pan on the stove. Lennix sat on one of the barstools on the other side of the island, chomping on a baby carrot while Dad stood behind her, his hands resting on her shoulders and Pop sat beside her, sipping on a beer that looked like Lennix had brought over from the Tap Room.

That was always her contribution to family dinner, a new brew she wanted to taste test before selling it at the family bar. She had a good nose for good beer, for damn sure.

Mom's head came up, her expression softening as she smiled at me. That smile was always a punch to the solar plexus. It was the very same smile she'd given me when she brought me home for the very first time. At first, I didn't understand the meaning behind the gentle look, but now I got it. It was love. Pure, unfiltered, and unconditional. "Hi, honey. You're just in time, it's almost ready."

"Would have been ready sooner if your grandfather would stop cutting in, trying to steal a bite of everything," Grandma grumbled, but it was all in good fun. She and my grandpa had been giving each other shit their entire lives. Pop once said it was how they kept their relationship from becoming dull. Mom said bickering was their love language. I knew it to be both.

"Wouldn't have to steal food if you weren't always tryin' to starve me to death, woman."

Grandma hooted out a laugh. "Please, I'm not going to take the time to starve you to death. If I wanted you dead, I'd do it quickly. I have a nice, firm pillow at home that's perfect for the job."

I let out a bark of laughter as I moved to Lennix, placing a kiss on the top of her head before moving around the island to do the same to Mom and Grandma. Dad got a quick, back-slapping hug. Same with Pop, only not as hard.

"Smells great in here. Can't wait to dig in."

Dinner went the same way it always did, with good conversation, a lot of laughs, and incredible food. Although, I didn't miss the way my mother's gaze kept drifting in my direction every few moments as we ate. I could sense her worry, and I hated that I couldn't fake it well enough to put her at ease.

Fortunately, she seemed content to wait until we had a bit of privacy before starting her game of twenty questions to make sure I was all right.

"I spoke to Alma earlier today," Mom said as everyone tucked into their desserts. "She asked after Rae, wanted to see how she was doing."

Something about that didn't sit right with me, twisting my stomach into an uncomfortable knot. "If she wants to know so bad, why not ask herself?" The words came out a little harder than I'd intended.

She arched a single black brow, that creepy mom intuition of hers always seeing more than I was comfortable with. "She has. She was just concerned that Rae wasn't being completely honest is all."

I shrugged, trying to rein my temper in. I reminded myself that Alma and Roan weren't bad people. I didn't know them well, they'd moved away when I was a teenager, but I knew enough to know they loved their daughter. I also trusted Rory and Cord's opinion above all else, and there was no way they'd be friends with shitty people. My gut reaction to think they'd dumped their problem child off on us because they didn't want to deal was off the mark, but it was difficult to remember that when every goddamn time I closed my eyes, I saw her crying that first night.

"Hal says she's good, so I guess she's good," I answered with a shrug.

"*Hal* says?" Mom asked, pinning me with a look that had the hairs on my arms standing on end. "You aren't working with her?"

Damn it.

"I've been drownin' in paperwork this week," I defended. "It's not like I can keep an eye on her twenty-four seven." But I could have at least watched out for her a *little*. "I trust Hal. He's a good guy, and he's taking care of her." A whole hell of a lot better than I probably would have, considering I couldn't seem to quit snapping at her.

She hit me with a disapproving glower that I'd seen more times than I could count, and each time, that look had my nuts shriveling back up into my body.

Fortunately, before she could jump down my throat, my little sister spoke up, directing everyone's attention to her. "I've met her. Talked to her a few times. She's really sweet."

Lennix's excitement at having another woman around the ranch was palpable. Sure, she was friends with most of the ladies who worked at the lodge, but at the end of the day, they all went home. Rae actually lived on the same land.

"Kind of nervous," she continued, and I couldn't help but get sucked in as she gave her impression of the woman. "A little unsure of herself, but I think she's tougher than she gives herself credit for. And she's *really* pretty," she tacked on, looking straight at me and waggling her brows. "Bet it's only a matter of time before all the cowboys start asking her out."

That coal in my gut that had been smoldering since she showed up here caught fire. Something sharp and uncomfortable slashed through my insides. "She's here to work, not date. This isn't one of those bullshit reality dating shows you love so much."

"Don't be such an asshole," Lennix threw back, ripping off a chunk of her dinner roll and throwing it at me, bouncing it right off my forehead with perfect precision.

"All right, that's enough." My father's deep, commanding voice cut through the air, effectively stopping our arguing, like it always did. Lennix and I didn't fight often, but when we did it never lasted more than a handful of minutes thanks to Cord's authoritative tone.

"She calls Zach Grumpy Cowboy," she added, and that goddamn twist in my gut got even tighter.

Both my Mom's and Grandma's heads whipped

around in my direction. "You've been mean to her?" Mom asked in that universal *mom* voice that made all kids, no matter their age, feel like shit.

"No, I haven't—that's not." *Fuck my life.* "I'm gonna fix it, all right?" What else could I say? It wasn't like I could defend my shitty behavior. I knew I'd been acting like a dick and it ate at me. "I've just been dealin' with a lot," I admitted, finally saying the words out loud. It wasn't an excuse, but the truth that I was willing to stop avoiding. I gave my mother my full attention, my gaze drilling into hers as I confessed, "I see what I've been doing, and I'm gonna correct my behavior, I promise."

There had been a lot of growing pains between me, Rory, and Cord the first few years after I came to live with them and the adoption went through. It wasn't that I was a bad kid, but twelve years of abuse and neglect, of fending for myself, had created barriers inside of me that weren't easy to break down. I could snap when I didn't mean to, say something rude without thinking, and hurt their feelings, which inevitably led to me spiraling because I hated hurting the people I loved.

It took some time, and I had to relearn a lot of the things I'd been forced to teach myself, but one lesson Rory taught me that always stuck was that I was allowed to fuck up. It was human nature. But I was always supposed to take responsibility for my mistakes and do what I could to fix them.

The anger faded from her expression and her features went soft, a lot of the worry she'd been trying— and failing—to mask melting away. I wasn't hiding from her anymore, she could see that, and she knew there was no reason for her to be concerned. "That's all I ask. I know my boy, and he's nothing but good."

That was something she started saying in the very beginning and had never stopped. She believed it whole-heartedly, and it was that faith in me that helped me become a man worthy of the family I'd been lucky enough to find.

Chapter Nine

Zach

I stood out on the deck, staring out into the backyard that was like a giant pasture that had been fenced in years ago. The tree fort my dad had built when Lennix was little was still there, as was the swing set and slide they'd gotten for her fifth birthday. Neither had been used in years, but they refused to get rid of either of them, stating that it was only a matter of time before we started having kids of our own, and they wanted their grandbabies to be able to enjoy those as much as my sister and I had.

I'd been too old for a fort and a swing set by the time Lennix came around, but my enjoyment came from spending time with her, reading her stories up in our special place, and pushing her on the swing. I'd been her favorite person when she was a kid, a role I'd never taken lightly.

"I was starting to worry." At the sound of my mother's voice, I lifted my beer and drank, waiting for her to join me at the deck railing. Lennix had nailed it again, bringing a dark, rick stout tonight specifically for me. "Glad to see it wasn't necessary."

"It won't stop you. You'll find somethin' else to worry about eventually," I teased.

She bumped my shoulder on a quiet chuckle then brought her wine glass to her lips. Rory might have run the Tap Room for decades, happily carrying on yet another one of our family's legacies, but if she had to choose between beer and wine, it would be wine every time. "It's called being a parent. I'm hoping you'll get to experience it yourself one day."

I let out a snort, giving my head a shake. "I wouldn't hold my breath on that if I were you. I'm perfectly content just as I am."

Mom leaned against me, lowering her head onto my shoulder. "There's a big difference between content and happy, honey."

And just like that, her worry was back. I wrapped an arm around her shoulders and pulled her against me. There hadn't been much time before I outgrew her, but I could still recall when the roles were reversed and *she* was the one to hold *me* reassuringly for that short amount of time.

"I'm happy, Mom. I swear." I waved my arm out in front of me. "I've got everything I could possibly need or want right here. I have you and Dad, Pop and Grandma, Lennix when she isn't being a gigantic pain in my ass."

She let out a long, deep breath. "We're not always going to be here, you know," she said, her words like a knife straight to my heart.

"Christ, don't remind me. Talk about a downer."

She pulled back so she could look up at me, her ebony brows furrowed. "I'm serious, sweetheart. What's going to happen to this place when you're too old to run it? Who's it going to go to if you never have a family of your own?"

My heart sank into the pit of my stomach. This really wasn't the kind of shit I wanted to be thinking about. "I'm sure Lennix will pop out a whole mess of kids eventually. She's still got plenty of time. You don't need to worry about the ranch. It'll stay in the family."

She shook her head. "That's not what I'm talking about." Her hand came up and rested against my cheek, twisting my face so I was looking down at her. "This ranch is *yours*, Zach. Forget about the Hightower name that came before. Or Paulson. It's not that anymore, it's Safe Haven. *Your* safe haven, son. It should be that very thing for the next person, and I know you'd raise your kids to look at this place like that."

I heaved out a breath and tried to look away, but she wouldn't let me.

"If you really and truly don't want kids, that's fine. I'll respect that decision. But if you're dragging your feet and settling for content instead of happy because you're scared or because you think you don't deserve it, well . . . that would break my heart."

Christ, talk about a kill shot.

"When the hell did you get so good at mom-guilt, huh?" I asked, desperately needing to lighten the mood. "You been takin' classes from Grandma when no one was lookin'?"

She pulled back and batted at my arm playfully. "I see what you're doing, and I'll let you get away with it this time."

"Oh really? What am I doing?"

"Changing the subject," she stated, hitting the nail on the head. "But I wouldn't be doing my job as your mother if I didn't point out that you got jealous in there when your sister mentioned Rae dating the ranch hands."

My fingers around my beer bottle tightened danger-ously, but I fought not to let anything show on my face. "You're way off-base, Mom. I wasn't jealous. I was annoyed. Last thing I need to deal with is fraternization between my crew." Maybe I should write up a new rule, forbidding any of them from hooking up. The more I ran that idea through my head, the more I liked it. It was what was best for the ranch, after all. We didn't need the drama.

"Whatever you say." Mom didn't bother hiding her eyeroll.

"What about the fact that she's barely legal, huh? There's, what . . . a twelve-year gap between us? She's too damn young. Or I'm too damn old, not sure which one's worse."

She waved me off. "Oh, please. No one is thinking about that but you. She's a fully grown, capable adult. Aside from the little bit of trouble she got herself into back in Los Angeles, she's been living on her own for years. I'd say she's more than old enough."

I stared at her in wide-eyed bewilderment. "Christ, when did you become a matchmaker? Fine, how about this? Did you forget the little fact that she's not from here? That when all of this is over, she'll be going back home? To *Los Angeles*?"

Mom's shoulder came up in a shrug. "This place has a habit of growing on people." She downed the last sip of her wine before adding, "Lennix was right, you know. She's very beautiful. Only a matter of time before someone comes in and sweeps her off her feet. Just remember that."

She gave me a pat on my back before turning and heading back into the house, leaving me to stew at the thought of Rae getting close to any of my guys. But it wasn't jealousy, damn it.

I quickly finished my beer and called it a night, saying goodbye to my family before jumping in my truck and getting the hell out of there before my mom got any other crazy ideas in her head. The empty ranch house loomed ahead of me, its solid shape a dark mass against the star-speckled sky. I still wasn't used to seeing it so dark. Until my grandparents moved out, it was always so full of life. It was where everyone gathered. Family gatherings were always in the big house. There was no shortage of friends swinging by for a quick visit that usually turned long.

I understood that it had become too much house for my grandparents, but I missed it. I just couldn't bring myself to move in there.

As I passed, my attention caught on the barn beyond. All the lights inside were on. It wasn't like Hal or one of the crew to forget to shut the place down at night. We kept a few on for the horses, but the place was currently glowing and the doors were still open. With a muttered curse, I turned the wheel, guiding my truck toward the barn instead of home. I climbed out of my truck and stomped to the barn, thinking over what I was going to say when I ripped my crew a new one in the morning for forgetting to shut the place down. Only, my boots skidded to a stop right as I entered and spotted the last person I would have expected standing at the stall of that red roan mare.

The horse's head was hanging over the stall door, her nose twitching as she sniffed around Rae's waist. The woman in question giggled as she ran her hands over the temperamental horse's mane.

"I told you to hang on," she told the horse, her voice coming out soft and sweet. "Man, you're impatient, aren't you?"

My heart lodged in my throat when the horse's head came up, her lips pulled back from her teeth like she was prepared to take a chunk out of the woman standing in front of her. I took a step forward, my mouth dropping open to shout at her to step back before she got hurt, but before I could get a word out, Rae reached into her pocket and pulled out a peppermint, holding it just out of the horse's reach.

"Ah-ah. We've talked about that, haven't we? No treats for you if you can't be nice."

The horse tossed her head, shaking her mane like she understood everything Rae was saying.

"If you want the peppermint, you have to behave. We agreed." My heart skipped two solid beats before flipping over and taking off like a rocket as she extended her hand slowly, palm up, offering the piece of candy.

The horse took it far more gently than I thought her capable of, causing Rae's entire face to break out in a beaming grin. "There you are. See? I knew you were a sweetie under all that sass," she cooed as she stroked lovingly between the animal's eyes. "You just need someone who gets you, huh?"

To my shock, the horsed extended its head, hooking its chin over her shoulder and pulling her in, as if to hug her. Rae laughed again and wrapped her arms around the horse's neck.

"There's my sassy, beautiful girl." I caught her pull back, her eyes darting to either side of the stall door like she was looking for something. "What's your name, huh? All the other horses have their names on their stall doors. A pretty girl like you should have an awesome name."

"She doesn't have one yet." My mouth opened and the words came spilling out without any input from my brain.

Rae startled at the unexpected sound of my voice, whipping around and taking two huge steps back from the stall. "I-I'm sorry. I know it's late. I probably shouldn't be in here—"

Damn, I felt like shit, knowing I'd been such a prick that she felt she should apologize for being nice to the animals. I held up a hand to stop her rapid-fire apologies. "It's fine, really. I was on my way back from dinner with my family, and I saw the lights on. Figured I'd come and see what was up, that's all." Her shoulders drooped on a breath of relief. "You can be in here as late or as early as you want, just as long as you close up."

She bobbed her head vehemently. "Oh, I will. I promise. I just . . ." She trailed off, pulling her bottom lip between her teeth and twisting her fingers together in front of her. "I'd never been around horses before I came here." Her gaze returned to me, a shy smile pulling at her lips. "They really are amazing. So big and intimidating. But so sweet underneath all that."

I moved closer slowly, feeling drawn to her in a way I couldn't ignore but also not wanting to spook her and send her running off. "That's a pretty accurate description. Well, for most of them anyway." I jerked my chin toward the horse she'd just been loving on. "I think you're the only one on the ranch who would call that one sweet."

Rae's face fell, a deep frown marring her beautiful features as she reached out to caress the mare's cheek. "What? She's a big old teddy bear! She's just misunderstood."

Something about the way she stared at the horse while saying that led me to believe that was something they shared, a connection that bonded them. It would definitely explain why the damn animal seemed more than happy to stand there with her chin resting on Rae's shoulder.

"Tell that to all the cowboys she's sent airborne any time they try to ride her."

She looked back at the animal with a thoughtful hum, absentmindedly stroking her. "Huh. Maybe she's just not ready?" she offered hesitantly, like she was afraid of sounding ridiculous. But she might be on to something.

"How do you mean?" I asked curiously.

"Well, Hal told me she's new here, right? You guys only just got her? Maybe she's not comfortable with her surroundings yet." It sounded as though she was speaking from experience. And I hadn't done a damn thing to make her transition here any easier. "Maybe all she needs is a little more time."

And the right person, I thought to myself. "You know what? I think you may be right."

Her eyes lit up in a way I'd never seen before, her smile so fucking brilliant it nearly blinded me. "You think so?"

I nodded, something in my chest feeling heavy and

warm at the same damn time. I was hit with the realization that I would do anything to keep that smile on her face. "Yeah. She seems to like you, so maybe you should be the one working with her for now."

Her mouth fell open. "Oh, no. I can't. I don't know the first thing about horses."

"I'll teach you." The offer spilled out before I could think it through. There was a huge difference in making things right by helping Rae feel welcome and throwing myself in front of her every chance I got. But I was in it now. There was no going back. "Look, I know I haven't exactly been the most welcoming—"

I knew she didn't mean to let out a snort when my eyes jerked up at the same time she slapped a hand over her mouth and bugged her eyes out. "Oh my God. I'm so sorry. I didn't mean to make that noise."

One corner of my mouth hooked up in a smirk I couldn't hold back. "Yes, you did."

She slowly grinned, giving me a nod. "Yeah, I did. But still. You're my boss, and I should be more respectful."

I waved a hand. "Don't worry about it. How about this? How about we start over?"

She beamed again and I thought I might go blind from the sight of that incredible smile. "Okay. Yeah. I'd really like that."

I moved closer, extending my hand. "Welcome to Safe Haven. I'm Zach, and I run this ranch."

She bit down on her lips like she was trying to mask her smile as she lifted her hand and placed it in mine. "I'm Rae. It's really nice to meet you."

Her hand felt soft in mine, small and delicate, and I had to work to ignore the tingling sensation that touching her shot up my arm. "Nice to meet you, Rae. You like horses? 'Cause we have this one that's full of attitude. Doesn't seem to like anybody, but I think she just may like you."

"I *love* horses," she exclaimed on a giggle. "I'd be happy to help you out, but I'm working the lodge tomorrow. How about the next day?"

I told myself the sinking sensation in my stomach had to have been a reaction to something I ate. It had nothing to do with the fact that I wouldn't be seeing her around the ranch tomorrow. "Sounds perfect. It's late. You should probably get some sleep."

Her features softened as she released my hand and stuffed both of hers in the front pocket of her jeans. "Okay, Zach. Goodnight."

"Goodnight, Hollywood."

She shot me a grin over her shoulder. "Grumpy Cowboy," she said with a nod before stopping like a thought just occurred to her. "Hey, Zach? Why doesn't she have a name?"

"Because I hadn't been able to think of one that fit her. But I think you landed on it."

She cocked her head to the side. "Me?"

"Yeah. When you called her sassy. Feels like the perfect name to me. What do you say?"

She nodded happily. "Yep. It's perfect."

"Then I'll get her nameplate ordered tomorrow. Get some sleep."

I watched as she left the barn, only pulling my gaze from where she disappeared when Sassy let out a short whinny as if you say: *you really are a sucker for that girl.*

"Don't look at me like that," I grumbled at the animal's judgmental stare. "I'm thirty-five years old, for Christ's sake. I can exercise self-restraint. Besides, she works for me."

But why the hell did that make it seem even hotter?

Chapter Ten

Rae

Working in housekeeping at the lodge was a totally different world than ranching, but just as exhausting in its own way. After half a day of stripping beds, vacuuming, dusting, and scrubbing toilets, the place was starting to feel endless, like no matter how many beds I made, there were still a million other rooms waiting.

There was one thing I learned in this job that I'd never taken into consideration until today. People on vacation were terrible at picking up after themselves. A ball of shame swirled around in my stomach at the realization that my friends and I had been guilty of that very thing. Actually, we were probably worse than the people staying at Second Hope Lodge whenever we'd gone on vacation. All form of manners had been thrown right out the window. We trashed hotel rooms and villas because it was expected that someone else would pick up after us while we were busy working on our tans out by the pool or sipping fruity cocktails on the beach. We hadn't given the poor people whose job it was to clean the disasters we left in our wake a single thought.

If my parents' plan was to send me here to humble me and make me see the error of my ways, they had succeeded brilliantly. I'd been here less than a week, and I already knew I'd been the worst kind of asshole back in L.A. I was determined to change that.

"Hey, how's it going?"

I looked up from the trash can I was emptying into a larger garbage bag and smiled brilliantly at Ivy, the pretty woman a few years older than me with pale strawberry blonde hair who was my boss for the day. She was the head of hospitality for the lodge. I wasn't exactly sure what all that job entailed, but apparently that put her over the housekeeping staff. "Great," I chirped, lying through my teeth. The work wasn't easy, that was for damn sure, and before coming here, I was a pampered little brat. But I would be damned if I didn't pull my weight or complained about it being hard when all the people around me did this day after day. The longer I was here, the more I realized I wasn't the person I had pretended to be back in California. I'd been faking it, wearing the layers of a vain, self-absorbed mean girl in order to fit in.

I wasn't exactly sure *who* I really was, but I knew I wanted to do everything in my power to find out, and I was starting to think this was the place to make that happen.

"Lucinda says you've been doing great." My chest started to feel warm, pride swelling inside me and filling the space at finding out I was doing a good job. I hadn't been sure what Lucinda, the head housekeeper, really thought of me. The woman wasn't exactly easy to read. She was an older woman, probably somewhere in her late forties, if I had to guess, who grunted one-word answers and wore a perpetual frown. I'd worried at first that she hated me on principle alone. That she didn't want to waste her time with a spoiled socialite. However, a couple of the other lodge staffers had pulled me aside to assure me it wasn't personal, that it was just how she was.

"I appreciate that."

"It's time for your lunch hour. Do you have any plans?"

"Oh," I started, caught off guard by yet *another* friendly person. Seemed like Hope Valley was full of them. "Um, no. I was going to eat the sandwich I packed." I *really* needed to get to a grocery store. If I had to eat one more peanut butter and jelly sandwich, I was going to scream.

"Forget about that. I should have told you, the restaurant kitchen holds back meals for the staff. You finish up here and I'll grab us a couple plates and meet you in the employee breakroom. Sound good?"

It sounded great, actually. A hell of a lot better than sitting by myself. "Yeah, that's perfect," I said with a genuine smile.

"Great! See you in a bit."

She took off, and I got back to work, an added layer of excitement falling over me as I worked at my new lunch plans. I finished scrubbing the bathroom and pulled off my rubber gloves, tossing them onto the housekeeping cart before wheeling it out into the hall. I returned the smiles of everyone I passed on the way to the storage room to drop off the cart, still a little thrown at how nice the people here were. Guests and staff alike.

I took the elevator to the first floor and turned left at the hallway right off the lobby. Instead of having guest rooms down this hall, there were offices, a couple conference rooms, the break room, and a locker room for us to use to change from our own clothes into our uniforms if needed. By the time I made it into the breakroom, Ivy was sitting at one of the round tables for four that filled the space, along with a few vending machines, a fancy coffeemaker, and a fridge.

She pointed to the plate in front of the empty seat across from her and waved for me to sit down. "Hope you like chicken. The other options were meatloaf and turkey pot pie. All of it is delicious, because Daniel doesn't know how to make a bad meal, but his grilled chicken breast is the best."

"That's perfect. Thank you so much." I sat down and inhaled deeply. I didn't know what he seasoned the chicken with, but it smelled downright heavenly. The chicken looked juicy, the side salad was fresh, with fat, ripe cherry tomatoes, and the roasted potatoes looked perfectly crispy. My stomach let out a low growl, reminding me how hungry I was. I picked up my knife and fork, not wasting a second, and dove right in, shoving a huge bite into my mouth without an ounce of shame.

When I used to go to restaurants in L.A., I'd push the tiny bits of food I paid an arm and a leg for around on the plate, maybe taking a bite or two so I could rave about how delicious the food at the over-priced five-star hotspot was. If any of the people I hung out with back then could see me now, they would curl their overly-plumped lips and look down their surgically straightened noses at me.

But I couldn't find it in me to give a damn how I looked shoveling food into my mouth. First, because everything I'd eaten since getting here—peanut butter sandwiches aside—was delicious. And second, because I'd never worked so damn hard in my life, and I needed food to keep me fueled or I was liable to pass the hell out. Fainting due to starvation would have been three gigantic steps back from where I was trying so hard to get to, proving to myself and others that I was better than I had been.

"How has your first day been so far?" Ivy asked, her gaze steady on me, genuine interest staring right into me.

"It's been really good," I replied, somewhat surprised to find that my answer wasn't a lie. I might not have been used to the work, but I was quickly coming to learn a sense of accomplishment from hard work that I had never experienced before. "Everyone here is so nice. And this place is beautiful," I said. Even the room I had been cleaning earlier, one of the smaller ones, had been warm and cozy and inviting. Like all the rest, it had gorgeous views of the ranch, with the foothills and mountains beyond.

The lodge itself was built to look like a gigantic cabin. The interior was designed in a rustic ranch style with wooden walls, thick, raw beams along the ceilings, and sturdy furniture covered in rich tones of buttery, studded leather. The fixtures were brass and high-end, complimenting the deep wood throughout. It was a place I would have gladly shelled out a pretty penny to stay at in my previous life. "I can see why it's booked solid for the next three months."

"Thanks," she chirped happily. "We try to make this place a great experience for everyone. People from the city love to come out here and decompress, you know? Go fishing, trail ride, hike. You'd be surprised how much of our business is repeat."

"I'm almost embarrassed to admit this, but I'd never been around a horse before I came here."

Ivy's eyes went big as she chewed the bite she had just popped into her mouth. "Really? I love horses. Does that mean you've never ridden before?"

I gave my head a shake and forked up some of the salad. "Nope. Never."

She sat up straight, excitement radiating from her. "You should totally talk to Raylan. He runs the trail rides and horseback riding lessons for the lodge. I bet he'd be happy to teach you."

A little flutter moved through my belly at the idea of getting on the back of one of those big, beautiful creatures. Zach had said he'd teach me how to work with Sassy, but I wasn't sure she was ready to have a rider yet. That didn't mean I hadn't been bitten by the bug since getting here. And learning to ride was crucial when it came to the ranch work I'd started doing. It was only a matter of time before it became necessary.

At the mention of riding, a thought popped into my head.

I wonder if Zach would be willing to teach me instead. But I quickly snuffed that idea out, doing my best to ignore the little tingles starting to dance up my spine and along my skin. It wasn't the first time I had thought about him since our interaction the night before, and every time the image of him popped in my head, that tingle started.

Zach was, hands down, one of the sexiest men I'd ever laid eyes on. I'd realized it that first morning when he showed up at the cabin in a bad mood and threw a ton of attitude at me. But last night, I'd gotten an up-close-and-personal look at him for the first time. Without the cowboy hat, I'd been able to see he had dark blond hair that matched the whiskers on his cheeks and chin. He wore it cropped close to his scalp so there wasn't enough for a woman to clutch in her fist, but it was still long enough to slide your fingers through. His eyes made me think of warm, decadent dark chocolate when they weren't glaring at me. But the main thing I noticed from the night before was how perfectly he filled out his worn, faded Wranglers. The man had an ass that just . . .

wouldn't . . . *quit*! A perfect bubble butt that men who spent years doing squats and lunges would never be able to replicate. It was round and looked firm as hell, and my mouth watered at the thought of taking a bite out of it.

I'd never considered myself an ass girl before. I liked a strong set of shoulders and a long, thick neck—both of which my new boss had—but I was officially the number one fan of Zach's ass. Hell, I would gladly start a fan club dedicated to it.

But looks aside, I couldn't stop thinking about the sparks that had shot up my arm the moment his big work-roughened hand had closed over mine. My entire body lit up at the simple touch, like I'd grabbed hold of a fallen powerline.

In the blink of an eye, a crush had formed. I was attracted to my boss in a way that made my skin feel tight and my breath quicken. And nothing could ever come of it. I spent way too many years making shitty choices and giving in to every selfish desire. I couldn't be that woman anymore. I needed to make better decisions. I needed to show that I could be responsible, and crushing on Zach was the very definition of irresponsible. My parents had sent me here for a reason, and that did *not* include trying to seduce their friend's much older son.

None of that mattered anyway, because I was sure

he wasn't the least bit interested. Despite his change in attitude last night in the barn, he'd made his opinion of me crystal clear. I was just a spoiled little girl in his eyes.

And no matter how badly I might want to make him see me differently, it was probably safer if his opinion didn't change.

I pushed the intrusive thoughts of Zach to the back of my mind and smiled at Ivy. "You know what? I might just do that. Sounds like fun."

Chapter Eleven

Zach

It was usually no problem to clear my mind and get through my day, but as I worked alongside Hal and my men, my mind kept drifting off. I kept going back to that conversation in the barn the night before with Rae. She really had surprised me.

I was willing to admit I'd made a snap judgement, painting her as a spoiled little socialite who thought she was better than the rest of us. That one single interaction had changed my mind completely. I knew I was wrong the instant I walked in and saw her with that horse. Selfish people were usually selfish with *everyone*, humans and animals alike. They didn't discriminate. But she'd won Sassy over in less than a handful of days.

She'd come up in conversation more than once among the other hands, and it was easy to see she was quickly starting to win everyone over. Then there was that smile. God*damn*, but I hadn't been able to get that smile of hers out of my head. I was surrounded by the beauty of this place day in and day out, still, I wasn't sure I'd seen anything more beautiful than Rae Blackwell's smile. It had the power to light up an entire block during a blackout.

Damn it. I caught myself getting lost in thoughts of her again as I finished brushing Roam down after a long day's work. I walked him to his stall and tossed him a flat of hay before shutting him in for the night.

I headed in the direction of the office, deciding my time would be better used getting some paperwork done than it would be going home, where I'd most likely stand at my living room window and stare out toward that damn cabin before finally taking my sorry ass to bed or into the shower where I would undoubtedly beat off to the image of a certain city girl, just like I had the past couple nights.

Christ, I was pathetic.

As I reached my office door, the sound of large tires crunching on gravel caught my attention and pulled me in the opposite direction, toward the open barn doors. I stood with my feet braced and my arms crossed as the unfamiliar pickup eased off the gravel road and came to a stop beside my truck. My shoulders tensed and the muscles in my back knotted up as I waited to see who was behind the wheel. The last time I'd gotten an unexpected visitor, the news had been far from good. However, when the driver's side door was thrown open and the man stepped out, all the anxiety that had started to sprout like weeds overrunning a flowerbed died off and a smile tugged at my face.

"You gotta be shittin' me." I let out a bark of laughter while the man threw his arms out to his sides, closing the distance between us.

"Surprise!" Connor Bennett exclaimed, the very same shit-eating grin he always wore stretched wide across his face.

"It sure as hell is." I pulled him into a quick, back-slapping hug before letting go and taking a step back to get a good look at him. "Not that I'm not happy to see you, but what are you doin' here, man?"

I met Connor on the rodeo circuit years ago, long before I took over Safe Haven. I did a little tie-down roping when I was younger, just for fun, but I'd only been okay at it. I knew I'd never make a career out of it, and hadn't really wanted to. Unlike Connor. He was a nationally ranked bull rider. He was a legend on the circuit and a celebrity in the world of rodeo. He had more sponsorships than I could count, and a face made for PBR to plaster on all their promotional materials.

The man made a living on the backs of some of the rankest fucking bulls alive, and he was damn good at it. He'd even come in second at the World Finals the year before. Not that he was happy with that. The man wasn't going to be satisfied until he was the champion. No matter the beatings his body had to take.

"Shouldn't you be somewhere in Wyoming right now, gettin' your ass tossed off a bull or beddin' down with a handful of buckle bunnies?"

"What? You haven't been followin' along with my career?"

I lifted my arm and waved it out. "Been a little busy here makin' a living for myself, brother. I don't have time to stare at your pretty face on the TV screen."

He pulled off his ball cap and swiped a hand through his hair before slapping it back on his head with a sigh. "Busted up my knee a couple months back, had to take a little time off. Headed home to rehab it for a bit, but you know how I am."

I sure did. The man had the attention span of a toddler in the middle of a sugar high. Couldn't sit still for long to save his life. Originally, he was from a small town in Texas called Cloverleaf, but seeing as his career took him all over, basically year-round, he didn't really have roots anywhere. He'd visited here more than once, staying a few days at a time over the years, but I wasn't sure the man could be content settling down in any one place.

"Shit man, I didn't know. You okay?"

He balled his fist and knocked on his right thigh above his knee. "I'll be good as new. Don't worry about me. But until I can get back on a bull, I figured I'd come see your ugly mug for a bit, maybe give you a hand on the ranch for a while, if you need it." His mouth curved up in a grin. "Maybe spend some time with that beautiful sister of yours," he added, earning himself a punch to the arm.

I jabbed a finger in his laughing face. "You go near my sister and you'll never get on the back of another bull, 'cause I'll kill you," I warned, even though I knew he was just talking shit.

He chuckled, holding his hands up in surrender. "Okay, okay. Message received loud and clear." He pulled his cap off again, going through the same motions as before: dragging his hand through his hair before yanking it back on again. It was a tell of his, a nervous tick he couldn't control, letting me know he wasn't as okay about his injury as he claimed to be. But I wouldn't push. If he wanted to talk about it, he would. Until then, I'd give him that play.

"Does your offer to help around here mean you're plannin' on staying for a while?"

He lifted his shoulder in a careless shrug. "It does if you're cool with it."

"Hell, Connor. You know the answer to that. You're always welcome here. You need a place to stay or did you already book yourself a room at the lodge?"

He shook his head. "Lodge was all booked up. Figured I'd find something in town if I needed to. Or, hell, I'd even be willing to crash in the bunkhouse if I have to."

I clapped him on the shoulder and used my grip to spin him around and start us in the direction of our trucks. "Like hell, I'm puttin' you up in the bunkhouse. You'd corrupt every damn one of those cowboys in no time. I'm sure we can find you somethin' fast enough."

"Sounds good to me. Then we're going out for a beer. It's been too long, man."

It sure had. And a beer sounded a hell of a lot better than paperwork or pining over the new girl, which were the only other options I had until Connor showed up.

"Damn, I missed this place," Connor said as he looked around the Tap Room from his stool at the high-top table we'd commandeered as soon as we arrived. For being the middle of the work week, the place was hopping. Then again, that was always the case.

The bar had been a fixture of Hope Valley for generations, and Lennix had made it even more popular when she expanded it, turning it into an actual brewery, complete with its own brewmaster and everything. The old bones of the bar were still there, but there was also a space for people to come in for tastings and tours. Where the ranch was in my soul from a young age, this place was all Lennix's, and our parents hadn't batted an eye when they retired from here and handed the reins over to her and let her run with her vision for the place.

I sipped a new pilsner that had just been put on tap as I proudly observed all the work my little sister had put in. "Yeah, it's not so bad."

Connor scoffed. "Not so bad? You kiddin' me? You got great beer, great music, and more gorgeous ladies than any one town has the right to have." He looked at the group of women a few tables down from us and winked, sending them into a fit of giggles and whispers. Connor Bennett had a reputation throughout the rodeo circuit as a ladies' man. He'd been dubbed the bull-riding playboy years ago, and there couldn't have been a more fitting moniker. I wasn't sure if the reputation came honestly or if he was doing his best to live up to it, but I couldn't recall a single time we'd gone out together that he didn't leave with a woman on his arm. Christ, some nights he had two.

He let out a low whistle, lifting his beer in salute in the women's direction. "Damn, would you look at them?" He jabbed his elbow into my arm. "Which one's caught your eye, wingman?"

I shook my head and took another pull of my beer. "None of them. You're on your own tonight, buddy."

Connor bugged his eyes out dramatically and sputtered. "What the hell are you talking about? We're always each other's wingman. Don't wimp out on me now."

"Not wimping out," I said with a shrug, a long day of ranching finally catching up with me. I was exhausted, it was getting late, and I had to get up early to do it all over again. "I'm just not in the mood."

His chin jerked back in surprise. "You settle down while I wasn't lookin' or something?"

I snorted into my beer, shoving the image of Rae that popped up away as fast as I could. "No, I haven't settled down. I'm just not feelin' it. Nothing wrong with that."

I tried my hardest not to squirm as he studied me like I was a specimen beneath a microscope. "You're so full of shit." He barked out a laugh. "Who is she?"

Ah fuck.

"Who's who?"

And double fuck.

"Well, if it isn't my girl, Len." Connor grabbed hold of my sister and pulled her into a tight hug that eventually morphed into a headlock. She batted at him until he released her, then slugged him in the shoulder once she was free.

"Thought I saw my brother sitting over here with an asshole." She shot Connor a cheeky smile. Despite my earlier warning, I knew I didn't have anything to worry about when it came to my friend and my sister. Their relationship was a lot like my relationship with her. They gave each other shit, but there wasn't a single spark to be found. She knew his reputation, and while she held affection for him, she thought his man-whore ways were beyond pathetic.

"It's good to see you too, sunshine. I've missed you. You decide to leave all this behind and run away with me yet?"

Lennix laughed, a deep, rolling belly laugh. "Man, you're a looker, Con, but I wouldn't let you near me like that if you bathed in an entire tub of hand sanitizer first."

I chuckled as he smacked a hand to his chest. "You wound me. I thought we were destined to be soulmates."

Lennix rolled her eyes before turning back to me, resting one hand on the table and the other on her hip. "What were you guys talking about before I walked up?"

"Nothin'," I said at the same time Connor answered, "The chick your big bro is sprung on."

Lennix widened her eyes, gaping at me. "You're into someone? Who? How did I not know?"

I let out a low growl, scowling at Connor and silently promising payback. Maybe I'd release Gretel in the cabin he was bunking in—a cabin that happened to be nowhere near Rae's. I could let her take a chunk out of *his* ass for a change. "Because there's nothing to know. There's no woman."

Connor coughed *bullshit* into his fist. That did it. I was going to commit murder. "There's a whole table of lovely ladies right over there, and your brother hasn't so much as glanced in their direction. That can only mean one thing." He waggled his brows for dramatic effect. "He's got his eye on someone else."

Lennix watched me closely for a second before sucking in a gasp. "Oh my God. It's Rae, isn't it? It is! It's Rae!" She let out a squeal and did a little happy dance as I felt the tips of my ears start to burn red.

"Who's Rae?"

"Rae's no one," I ground out.

"She's new on the ranch," my sister continued, not giving a damn about my level of discomfort. "And she's totally beautiful."

They both turned to face me, matching asshole grins

on their asshole faces. "Well, well, well. Isn't this an interesting turn of events?"

I was officially done. Standing from my stool, I removed my wallet from my back pocket and pulled out a few bills without counting and tossed them on the table. "I'm out," I stated gruffly, sending murderous vibes at a laughing Lennix, not that she cared. She'd stopped being scared of me around the age of five when she turned into a little demon who started fighting dirty. She'd rip the hair from my arms or legs, scratch, bite, or pull my hair. I pointed my finger at Connor's face. "And for being a dick, you can walk back to the ranch."

He grinned unrepentantly. "I don't think that'll be necessary," he said as he faced the table of women once more, shooting them a wink. "I don't think I'll be returning to the ranch tonight either."

I shook my head as Lennix curled her lip in disgust. "Suit yourself. See you guys tomorrow."

"Goodnight, big brother," Lennix called as I started out of the bar. "Tell Rae hi from me."

Fucking hell.

Chapter Twelve

Zach

The warm breeze filled the cab of my truck as I turned the wheel and pointed it back toward the main part of the ranch. Usually I was tired after a long day of work, my body worn out, but spending the day driving around in my truck, counting cattle and checking the herd, was peaceful as hell. Relaxing, even.

"This is the life," Connor said from the passenger seat. The aviator sunglasses covering his eyes pointed out his open window at the view beyond.

"It doesn't suck."

He chuckled and slumped down low in the seat, pulling the brim of his baseball cap low over his eyes like he was gearing up for a nap. "You sure got it good out here, man. If I were to ever retire, this is what I'd want to do."

In all the years I'd known him, Connor Bennett never even uttered the word retirement. I always assumed he planned to go out still clinging to the back of an angry bull in his old age. "What, you want to be a rancher?"

He lifted his shoulder in a shrug. "Doesn't have to be *my* ranch. I just like the work. It's honest. I feel useful here."

I couldn't help but think long and hard about the things he'd said the past few days since his unexpected arrival. It didn't take a genius to realize my friend was struggling, but I knew if I voiced my concern—or, hell, even showed it—he'd shut down or possibly leave, and I had a feeling he needed this place at the moment. It came by its name honestly, after all, and I didn't want to take that away from him.

"Yeah, well, you know you're welcome here any time, man. There's more than enough work to keep you busy."

I looked over and caught the smallest vestige of a smile on his face before we lapsed back into a comfortable silence for the rest of the drive.

"Jesus," he said as the lodge came into view a while later. "This place is impressive."

I let out a chuckle and shook my head. "You act like you haven't seen it before. You were here for the grand opening."

"I know, but it's been more than a few years, and the mind tends to forget the details after a while."

I took in the large structure, pride at what my family had built and all the legacies they'd created swelling in my chest. "It's kind of taken on a world of its own. The woman we have running hospitality got the idea for all these tourist events, stuff like fly fishing, trail riding, hiking. There's even an archery range beyond that grove of trees there." I pointed past the few cabins behind the lodge that we rented out to our longer-term guests to a grove of trees. "As soon as we started offering up that stuff, our bookings nearly doubled. She's really built this place up. Made it even better."

"You guys have been busy," he pointed out as I guided the truck around to the back of the lodge where our family and staff parked, leaving the front open for guests. The second I pulled into an open spot, the back door of the building opened and a familiar head of light brown hair came into view, the honey colored highlights liberally laced throughout the silky strands shimmering beneath the sun.

My body reacted instantly. My heart rate increased and all my blood traveled south, gathering in my groin and making my pants uncomfortably tight. I could barely hear anything over the sound of my heart pumping in my ears.

One of the housekeepers had come down with the flu, so she'd been filling in. This was the first time I'd laid eyes on her in nearly three days, and just a small glance made my lungs constrict like someone reached into my chest and wrung them out like a wet washcloth.

Her jeans hugged her body to perfection, giving every man in the vicinity a perfect view of that ripe peach ass and mile-long toned legs. She was wearing boots and a simple white T-shirt fitted to her trim waist and round tits, which looked to be the perfect handful, but even dressed to do ranch work, she held my attention and refused to let go. Whether she was dressed like some SoCal socialite or a farm girl, she stood out. It wasn't about what she was wearing, it was just . . . her.

I sat immobile as she looked back over her shoulder at something, her smile lighting up her entire face. I felt my lips begin to curl up at the sight of it, only to have them fall in the opposite direction as I caught sight of who she was gracing with that gorgeous smile.

Jealousy stabbed at my insides and crawled beneath my skin, making it feel like I was covered in fire ants as Raylan, the guy in charge of all the horseback events for the lodge, stepped onto the deck with her.

I'd known him since we were kids. Hell, up until two seconds ago, I'd considered the guy a good friend. His sister and Rory were tight, so we'd been raised close, but as I watched Rae reach out and place her hand on his forearm, giving it an affectionate squeeze, I wanted to rip his goddamn throat out.

"Yo, Zach." The slug to my arm yanked me out of my murderous thoughts and back into the present. "I said your name like ten times."

I blinked, trying to clear the red from my vision. "What?"

Connor's brows pulled together as his gaze bounced between my face and the chokehold I had on the steering wheel. A few more seconds and I might have ripped the damn thing right off. "What's with you? You look like you want to rip somebody's spleen out through their eye socket all of a sudden." He wasn't too far off the mark. He turned to look out the windshield. "What's gotten into—oh shit," he said as soon as he spotted Rae. He ripped his sunglasses off and scooted forward in the seat to get a better look. "*Damn.* That's her, isn't it?" He let out a sharp whistle, twisting his neck to shoot me a shit-eating grin. "Can't fault your tastes, brother. She's gorgeous."

The muscle in my jaw was ticking like crazy. "Shut

the fuck up," I ground out as I worked to unlock my molars. "And get the hell out of my truck."

Connor climbed out, the asshole laughing as he slammed the door, drawing the attention of Rae and Raylan. My focus was so consumed with the woman that it was impossible for me to miss the way the color rose in her cheeks when she spotted me. I also didn't miss the way she quickly dropped her hand from Raylan's arm and took a step backward as I got closer. It helped to settle some of the irrational anger that had started churning inside of me. But not all of it.

Raylan, clueless to just how close he'd come to being physically maimed, recognized Connor as he bounded up the back stairs. The few times Con had come out to the ranch for a visit, Raylan had joined us for a couple beers, and the two of them had hit it off. "Hey, man. Didn't know you were in town." He clapped Connor's offered hand and pulled him in for a quick slap on the back.

"No one did. Surprised this one the other day when I showed up out of the blue." He hiked his thumb over his shoulder in my direction as I climbed the three steps up to the deck at a much slower pace.

"Well, it's good to see you."

"You too. It's been too long." Connor turned his attention to Rae, offering her that charming-ass smile of his that earned him countless ad campaigns and no shortage of bedmates. "I'm Connor." He extended his hand toward Rae.

The acid in my stomach threatened to travel up my throat as she reached out and wrapped her fingers around his, giving his hand a shake. "Rae. Nice to meet you."

"Oh, the pleasure's all mine, I assure you."

Christ, what was the deal with all my friends wanting to die today?

A low growl worked its way up from my chest, and I swear, it only made him grin that much bigger.

Raylan jerked his chin up at me in silent acknowledgement as I joined their little huddle. "We should hit up the Tap Room tonight," Raylan said, clapping Connor on the shoulder again and giving him a little jostle. "You know you can always count me in for a good time. Matter of fact, I was trying to talk Rae here into hitting town later on to cut loose for a bit."

Her blush grew, staining her cheeks an even deeper red. "Oh, um, I don't know." She danced around the invitation, her gaze darting all over the place, almost as if she were too nervous for it to land on me. "I'm kind of tired."

"Come on, boss." Raylan grinned and nudged me with his elbow like it was a given that I'd side with him.

"Tell her she should go out with us. We're a hell of a lot of fun."

Normally I would have agreed. Raylan knew how to have a good time, that was for damn sure, but as I forced myself to look away from a blushing Rae, my eyes narrowed menacingly. "If she said she doesn't want to go, she doesn't want to go. End of discussion."

His chin jerked back at my tone, his brow furrowing in confusion. I couldn't really blame him. To most of my friends, I was known as the easy-going one. I'd rid myself of the habit of being quick to anger a long time ago, but something about the woman standing less than three feet away threw me so off balance, I couldn't tell which end was up.

Sensing shit was spiraling out of control, Con finally decided to stop being an asshole and cut me some slack. "Come on, man," he said to Raylan, leading the way back toward the door he'd exited only a minute ago. "I don't know about you, but I'm starvin'. Let's get some grub."

Raylan shook off the awkwardness easily enough. "Sounds good." They started back into the lodge, but stopped so Raylan could look back over his shoulder. "Hey, Rae, just let me know what time works best for you."

She graced him with another smile that I had no

reason to be pissed about, but I wasn't feeling particularly rational at the moment. "Thanks. I really appreciate that, Raylan. I'm excited."

My gaze ping-ponged between the two of them. "What's going on? What are you excited about?"

"Ivy suggested I ask Raylan for horseback riding lessons." She bounced on the tips of her toes, her excitement palpable.

"I can teach you." The words spilled out, sounding a lot more like an order than a suggestion.

Rae's eyes went big, her lips parting to form an O. "I-I couldn't ask you to do that. Really. You're so busy—"

"It's no problem."

Raylan cut in, taking his life into his own hands as he said, "I really don't mind. It's kind of my job."

For some reason, the thought of letting another man teach Rae to ride a horse made my skin prickle uncomfortably. If Raylan did it, he'd get to touch her. He'd get to spend time with her, just the two of them and the animal. It set my teeth on edge.

"You got guests to take care of," I clipped before getting a hold of myself and pulling in a deep breath, hoping to calm the raging waters inside of me. "You focus on the paying guests. I can take care of Rae," I said, the finality in my words leaving no room for argument.

One thing was for sure. Connor was never going to

let me live this shit down. He'd hold my crazy-ass behavior over my head for eternity. He'd probably even tell Raylan why I was acting like a jackass, and the two of them would enjoy giving me hell together.

But as I finally caught Rae's gaze, her excitement still showing in the beautiful curl of her lips, I really couldn't find it in me to care.

Chapter Thirteen

Rae

I regretted my decision to take up horseback riding as soon as Zach adjusted the stirrup and helped hoist me onto the back of his horse, Roam.

"You have to try to relax," he said for the third time in less than a minute. His voice was low and soft, and would have been soothing if I wasn't currently freaking the hell out.

Roam shook his head, tossing his mane, and made a noise that sounded distinctly unhappy. He wanted me on his back about as much as I wanted to be there.

"That's really easy for you to say when you're all the way down there, and I'm *all the way up here*." No one told me I would be so high off the ground when I got on the back of this damn thing. I took my eyes off the horizon and looked down the three stories to the ground where Zach was standing at my side to see him fighting a smirk. My eyes bulged out of their sockets. "You think this is funny? I'm like, a bagillion feet off the ground! If I fall off, I'm going to break my neck."

"You're not gonna fall, I swear. I won't let you, Hollywood." His hand came up and rested on my knee, the touch was meant to be grounding, but instead, a shock of static electricity bolted through my system. When I'd shown up at the corral for our riding lesson and found him waiting for me, my heart took off at a dangerously fast gallop. It had done the same thing the day before when he showed up at the lodge just as Raylan and I were discussing my taking riding lessons.

I had hoped that the few days away, working at Second Hope, would have been enough to tamp down the juvenile high school crush I'd formed on the man, but no such luck. Being close to him made my mouth dry and my brain fuzzy. It had been difficult to focus on anything else, especially when he'd grabbed the brim of the baseball cap he was wearing and spun it around so the ranch logo on the front faced backward. I was convinced that the most evil thing a sexy man could do was twist his ballcap backward. It hit a lady right in her nether regions.

I'd been struck dumb the moment he'd done it, at least until I threw myself up onto Roam's back. Then all my focus shifted from Zach to center on the ground that looked really hard and unforgiving from my incredible height.

"You can't promise that. This horse doesn't feel like he's a fan of me being up here. What if he throws me? Human bodies bounce, Zach. They bounce!"

"Roam isn't going to throw you, sweetheart. It's why I chose him. And no, he's not real happy with you at the moment, but he's makin' that known by pawin' at the ground. See?"

I leaned over just a few centimeters to watch as Roam dug at the dirt with his front hoof.

"He's communicating with you, Rae, tellin' you to calm down and quit squeezin' him to death."

I let out a shuddered breath. "I'm not squeezing—"

"With your thighs. You need to unclench."

I tried to do as he said, but panicked when Roam shifted his big body. "If I loosen up I'll slide right out of the saddle the first time he takes a step."

Zach looked at me consideringly before ordering, "Move forward."

"*What?*"

His eyes met mine, that decadent, rich brown penetrating so deep it felt like he was seeing every little thing I tried so hard to keep hidden. "Trust me, Rae." It wasn't an order or a command, it almost sounded like a plea. "I won't let anything happen to you." Every instinct told me I could believe him, that he meant what he said. He must have seen it on my face, because his features grew gentle, almost tender, as he repeated, "Now, move forward and take your feet out of the stirrups."

I did as he said, shifting closer to the saddle horn until I had nowhere else to go. A moment later, Zach was lifting himself up and coming to rest right behind me, so close his body heat sank through the clothing separating us and soaked into my skin. His scent filled my nostrils. Clean cotton and leather and earth, along with something spicy and decidedly male. I wanted to twist around in the saddle and bury my face in his neck, breathing deeply until I could identify the smell.

He reached up and placed his hands on my ribs on either side, his big hands wrapping around me. "How does this feel?" I had to try really hard not to focus on the way his breath skated across my neck and stirred my hair as he spoke close to my ear and concentrate on the pressure he was applying.

"It . . . it doesn't feel like much of anything."

His grip grew a little tighter. "Okay, and what about now?"

"It feels like you're trying to hold on."

In the next breath, his hold grew so tight it threatened to squeeze the air from my lungs. "And now?"

I pulled in a sharp gasp. "Like you're trying to crush my ribs."

As fast as it came, the pressure disappeared, but instead of removing his hands completely, Zach trailed them downward until they settled in the dip of my waist. I bit down on the inside of my cheek to keep in the whimper that wanted to break free at his touch.

God, I *really* needed to get it together.

"Exactly. See how tense you are right now, Roam can feel every single bit of it. If you want to get him to trust you, you have to put your trust in him. Now, I want you to loosen your hold." His hands came down on my jean clad thighs, causing my breath to hitch. There was no way he could have missed the shiver that worked its way through my body, but he was gentleman enough not to point it out. "Only put as much pressure as I did that second time. That and the stirrups are all you need in order to hold on."

I did my best to loosen my muscles, easing the tension in my legs. Just like he had the last time I loosened up, Roam shifted his considerable weight, but with Zach behind me, it was easier to not be so scared.

"Good. That's him telling you he likes this better.

He'll communicate with his body. It's your job to listen. Now, put your feet back in the stirrups."

"A-are you sure?"

Zach's hands traveled around to my front, his arms surrounding me completely as he pressed his palm into my belly, bringing my back more firmly against the solid mass of his wide chest. From this position it was impossible not to feel every dip and ridge of the countless muscles beneath his shirt. The man's body felt like it had been chiseled out of marble.

"I've got you, Rae," he assured me quietly, speaking against the shell of my ear. "I'm right here. I won't let anything happen to you."

I didn't have a doubt in my mind that what he said was true. He wasn't going to let any harm come to me on top of this horse. I felt the certainty of that in my bones as I shifted my legs to hook my feet back into the stirrups.

"Good girl," he breathed, and something about those words, the praise behind them, lit a fire deep in my belly. "Now give him a light tap against his ribs with your heel."

I did as he said, setting Roam into motion, and even though we'd only started at a slow canter, my heart felt like it had taken off at a sprint.

I GUIDED Roam back toward the barn, the same smile I'd been wearing the past half hour still stretched across my face. I was starting to think the smile was permanent.

Once I'd gotten over my initial fears, I'd quickly discovered a newfound love for riding. By the end of the lesson, Zach had taken the reins and kicked Roam off into a full gallop. It felt like I was flying.

I'd never felt anything more freeing, more exhilarating in my entire life. With Zach holding on to me, keeping me safe, I'd been able to truly let go and put all my faith in the animal beneath me. Zach had been right. Roam was a sweet and gentle horse, and as we made our way slowly back to the barn, with Zach back on the ground, leading me and Roam by the reins, I felt comfortable on his back by myself. Not enough to take off at a fast run, mind you, but I could have gone a few laps comfortably, just the two of us.

I leaned forward in the saddle as Roam's hooves slip-clomped against the floor of the barn and gave his neck a gentle rub.

"You really are a good boy, huh?" I crooned softly. "Such a good speckled-butt boy."

Zach's chuckle carried up to me as he brought us to a stop. "He's an Appaloosa."

I sat up tall and looked down at him in confusion. "Huh?"

"The markings. He's an Appaloosa."

"Oh." I curled my lips between my teeth to hide my smile. "Got it. But I still think I prefer speckled-butt. What do you say, Roam?"

He let out a gust of air from his nostrils that sounded an awful lot like a harrumph. Zach's lips curled up into a grin as he arched a brow. "Pretty sure that means he's not a fan."

"Whatever," I said with a teasing roll of my eyes. "I'll save my affectionate nicknames for Sassy then. At least she seems to enjoy them."

Each evening after getting off work, I'd come down to the barn to see the horses, but to spend time with Sassy in particular. I wasn't sure what it was about her that I was so drawn to, but I felt a kindred spirit in the animal that I almost swore she felt as well. From what I heard, she was still full of attitude with all the other hands, and while she didn't hesitate to show me a bit of the fire that earned her name, she was never anything but affectionate. My favorite time of day was that quiet hour in the barn, just the two of us. Whether work had been good or bad, she made it all disappear.

"She does seem to be a fan," Zach said with a jerk of his chin. I followed his line of sight to Sassy's stall, and sure enough, her head peeked over the door, her big black eyes trained in my direction. She let out a chuff and tossed her mane as if to say *"What the hell, lady?"*

"I think she might be a little jealous I went out on Roam today," I said with a laugh.

"Probably," Zach agreed, humor in his voice. "She doesn't really strike me as the kind of animal who's big on sharing. "Come on. I'll help you down." He reached up, circling my waist with his large hands. Sparks went off in my belly like I just ate a whole bag of pop rocks as the rough pads of his fingers brushed the patch of exposed skin on my side where my T-shirt had ridden up. There was nothing sexual about the touch whatsoever, yet it still lit me up in a way no other man's touch ever had.

My breathing grew choppy as he slowly lowered me, the soft curves of my body dragging across the rock-hard wall of his. My nipples pebbled. My core twisted. I wasn't sure my knees would be able to hold me once he let go, and it had nothing to do with being on horseback. Sure enough, my legs wobbled beneath me as soon as my boots hit the ground, and had Zach not been holding onto me, I wasn't sure I wouldn't have landed right on my ass on the dusty floor.

Zach's fingers pressed deeper into my skin as his eyes darted between mine, drilling impossibly deeper before traveling down to my mouth. The brown of his eyes grew even darker as his pupils expanded, the black swallowing up all color. I'd seen that look on men's faces before. I knew when they were attracted to me, desired me. But it had never felt this intense. This . . . combustible. It felt like one move would be all it took to set the world around us ablaze.

I was lost in his gaze, happy to stay locked inside of it. Unfortunately, whatever spell weaved around us was broken when Roam, having apparently had enough of being ignored, butted Zach in the back with his nose.

I cleared my throat, blinking back into reality quickly as I took two shaky steps back. Nerves suddenly gripped me tightly as I forced my gaze from his, letting it bounce around the barn. "Uh, th-thank you. For the riding lesson. It was . . . I had a lot of fun."

He pulled his hat off, smacking it against his strong thigh as he raked a hand through his short hair. "Yeah. No problem," he muttered before putting it back on, brim forward this time. "Just let me know when you want to go again."

I wasn't sure if continuing our lessons was the smartest thing, but I also knew I didn't want them to stop. I *liked* spending time with him. We might have gotten off to a rocky start, but I was finally seeing the side of him that Hal and Lennix had both assured me was there. He was funny and clever. He was smart and kind, hands down the hardest worker I'd ever known. He cared for the people he employed, for his family, for the animals on his ranch. The more I got to know him, the more I discovered there was a lot to like. The more I realized he was all good, down to his very core.

"Yeah, okay. I will. Thank you."

I took another step back, prepared to turn and hightail it out of the barn when he spoke again. "Will you be at dinner at the lodge tonight?"

"Oh, no. I've been meaning to go into town for a few days now to get groceries and some other stuff."

He took a step closer. "Do you need me to come with you? I know you don't really know your way around town."

He was right about that, and while I would have loved to spend even more time in his company, I knew I needed to put some space between us until I could get my head on straight. I'd made way too many stupid decisions in my life, and I didn't want Zach to be another. He was too good a person. He deserved better than me.

"No, thank you. Lennix gave me directions." I offered him a small smile as I slowly pivoted on the heel of my boot. "But I appreciate the offer."

"Yeah, of course."

I told myself I was only imagining the way his expression seemed to fall before I turned away and headed toward the row of ranch trucks parked along the side of the barn . . . it was all in my head that he seemed almost disappointed.

Chapter Fourteen

Rae

It was only after exiting the barn, the heat of the sun spreading across my skin, that I was able to pull in a full breath. There was something so damn potent about Zach Paulson, that it consumed everything. I needed to get the hell out of there.

I hustled toward the nearest truck, letting out a relieved sigh when I found it unlocked. Hopping into the driver's seat, I flipped the visor down and caught the key ring before it fell in my lap. I shoved the key into the ignition and twisted but nothing happened. "What the hell?" I tried again with the same outcome. "Oh, come on," I groaned. "Not now." Not when I was so close to escaping.

I looked around, finally noticing that the gearshift looked different and there were three pedals instead of two. "Just freaking great. How the hell am I supposed to drive this thing?"

"You have to push in the clutch."

I let out a startled shriek and whipped around to find Zach standing on the other side of the closed door, only just noticing the driver's side window was down. "What?"

"The truck. It's got a manual transmission. You have to push in the clutch to start it."

"Oh." My gaze bounced between the pedals trying to understand what he was attempting to explain to me. "Um . . . okay." I recognized the gas pedal and the brake, so I could only assume the pedal on the far left was the clutch. I pushed it in and twisted the key again. This time, the truck started up on a deep rumble, the engine so powerful I felt the seat vibrate beneath me. "Got it."

I grabbed the gearshift and tried to move it only for it to make the worst screeching sound imaginable. "Jesus! What was that?"

Zach didn't bother hiding the smile on his face. "Never driven a stick before?"

I shot him a side-eyed look, lifting my brows high on my forehead. "Is that supposed to be a sex joke?"

His head fell back on a deep laugh, the pleasant sound causing my core to clench. On top of having the best ass I'd ever seen on a man, he also had the sexiest throat. Until that very moment, I hadn't even known it was possible to consider a throat sexy, but his was. All thick and strong and corded, in perfect proportion with his broad, solid shoulders. Honestly, *everything* about the man was sexy as hell. "No, it wasn't a sex joke. Come on." He grabbed the handle and pulled my door open. "Scoot over. I'll drive you."

Damn my heart and its inability to maintain a normal rate in this man's presence. If it kept up like this, I was liable to have a heart attack before I reached twenty-five. "You don't have to," I blurted out quickly. "I mean, it's really not necessary. I'm sure I can figure it out." To prove my point, I grabbed the shifter again, only to grind the gears for a second time.

"I'll teach you to drive a stick, but it'll take some time for you to get it. And I thought you needed groceries," he challenged with cocked brow.

I shot him a glare for being so damn smug and grumbled, "Fine. But I want to learn. I don't want to be dependent on everyone here. People will get sick and tired of me coming to them for every little thing I can't do." I hadn't meant for all of that to spill out. I'd let my frustration at feeling helpless get the best of me and showed more of my hand than I'd intended.

His brow furrowed as he shook his head. "I don't know what it was like back in California, but that's not how it works here. We take care of each other here. If someone needs help, we help. That's all there is to it."

I narrowed my eyes, my turn to issue a challenge as I replied, "Like you did when I first got here?" He broke eye contact, dropping his head as if in shame, and I instantly felt bad for throwing that in his face. "I'm sorry. I shouldn't have said—"

"Stop." My mouth snapped shut. "Don't apologize to me. You weren't wrong. I was an asshole when you first got here. If anyone needs to apologize, it's me."

"It's forgotten," I stated quickly, kicking myself for even bringing up the past.

"But is it forgiven?" he asked quietly.

I swallowed, my mouth suddenly feeling like it was full of cotton. "Of course. It's all forgiven. I won't bring it up again." I shifted over on the bench seat of the truck, eager to disable the tension swirling around us. "Now, get up here and drive me to the grocery store already." My lips curved upward into a grin. "I don't have all day."

The drive to the grocery store was made in silence, but there was something companionable about it. It wasn't awkward or charged. It was as if we were comfortable enough with each other to be in the present, no need for mindless chatter to fill the minutes. It was nice, being able to watch the landscape, so different than what

I was used to, pass by as we left the ranch and headed into town.

We rode with the windows down, the fresh, pleasant breeze filling the cab as some country song played at a low volume on the radio. I couldn't remember a time in my life when I'd felt so content, so at peace. Back in L.A., it had been a constant battle with my so-called friends to constantly one-up each other, to always be on top. There was nothing calm or settling about that life. You were either planning how to bring someone down or constantly looking over your shoulder, waiting for someone to plunge a knife in your back.

I was finally starting to understand why my parents sent me here and what lessons they were hoping I'd learn once I got away from that viper pit I'd been living in for so many years.

I couldn't help but smile at the number of people who waved at our passing truck as Zach wound it through the streets of downtown Hope Valley. "Man, you're really popular in this town, aren't you?" I observed with a small laugh after Zach lifted his hand from the wheel to return a wave for the tenth time.

"It's more my family than me. They've been here for generations."

I gave him an assessing glance. "I don't know about that. I think you might be selling yourself short." He let out a hum, but didn't say anything more about it as he guided us toward the local market.

Fresh Foods wasn't some big chain grocery store like you'd see in the city. It was much smaller, but as I slowly perused the aisles, scanning the shelves as Zach pushed the cart behind me, I was happy to see that the selection wasn't lacking just because it wasn't some huge warehouse that sold everything from women's sandals to potato chips.

The wine selection was surprisingly good, and I was excited to find they even had a section of different kinds of artisan cheeses.

"You know you're gonna need more than just wine and cheese, right?" Zach pointed out as I tossed a wedge of Manchego and a wheel of a delicious looking white truffle goat cheese.

I shot him a look over my shoulder. "Says who?"

"Doctors and dieticians, I'm sure." He grinned and shook his head as I placed a bottle of cabernet into the cart gently, like it was my most prized possession. And after so many days of peanut butter and that god-awful bourbon, it really was. "You're either going to clog your arteries or develop a drinking problem at this rate."

"Okay, fine, bossy. I'll get other stuff too." With a huff, I forced my feet to move out of what would undoubtedly be my favorite section of the store.

"Do you have a list?" he asked as I started pulling random things from shelves as we moved along the aisles. So far I had a box of dried pasta, a loaf of sourdough bread, a single can of green beans, a bag of trail mix, and a couple boxes of cereal. I turned to find him staring down at the contents of my cart in confusion.

"A list for what?"

He lifted those chocolatey eyes to mine—which reminded me, I needed to grab some chocolate too—and raised his brows high on his forehead. "A grocery list. So you know what you need." He waved his hand over the cart. "I'm not sure what the hell you're plannin' on making with all this, Hollywood, but I don't think it's gonna taste very good."

I stared at the items I'd thrown into the cart. Honestly, I wasn't sure what the hell I was doing. I didn't know how to cook to save my life. Back in L.A., I lived off takeout and dining out at whatever restaurant was the hot spot to be seen in at the moment. I paid someone else to handle the shopping whenever I needed my fridge or pantry stocked.

A blush crawled up my cheeks and the tips of my ears started to burn. Curling my lips between my teeth, I looked up at Zach from beneath my lashes and shrugged. "I've never shopped for my own groceries before."

His mouth dropped open wide enough for a family

of flies to move in. "You're kidding me." He let out a bark of bewildered laughter. "You've never grocery shopped before?"

My expression fell into a frown as I crossed my arms over my chest defensively. "Don't make fun of me."

His smile fell instantly. He released the cart handle and rounded it, heading right for me. "Hey," he said quietly, reaching up and taking me by my upper arms. His gentle touch was a contrast to his work-rough palms. In that moment I realized every man who'd touched me before Zach—not that there were many at all—had soft, perfectly manicured hands. My skin broke out in goosebumps as he trailed those hands down to my elbows and back up in a tender caress, a shiver working its way across my spine. I was pretty sure that one touch had ruined me for all soft-handed men from here on out. "Never." He said that one word with such earnestness that it rattled through me. "I would never make fun of you, Rae. I'll tease you, sure, but I will *never* make fun of you. You have to believe that."

I did, actually. I wasn't sure if it was the passion of his declaration or the intensity in his gaze, but I believed him.

I swallowed in an effort to ease my dry throat. "Okay," I said on a croak. "I believe you."

God, this man really wasn't helping me get over my

crush. Especially when he smiled like I'd given him the best gift ever. Like how he was smiling at me just then.

"Good. Come on, then. I'll help you out. We'll get you set up with some staples every house should have, and I'll show you some quick, easy-to-make meals that consist of more than just wine and cheese."

He could knock my wine and cheese all he wanted, but there was nothing better at the end of a long day than a bubble bath with a glass of wine and a cheese plate, and that was a hill I was willing to die on.

We went aisle by aisle, filling the cart with enough food to hold me over for a while. He tossed out my canned vegetables in exchange for fresh produce. When I argued, he simply gave me a look—the one that looked a whole lot like the look my mom used to give me when I was little and bitched about eating my vegetables—and kept on walking, tossing in more fresh, leafy greens as he went.

In the past twenty-four hours Zach Paulson had insisted on teaching me to ride a horse, promised to teach me to drive a stick shift, and was now talking about how he'd help me learn my way around the kitchen so I could cook for myself.

Given his gift for filling out a pair of faded Wranglers and all those hard, defined muscles, it was clear that if ever there was a perfect man on this planet, Zach was it. The fact that he looked the way he looked *and* could cook was enough to seal it, even if he didn't have the world's most incredible ass.

And speaking of his ass . . . he'd trailed ahead of me in the produce section while I pouted over a head of broccoli, and now that it was in clear view, I was tush-struck.

"It's not gonna kill you to eat more fruits and—" He turned around mid-rant and caught me red-handed, so to speak. A cheeky smile tugged at his lips. "Were you just staring at my ass?"

My entire face caught on fire. My eyes bugged out, and every word I'd ever learned fell right out of my head. "I—what? *No!* Of course not. I wouldn't. That's not—" I blew out a raspberry before a hysterical cackle burst past my lips. "Please. Get over yourself."

"You were! You were totally checking out my ass." His laugh filled the produce section. I would never get tired of hearing that sound.

"Shut up," I grumbled, embarrassment heating my entire body from the inside out. "You know, a gentleman wouldn't make a big deal out of it."

His grin grew cheeky, causing my thighs to clench involuntarily. "That's your mistake for thinking I'm—"

I wasn't sure what he'd been about to say, but whatever it was, the words died on his tongue at the same time all the color drained from his face, leaving him looking a sickly shade of white. His gaze shifted from me to something over my shoulder, and it was as if he suddenly disappeared on me. Like his mind had taken him somewhere else.

He went from laughing one second to looking like he'd come down with the flu the very next. His skin even had a slight sheen to it, like sweat had beaded along his forehead.

"Zach?" I said his name quietly, carefully taking a step in his direction. "Are you okay? What's going on?"

His throat worked on a thick, audible swallow as he kept his gaze trained behind me. I turned to see what he was staring at, but other than a wall of fresh produce, all I caught a glimpse of was a person's back as they disappeared around the corner.

I shifted my focus back to Zach, worry prickling my skin at the way his chest was heaving like he was struggling to take in a full breath.

"Zach," I tried again, but it was as if an empty vessel was standing in front of me. "Zach!" I gripped his arms and gave him a shake, letting out a breath of relief when he finally blinked, the focus returning back to his eyes as he looked down at me. "Are you okay? What just happened?"

"Nothing. I-I have to go," he said, taking two steps

backward, like he was preparing to take off at a dead sprint.

My chin jerked back in shock. "What?"

"I just remembered, I have somewhere I have to be. But I'll call Lennix and have her come pick you up."

"Wait. Zach." That didn't make any damn sense. I didn't know who or what he just saw, but whatever it was had been enough to scare him in a way I'd never seen before. "Talk to me. What's going on?"

"I'm sorry, Rae. I'll see you back at the ranch."

That was all he gave me before turning on the heel of his dusty boot and taking off toward the exit like the hounds of hell were nipping at his heels.

Chapter Fifteen

Rae

A small red two-door coupe pulled up to the curb in front of where I was sitting, surrounded by shopping bags I'd paid for on auto pilot after Zach ditched me in the middle of a grocery store I'd never been to before in a town I wasn't familiar with. The driver side door opened and Lennix climbed from behind the wheel. "Hey. Everything okay?" she asked as she rounded the hood and met me on the sidewalk. "Zach just called and said you needed a ride, but he hung up before I could get a word out."

I stood up and dusted the seat of my pants off, still trying to piece together what the hell had happened earlier. "I . . . don't know, honestly. He insisted on driving me here when we both discovered I didn't have a clue how to drive a standard transmission. Everything was fine, we were shopping and joking around, then it was like he just shut off."

Lennix's brow furrowed deeper, concern for her older brother carved into the planes of her face. "Shut off? What do you mean?"

I shook my head, not fully understanding it myself. I wasn't sure if I should be worried about him or mad that he'd bailed. "It was the strangest thing. He was fine one moment, and the next it looked like he'd seen a ghost."

She pulled her bottom lip between her teeth, biting down hard as the worry on her face grew. "But you didn't see anything out of the ordinary? He didn't say anything?"

"No. He just said that he suddenly remembered he had to do something, then he took off, leaving me here by myself."

I watched as she worried her bottom lip between her teeth. I could practically see the wheels turning in her head before she seemed to shake everything off and reach down to grab some of my bags. "Let's get this stuff back to your place before it spoils."

The two of us loaded my groceries into her trunk then made the drive back to the ranch. This time the silence was nearly unbearable. The tension was so thick it could have been cut with a knife.

With each passing minute, the uncertainty of how I

was supposed to feel swayed closer and closer toward concern as I recalled the fear etched into every line of Zach's strong frame.

As soon as Lennix parked in front of my cabin, I said a quick thank you for the ride and grabbed all my bags from the trunk, looping the handles over my arms so I only had to make one trip. I gave her a wave over my shoulder and rushed inside, making quick work of putting everything away. I stuffed the food into the fridge and cabinets in no particular order before heading out the door once again.

As I got closer to Zach's house, I noticed his truck parked out front. The windows were dark as I made my way up the porch stairs to the front door, but I knocked anyway, my heart racing and my throat growing tight. I needed to make sure he was all right. After a minute passed with no answer, I pressed my ear to the wood, straining to hear signs of life on the other side, but there was no noise coming from the other side.

"Zach?" I called out, anxiety gripping at my chest as I knocked again, but I still got nothing. With a sigh of defeat, I started back in the direction of my cabin, but instead of going inside, I passed right by it and headed toward the barn instead. I knew if I went home I'd just pace the floor and worry. Fortunately, Sassy had a way of leveling me out when my day wasn't going as planned.

Her head peeked over her stall door as I entered the barn and flipped the lights on, her big black eyes landing on me like she had been anticipating my arrival.

"Hey there, pretty girl," I said gently, rubbing a hand up her muzzle to her forehead as she snuffed around my waist, trying to get at my pockets for the peppermints I always kept on hand whenever I came to visit her. "I'm sorry. I forgot your treats today."

She made a chuffing sound like she understood what I said and was making her displeasure known.

I smiled when she butted me with the side of her head and tugged at my hair with her lips. "You really are living up to your name today, aren't you, sassy girl?" Another bump of her snout had me holding my hands up in surrender. "All right, fine. I give in. Let me see if I can find any peppermints around here."

I moved through the barn toward the feed room to see if Hal had anything stashed back there. Sure enough, there was a big bag of individually wrapped peppermints sitting on a shelf along the far wall. I grabbed a handful and started back out to Sassy's when a loud thunk from a couple stalls down drew me up short.

I moved in the direction the noise had come from, glancing over the door to Roam's stall. "Zach?" I grabbed the latch and yanked the door open. "What the hell are you doing?" I demanded at the sight of the man sitting on the floor of his horse's stall.

He looked up at me with a goofy grin on his face, his eyes bloodshot and bleary. "*Heeeey*, pretty lady."

I moved toward him, giving Roam a pat and a gentle shove out of the way so I could get to his owner. "Why are you on the floor?"

He looked around at his surroundings like he was just noticing where he was for the first time. "I think I fell down."

As soon as he spoke, I reared back at the stench of cheap, stale booze on his breath and leaching from his pores. "Oh my God, you smell like a dumpster that's been drenched in gasoline and set on fire."

Zach lifted the bottle clutched in his hand. It was that same brand of disgusting bourbon that I'd found stashed in my cabin. He put it to his mouth and took a giant swig before I was able to grab it out of his hands.

"All right, I think you've had enough." I gagged when I was hit with another whiff from the bottle. "I didn't take you for a fan of cheap booze that would burn a hole through your stomach lining." I shook the bottle in his face, my top lip curling up in disgust. "This stuff is terrible, Zach. If you're going to tie one on, at least do it respectfully. What, you didn't have any battery acid on hand?"

He lifted a shoulder in a shrug and listed to the side, nearly toppling over. "It's some shit Hal left in the tack room," he slurred. "Stuff's awful, but it'll get the job done."

I wanted to pry, to ask him why he felt the need to get shit-faced after running out on me in the grocery store, but there were more pressing matters at hand, such as getting him off the floor before Roam accidentally stepped on him and went out of the barn.

"How full was this when you got a hold of it?" I asked, inspecting the bottle that was barely a quarter full.

Zach's hands came up before flopping back down at his sides. "Dunno. A lot."

Something in his eyes tugged at my heart, creating an ache I couldn't rub out. There was a sadness lingering behind the haze of alcohol. A pain I couldn't even begin to understand.

"Come on, big guy." I pushed to my feet, holding my hand out to him. "I think it's time we get you to bed, yeah?"

He heaved out a sigh and dropped his head back, thumping it against the rough wooden wall. "You look like an angel," he slurred softly. "Did you come to save me?"

"Do you need saving?" I asked, tilting my head to the side in concern.

"Who the fuck knows? But I'll tell you what I *do* need. More booze."

He reached for the bottle I was still holding, but there was no way I was letting him have it. It was already going to be a struggle to get his drunken ass back to his house. One more sip and he was liable to pass the hell out. Sure, I had a crush on the guy, but that didn't mean I wanted to sleep in a freaking barn just so I could make sure he didn't choke on his own vomit in the middle of the night. I might not be living with the same comforts as I had in L.A. but a girl had to draw the line somewhere.

"Not a chance in hell." I exited the stall just long enough to throw the bottle in a nearby trash can before going back for my drunken boss. "You're done for the night." I grabbed his hand in both of mine and let out a grunt as I tried to pull his considerable bulk off the floor. "Work with me here, would you? I can't do this all by myself." I heaved again to no avail. Instead of trying to help, he started singing some country song, and even though I didn't recognize it, I was pretty sure he was getting at least half the words wrong. "Damn it, Zach." I let out a frustrated huff and blew a strand of hair out of my face. "Get your feet under you, or so help me God, I'll let you spend the night out here with Roam."

The horse in question whinnied like he wasn't a fan of the idea of sharing his bed with anyone else. And given the way Zach smelled just then, I didn't really blame him.

It took two more tries, but he finally cooperated and wobbled to his feet as I yanked on his arm. Roam nudged at him like he was worried for his owner. That made two of us. Still, I assured the big, gentle giant. "It's okay, big guy. He'll be fine. He just needs to sleep it off. He'll be good as new tomorrow." Depending on how bad the hangover was.

His arm lay heavy over my shoulders as I began to shuffle us out of the barn, nearly tripping over my own feet when I felt his nose nuzzle into my hair and inhale deeply.

"Mmm," he hummed pleasurably, a deep rumble that made my belly swoop and my core squeeze. "You smell so good." He inhaled again. "Always smell so good. It drives me crazy."

I let out a shaky exhale, telling myself that these were just the drunk ramblings of a guy who'd gone through something earlier that day and not to take anything he said to heart. It would lead nowhere good, that was for damn sure.

It took double the amount of time it should have to get from the barn to Zach's house, and more than once, I was afraid he was going to fall right over and squish me underneath him. "You know, when you decide to tie one on, you go big," I grunted as I struggled to keep us both upright and shuffling in the right direction. "You barely had an hour to get this drunk after you left me at the grocery store."

A pained sound expelled from his chest as he leaned harder against me. "I'm so sorry, Hollywood. Never should've left you there," he slurred.

I tried to remember to lift with my legs as I hefted his weight more firmly on my shoulders. "It's all right."

"It's not. Was a dick move."

I cut my eyes sideways to look up at him in the deepening twilight. The sun hadn't quite lowered all the way just yet, but the moon and the stars were already starting to put on their show. The whiskers on Zach's jaw were longer this time of day. His eyes were dark, smudges of purple underneath that normally weren't there.

"Stop being so hard on yourself. At least you called Lennix to come get me."

He grunted, but I couldn't tell if it was in agreement or if he was still beating himself up. My cabin came into view just then, and Zach nearly threw us off balance when he turned, heading in that direction instead of his own house.

"Whoa, big guy. Come on. I need to get you home."

"Don't want to go there," he grumbled, digging his boots deeper into the ground to fight against my pull. "I'll stay with you."

My mouth dropped open, a sputtering sound coming out before I was able to form words. "But . . . there's nowhere for you to sleep, Zach. There's only one bed."

"Then I'll take the couch."

It was as if he was going out of his way to make this harder on me. "My couch isn't big enough for a grumpy cowboy your size. You'll wake up with a sore back and neck on top of the hangover you've already assured yourself."

"Don't care," he grunted. "I don't wanna be alone tonight."

God, he really was breaking my heart.

Letting out a sigh, I set us on the path to my cabin. I could have kept arguing, but I knew he still would have won in the end, so I didn't bother wasting time. "Let's get you to bed, then."

The muscles that I had been pushing to their limit gave out just as soon as we shoved through the cabin's door. I held out long enough to dump Zach onto the couch before my knees buckled. I plopped down on the coffee table.

Zach let out a sigh. "Smells just like you in here," he mumbled. "Could drown in that smell."

I did my best not to let his words affect me as he rested against the back of the couch, snuggling in like he wanted to surround himself with my scent. Drown in it like he'd just said.

I bent forward, lifting one of his legs up to pull his boot off. Of course, he didn't make it easy. I got one off and moved onto the next just as he leaned in so close he was all I could see.

"God, you're pretty," he said with a dreamy smile. "So damn pretty. Thought that the day you showed up. So goddamn pretty it hurt to look at you."

A flush crawled up my cheeks at the same time a million butterflies took flight in my belly. "All right, smooth guy. Time to pass out. Let's lie down."

I tried to shift him, but his hand came up, tangling in my hair and holding me in place, our faces so close our noses almost touched. "God, I've wondered what you taste like every day since you got here."

"Zach," I said, my voice pleading, though, I wasn't sure what I was begging for. For him to stop, or to close the last inch between us.

"Been dyin' to kiss you. Don't think I can wait another second."

With one hand in my hair, he used the other to tilt my chin up and sealed his lips to mine.

Chapter Sixteen

Zach

It felt like someone was using the inside of my skull like a steel drum. The sun cut through the window, searing my corneas the moment I made the mistake of opening my eyes. It took a while for me to figure out what woke me up, the disorientation creating a fog in my head that didn't seem to want to clear. Finally it hit me, the sound of whispered curses. And the smell of charred bacon. That was what had woken me up, and the moment realization of what I was smelling penetrated my consciousness, my stomach lurched.

"Shit," I grunted as I pushed up to sitting, breathing in through my nose and out past my lips slowly, trying my hardest not to puke. My back screamed at the motion and my neck felt stiff as a board. The couch I'd been sleeping on was only half my size, and definitely not something I had in my own house. Then a voice spoke up that caused my lungs to seize.

"Good morning. How are you feeling?"

I made the mistake of jerking my head around toward the kitchen at the back of the cabin, causing my brain to rattle and bang around inside my skull. "Oh, fuck me," I grunted, slamming my eyes closed and pressing my thumbs deep into their sockets to try and stop the stabbing pain.

"If you're going to be sick, I'm going to have to ask you to do it in the bathroom. I'm kind of a sympathy barfer."

I peeled my eyelids back open on a soothing inhale and looked to where Rae was standing in her kitchen, wielding a pair of tongs. "Is that a thing?"

She nodded seriously. "Sure is. You puke, I puke. That's just how it is."

Christ, why the fuck did I drink so much last night? Then I remembered, and the urge to get obliterated again reappeared.

"Don't worry. I'm not going to be sick." At least I hoped not. With the smell of charcoaled bacon filling up the room, that was still up in the air.

"My attempt at cooking failed miserably," she said as

she moved to the small kitchen window and pushed it up to let the smoke out and fresh air in. "But I do have some coffee, if you think you can handle it."

I needed coffee desperately, especially after the bender I'd gone on the night before—and Christ, I'd be lucky if that rot-gut bourbon had left any of my stomach lining behind—but despite being so drunk I couldn't stand on my own two feet, I'd been cursed with a memory good enough to recall all the events that had taken place while I was . . . impaired. The smartest thing I could do was get the hell out of there before I did something I'd regret. Well . . . something *else*.

Fuck me, but I couldn't believe I said all the things I said. I couldn't believe I'd *kissed her*. And of course it had to be the kind of kiss that would have had the power to knock me on my ass—if the booze hadn't managed to do it first. But it never should have happened.

The fact was, I had seriously fucked up. I was her boss; I was older. I was supposed to be the responsible one, and no matter the shape I'd been in, I had taken advantage of her.

I let out a weary sigh. "Look, Rae," I started as I pushed to my feet, noticing for the first time that they were bare, "About what happened last night."

"Oh, Zach. Don't worry about it. You don't—"

I cut her off, forcing the words past my lips. "It was a mistake." She froze in the midst of grabbing a coffee mug from one of the cabinets. Her back was to me, so I couldn't see the look on her face. I wasn't sure if that was a blessing or a curse. On one hand, I wanted to know how she was feeling, what she was thinking, but on the other, I was scared of what I might see. If she hated me for the shit I pulled the night before I didn't want to see it. I wasn't sure I'd survive seeing her look at me with disdain. "I sincerely regret what happened, and it'll never happen again," I continued, the bitterness on my tongue having nothing to do with the alcohol and everything to do with what I was saying.

It took several seconds before she moved. Her shoulders raised toward her ears as she closed the cabinet and placed the mug she'd retrieved on the counter. When she finally turned to face me, the expression on her face was indecipherable. Usually Rae gave away everything she was thinking or feeling with a single look, but I got nothing. I'd never seen her look so blank, and I could only assume I was to blame.

"Let's just pretend it never happened."

I studied her closely, looking for anything at all that might tell me how she was feeling. "You're sure?"

Her lips curved upward, but the infinitesimal smile

didn't come anywhere near her eyes. "Absolutely," she assured me. "You were drunk. It was nothing."

Hearing her disregard a kiss I wouldn't be forgetting any time soon was a punch to the gut, but I appreciated her letting me off the hook. How I'd behaved the night before, kissing her without permission, taking advantage of my position of authority, was deplorable. I hated myself for it. The hangover currently splitting my skull and churning in my gut was the least I deserved.

"Exactly," I agreed, the words making the twisting sensation in my stomach even worse. "Nothing at all."

Silence enveloped the cabin, the atmosphere growing thick and tense. Finally, I couldn't take it any longer. I needed to do us both a favor and get the fuck out of there before I made everything even worse.

"I should head out. But I appreciate you taking care of me last night. You didn't have to do that."

She dipped her head like she was hiding from me as she spoke softly, "It wasn't a big deal."

Maybe not to her. But it was to me. "Anyway, I'll get out of your hair." I threw my thumb over my shoulder awkwardly. "Enjoy the rest of your day."

"Zach," she called out when I turned and started for the door.

Hand on the knob, I looked back over my shoulder. "Yeah?"

She pointed at something near the sofa I'd slept uncomfortably on last night. "Your boots."

"Shit. Right. Thanks." So much for a graceful exit, I thought as I snatched my boots up and made quick work of pulling them on before bolting out the door. I headed straight for the shower as soon as I got home, washing off the stench of bourbon, the remnants of Roam's stall floor, and the shame from my body, scrubbing until my skin was bright pink.

The hangover was still in full force as I got dressed and downed a couple pain relievers with a cup of black coffee before grabbing the keys to my truck and heading out. It was only a matter of time before word of my behavior at the store yesterday, then my bender in the barn, spread around, if it hadn't already. I knew my parents would be upset if they found out about it through the grapevine instead of from me, so as badly as I wanted to head toward my spot by the river, I guided my truck in the opposite direction toward their house.

As it always was, the door was unlocked, opening wide for me as soon as I twisted the knob. "Anyone home?" I called out, pausing at the entryway and listening closely before moving deeper into the house. I'd walked in on them doing things no son should *ever* see his parents doing one too many times in my life. I knew better than to barge in when it wasn't a planned visit.

"Hey, sweetie," I heard my mom call back. But that wasn't good enough.

"Everyone's dressed, right? I'm not gonna see anything that'll cause me to need even more years of therapy, am I?"

Rory appeared in the entryway—fully clothed, thank the Lord above—drying her hands on a dishtowel. "Hi, honey. This is a nice surprise." She moved toward me, raising on her tiptoes to press a kiss to my cheek. I returned the gesture, pressing an affectionate kiss to the top of her head. "I'm making breakfast. You hungry? It's blueberry pancakes."

Rory's pancakes were the first thing she'd ever cooked for me, and they had been my favorite since that very first day twenty-three years ago. No matter how sick I felt, there was no way I'd say no to those pancakes.

"You already know the answer to that."

She smiled and waved me in. "Good. Come on in. Want some coffee? Just finished brewing a fresh pot."

"Definitely wouldn't say no to that."

"Hey, bud," Cord greeted as soon as I entered the kitchen. I moved to where he was sitting at the island and leaned in to give him a hug.

"Hey, Dad."

He leaned back, his eyes drilling into me, seeing beneath the surface like he always had. The first time I met Cord Paulson, he'd been chasing me down after I threw that rock through the window of the Tap Room. I could still recall the very visceral fear I felt as he ran after me. Cord Paulson was the biggest guy I'd ever seen. Not only physically, but his presence as well. He was strong as hell in every single way, and he made sure he was that way so he could take care of his family. That had included me from the moment he pulled me back into the bar and I'd given him and Rory my story. The whole ugly thing. That was the moment I'd become theirs.

"You look like hell," he stated in a no-nonsense tone, letting me know it wouldn't do a damn bit of good to lie. "What's going on?"

I took the stool beside his as Mom stacked pancakes on a plate beside a couple strips of bacon. Fortunately it was cooked properly this time, so my stomach didn't have the same convulsive reaction it did at Rae's house.

"Is something wrong?" She looked on with concern as I poured syrup and cut into the stack of pancakes. I shoved the first bite into my mouth, the familiarity of my favorite meal helping ease the tightness clutching at my chest since running out of Fresh Foods.

I swallowed and let out a sigh. "I saw Charles Caswell yesterday," I said without preamble, ripping the Band-Aid right off.

Rory's fork clattered to the counter, her face growing pale. "What? H-how?"

The headache behind my eyes was growing. Merely speaking that name out loud turned the little bit I'd eaten to lead. I pushed the plate away, unable to stomach another bite.

"It was at the market, yesterday. I took Rae to get some stuff and I saw him there."

Dad's hand came down on my shoulder, that touch releasing even more of the pressure from my chest. That was what they did for me. What parents did. For the first twelve years of my life I didn't think that was something I'd ever have. I never wanted to take what Rory and Cord gave me for granted. I'd told myself that being a part of this family had healed me, so why the hell was I so affected by one of the two people who hadn't been part of my life for more than two decades?

"Did something happen?"

I wrapped my hands around my coffee mug, staring down at the dark liquid inside and letting the heat seep into my palms, hoping it would warm the coldness inside.

"Not really," I answered him, giving my head a shake before taking a sip of coffee. "It was only for a split second. He was turning to go down another aisle. He didn't see me, but . . ."

"Go on," my father coaxed, giving me the nudge I needed.

"I had a panic attack in the middle of the store. I ran out of there like my ass was on fire, leaving Rae behind, I was so desperate to get the hell out of there, away from him."

"Did she get home okay?" Rory asked, her heart so big it was impossible not to care about the wellbeing of everyone around her.

I nodded. "I called Len before I pulled out of the parking lot, made sure she could pick her up."

"That's good," Mom said with a nod of relief. "At least you made sure she was safe first. I can't imagine she'd be upset about that."

"If she was upset, it didn't stop her from helping me out when she found me drunk on a bottle of cheap bourbon on the floor of Roam's stall."

"Oh, Zach." The sadness on her face was like a white-hot poker to the chest.

Cord was still watching me closely. "Explains why you came in here lookin' like stomped on horse shit."

I shot him a flat look as I took another sip of coffee. "Thanks so much for the sympathy, Dad."

He didn't look the least bit impressed. "You know you'll always have that from me, when it's deserved," he stated in the *dad* voice he'd perfected over the years.

"You have that from me about running into that piece of shit yesterday. I understand how seeing him could set you off like that, and there's not a damn bit of shame in your reaction, so get that out of your head right now, because I know that's where your thoughts are going."

Damn it. Of course he was right. He understood better than anyone what it had been like for me back then, since he'd been there himself. It was his story, along with my own, that inspired my mother to start Hope House.

Shortly after they brought me into their lives, Rory and Cord had started a foundation, and from there, they'd opened a group home for foster children. Hope House was a saving grace to kids in the system. More kids than I could count had called that place home in the years since its inception, and they'd all been given opportunities most kids in foster care never got. My parents were determined to make it a safe place, an actual home instead of some stopping point before another shuffle, or worse, another hellhole, of which there were far too many.

They hand-picked every single person they brought on to help run Hope House and care for the kids, making sure they were people who could be counted on, who were reliable, and who would break their backs to give the children in their care good lives.

They cared for the children they were charged with. They treated them like they would their own kids. There was no aging out of Hope House. One of the cruelest things that could happen to a foster kid was to turn eighteen and be shoved out of whatever home they were staying in without any prospects or skills or a single opportunity to help them become something. The people running the home made sure these kids were looking at bright futures.

Cord hadn't been as lucky as I was or the kids taken into Hope House. He'd aged out of the system, and with no other choices, he'd enlisted in the Navy to keep from being homeless. So if there was one person on this planet who could relate with me, who could understand, it was him.

"I will have your back through anything, always, but you know as well as I do that you handled it badly. Using booze to numb the pain is taking a trip down a very dangerous road. You know that. You can't drink your problems away, son."

My chest heaved on a powerful exhale. "Yeah, I know, Dad. It was just a bad night. It won't happen again."

He reached out and grabbed my shoulder, giving me an affectionate jostle. "I know it won't. I trust you. And you know you can come to us if shit ever gets too heavy.

It's what we're here for. It's what we do, no matter how old you are. You find you're stugglin', you let your mom and me do our job and guide you through it to the other side. Deal?"

"Deal."

Chapter Seventeen

Rae

"**D**amn it!" I snatched my hand away from the cast iron skillet but it was too late, a blister was already forming on my palm. It was my fault for being distracted when I was trying to teach myself to cook.

No, that wasn't right. It was *Zach's* fault. He deserved the blame, and on his shoulders was right where I intended to place it.

"It was a mistake."

"It will never happen again."

"I regret what happened."

His words had been playing on a constant loop since he ran out of my cabin like he couldn't get away from me fast enough. The sting they caused still lingered, refusing to go away, even though nearly a week had passed. It was the kind of persistent, burning sting that felt like bees and fire ants swarming beneath my skin.

I pulled my head out of my unpleasant thoughts before the cabin could fill with the smell of burning and grabbed a dishtowel. Wrapping it around the handle of the skillet, I pulled it off the burner and dropped it into the sink with a heavy clang, the contents inside looking nothing like they had on the recipe currently up on my laptop.

I pulled in a steadying breath, determined not to sink into defeat. I'd learned a lot about myself since staying at Safe Haven Ranch, mainly that I was capable of a lot more than I thought. However, I also realized I'd depended on Zach for a lot as well, like teaching me to ride a horse, to drive a stick, to grocery shop for the first time. But I didn't want to have to rely on him anymore. I wanted to do something for myself, like learn how to cook.

"You will *not* win." I jabbed an accusing finger at the congealed mass in the skillet. "I'm going to defeat you, damn it."

My cellphone rang from my back pocket as I got to work scrubbing out the charred-on food. I reached for it with one hand, smiling at the picture of my mom that popped up on the screen. We'd been texting regularly, but with her and my dad being out of the country, it was difficult to get the timing right for phone calls or Face-Time. "Hi! Where are you calling from this time?" I answered excitedly, tucking the cell between my ear and shoulder to free up my hands.

"Hi, sweetie! I miss you! We're still in the Nether-lands, but we leave for Ireland tonight."

"How were the shows? Dad kill it like always?"

I could hear the smile in her voice as she replied. "You know your father, he's one with the music."

He certainly was. I'd seen my father perform a few times, and there was only one way to describe Roan Blackwell when he was up on the stage . . . pure magic. Then again, that was the case anytime he played his guitar and sang. Some of my best memories were of him holding me on his lap, strumming discorded notes and humming melodies that would eventually be twisted together into a beautiful song.

Every time the pieces of a new song would come together, he'd look at me and smile, placing a kiss on the top of my head and telling me I was his inspiration. That was what he always said. Mom was his muse and I was his inspiration. He still claimed to this day that his music had gotten a million times better after I was born, and he contributed it all to "the two most important women in his world."

God, I missed them both like crazy.

"I'm glad it's going so well. Be sure to take plenty of pictures for me."

"I will, sweetheart. But enough about all that. I want to hear all about you? What are you doing right now?"

I looked to the unidentifiable substance currently swirling down the drain. "Well, I was *trying* to cook, but so far it's not going very well."

"Wait. You're—you . . . you're cooking?"

I rolled my eyes to myself as I shut off the water and lifted the pan from the sink. I dried it off and seasoned it with oil like I'd seen on the internet before putting it aside. I wasn't ready to give up. I planned to try again, but not while I was on the phone. I couldn't risk the distraction. The last thing I needed to do was burn the Paulson's cabin to the ground.

"Yes, Mom. I'm cooking. Well, trying. But I'm getting better." At least that was what I had been telling myself over the past several days. I was attempting that whole manifesting destiny thing by saying I would learn to cook.

"Wow, honey. I'm—I'm really proud of you."

I smiled at the pride I heard in her voice, even if it was mixed liberally with humor. She was rooting for me, and that felt really good. "Thanks. Maybe by the time you guys are stateside, I'll be good enough to cook a meal for you."

I thought I heard a sniffle carry through the line. "We'd love that, Rae. More than you know. I'm so glad you're doing well over there. I know things were tense the last time we saw each other, but you have to know, your dad and I love you very much. We didn't send you there as a punishment."

"I know, Mom. I get it now. I'll admit, I didn't see the real purpose at first, but the longer I've been here, the more I understand why you guys did what you did."

"Oh, sweetie." There was another sniffle.

"I . . . I like it here, Mom" I admitted. It was the first time I'd said it out loud, even to myself, and the truth of how much I liked it caught me by surprise. The uncertainty and tension with Zach withstanding, I really *did* like being here. The work was hard, but meaningful, and I found I enjoyed falling into bed exhausted every night because it meant I'd had a hand in keeping the ranch and the lodge running. I loved the horses and chickens and cows. I even liked Gretel, when she wasn't being an asshole.

I loved the view of the mountains surrounding the town during the day and the starry sky at night. I was even coming to like my little cabin. There wasn't much to it, but it was starting to feel like home.

"That makes me happy," Mom said. "You sound, I don't know, different somehow. Almost . . . lighter."

"I feel different," I confessed quietly. I'd come here feeling like I didn't belong anywhere, like I didn't know who the hell I was, but I was slowly getting to know myself with each passing day. What I liked and what I disliked—not what I *pretended* to care about because it was what was popular at the moment. I was getting to know *me*. And I was liking the version of myself I was discovering. She was a hell of a lot better than the girl I'd been back in L.A.

We chatted for a few more minutes. I told her about my foray into horseback riding and my determination to learn to drive one of the ranch trucks. I talked about my growing friendships with Ivy and Lennix while she filled me in on everything happening with her and my dad. The one topic I made sure to steer clear of was anything having to do with Zach. Especially the kiss he'd so easily disregarded the morning after it had happened. Like he said, it was never happening again. I filed it away with all the other stupid things I'd done in the past, and I was determined to move on and forget it ever happened. So far, my plan to do that consisted of avoiding the man in question like the plague.

"Well, I don't want to keep you longer than I already have. Sounds like you were in the middle of something when I called, so I'll let you get back to your cooking," she finally said.

"Call again soon, Mom. And give Dad my love, will you? I miss you both like crazy."

"We miss you too, honey. So much." There was a slight pause before she asked, "I love you; you know that, right?"

"Of course I do, Mom." My voice came out raspy, full of emotion. "I've always known that. Never doubted it for a second."

There was a gust of air through the line as though she let out a breath of relief. "Good. That's good."

"And I love you too. Both of you. Very much. I'm sorry if it ever felt like I took that for granted." I *had* taken it for granted. I'd taken so much for granted. But not anymore.

We disconnected, and I stuffed my phone back into my pocket, but before I could get back to work on the dish I'd been trying to perfect, someone knocked on the door to my cabin.

I whipped around, my heart in my throat at the idea that it could be Zach on the other side. I'd been doing my best over the past couple of days to pretend he didn't exist. It was easier said than done, especially since I was back to ranch-hand work, but I'd made sure to stick close to Hal the past two days, getting my assignments and such from him.

Before I had a chance to freak out too badly, the

person on the other side called out. "I know you're in there, Rae. I can smell the burned efforts of your cooking." My shoulders sank in relief at the sound of Lennix's voice. "Open up. I've got Ivy with me, and we have wine," she finished in a singsong voice.

I rushed to the door, throwing it open. "You should have led with that," I teased, waving the two of them in.

Lennix moved right to me, quickly pulling me into a hug before letting go and heading for the kitchen. Ivy followed after her, her nose scrunching up at the smell as she leaned in to place a kiss on my cheek. "What were you trying to make this time?" she asked as she grabbed hold of the door and swung it open and closed like she was trying to air the space out. "Maybe I'll leave this open for a few minutes."

I took the bottle of wine she offered with a laugh and followed after Lennix into my kitchen where she'd already pulled out three wineglasses—a purchase from my second trip into town, that time with Lennix to assure I wasn't left behind again.

"I was trying to make German pancakes."

"Aw, I love Dutch babies!" Lennix declared enthusiastically. Her smile fell a second later as she looked at my stovetop. "Uh, babe. Aren't you supposed to have an oven to make those?"

I shrugged as I pulled the cork from the wine bottle

and poured three generously-sized glasses. "That's what the recipe said, but I thought I could try and find a workaround by cooking them a little longer on the stovetop."

Ivy took the glass I offered her and sipped, one brow rising with a humorous look. "And how'd that work out for you?"

I shot her a flat look over my shoulder as I pulled out all the fancy cheeses I'd grabbed at the grocery store, finally excited to have a use for them. "You smell it in here, don't you?" I also grabbed some fresh fruit and some cured meats I'd gotten as well. I might not be able to cook yet, but I could whip together a charcuterie board better than anyone else. If I had a resume, I would have listed it under one of my special skills.

"You know, if you want to keep practicing, you're welcome to come over and use my stove any time."

I looked at her with wide eyes. "Really, you wouldn't mind?"

She lifted her shoulders in a casual shrug as she popped a cube of BellaVitano into her mouth. "Of course. I'll open all the windows beforehand." She dodged the cracker I threw at her head with a laugh. "I'm kidding! But seriously, you're welcome anytime. Just text me."

"I appreciate that." I nibbled nervously on my bottom lip as I took a seat in one of the chairs at the kitchen table. "I'm on the calendar to cook dinner for all the staff and hands next week, and I want to be able to cook without risk of burning down the kitchen and make something that won't give everyone food poisoning." My expression fell. "It would be my luck that the ranch would fall into dire straits when no one was able to work because they were all deathly ill from my cooking."

Ivy took the chair across from me while Lennix hopped up on the countertop across from me. I might not have had much in way of seating, but my new friends made it work.

"You'll do fine," Ivy assured me. "And we're more than happy to help if you need us. Just say the word."

"I appreciate the offer, but this is really something I want to do myself." I stared at the table top as I dragged my finger along the designs made by the woodgrain. "I've never really had to do anything for myself before. It was all done for me growing up," I admitted, a large dose of shame making my cheeks and the tips of my ears turn red.

I hadn't really gotten into all the reasons I'd been sent to the ranch in the first place, and I would have been lying if I said I wasn't worried about what Lennix and Ivy might think of me once they learned the truth.

Lennix eyed me thoughtfully over the rim of her

wineglass as she took a drink, and as I waited out her silence, my anxiety grew.

"We know why you're here, Rae," she said, her statement taking me off guard and causing my chin to jerk back.

The wine I'd sipped turned sour in my mouth. I forced it down past the painful tightness in my throat, swallowing audibly. "You . . . know? Like, everyone?"

She nodded.

The bites of cheese I'd eaten curdled in my stomach as I set my glass on the table and pushed it away.

"I knew who you were the moment I saw you," Ivy admitted, casual as could be. "I have an addiction to trashy tabloids." She shrugged unrepentantly and smiled. "I never claimed to have good taste."

"If you thought we were going to judge you because you made a few stupid mistakes, you don't know us very well," Lennix continued. Her expression had never wavered, never darkened or turned even the slightest bit judgmental with all the bombs she'd just dropped on me. She didn't look at me any differently than she had the day she showed up here to introduce herself. "You aren't your mistakes, babe. You might not have come here of your own free will, but from everything I've seen, you've made the best of it. You haven't complained or whined that it's too hard. You've worked hard and pulled your weight, busted your ass to do so."

Ivy held her hand up in the air like a middle schooler sitting at the front of a classroom. "I can confirm that." She looked at me, her expression dead serious. "Sure, it's only cleaning rooms and stuff, but when you've worked for me, you've taken every single aspect of your job seriously. You don't slack off, and you don't expect anything to be handed to you. You screwed up. Who hasn't? I know I've done my fair share of dumb things."

"Same," Lennix agreed resolutely. "I grew up on a ranch, for crying out loud. There was no limit to the amount of trouble I could get into. Not to mention I had a big brother thirteen years older than I was who was already an expert at mischief and shenanigans by the time I came along. He taught me well."

"Zach?" I let out a bubble of incredulous laughter. "You're kidding me? I didn't think he was capable of causing trouble. He always seems so . . . responsible."

Ivy and Lennix both burst out laughing. "You're talking about *my* brother?" Lennix squeaked. "Please! I think he spent most of his teenage years grounded. By the time I was old enough to cause trouble, there wasn't anything I could say or do that my parents hadn't already experienced. The most freaked out I'd ever seen my mom was when she caught Zach in the hayloft with a girl. I remember hearing her slam into the house, screaming incoherently about her eyes burning."

I ignored the sharp pang in my chest at the mention of Zach with another girl. It wasn't like I had any business feeling jealous. We'd only shared one kiss, after all, and that had ended disastrously. But it was nice to hear he wasn't as perfect as I had been thinking this whole time. And it was *really* nice to know my new friends didn't judge me for the things I'd done in the past.

For the first time in my life, I had real friends. True friends. And it was one of the best feelings I'd experienced in a really long time.

Chapter Eighteen

Zach

It had been a shit day. If anything could possibly go wrong, it had, starting with a call from the cops before the sun started to rise. Some kids had decided it would be fun to hotbox their car while cruising down some back roads around the ranch and ended up taking out a section of fence. A number of our cattle had gotten out and were blocking traffic.

That had been fun.

After getting the cows wrangled back where they belonged and fixing the section of fence, I got a call from Hal that one of our balers was busted. I'd spent the better part of the day trying to get the damn thing running, but it had been no use. It was the start of haying season, and being one baler short put us behind before we really had a chance to start.

I had to drive nearly an hour out of town to get a new one in Hidalgo, which cost precious time I didn't have. But none of that compared to the damage done from some kind of stomach bug that had run through the bunkhouse like headlice through a kindergarten class. We'd been short on manpower for a week and a half now. As soon as one man returned another two would get knocked on their asses.

The shitty mood I'd been in the past several days could have easily been attributed to the string of bad luck I'd been having, but the truth of my short fuse and surly attitude had started even before my crew began shitting and puking their guts out.

I'd been a miserable pain in the ass since the day after I ran out of Rae's cabin. Since then, she'd gone out of her way to avoid me like the plague. Even on the days she worked with my crew, she'd managed to keep her distance, refusing to look at me, and if I tried talking to her she'd either find a reason to get the hell away from me as quickly as possible, or give me short, clipped answers that left no opening to further the conversation.

At first I worried it was because I'd crossed a line with that kiss and made her uncomfortable, but the more time that passed, I had the feeling it wasn't about discomfort. She seemed mad . . . at me personally. One moment she'd be smiling and laughing with the other guys like there wasn't a thing wrong, but the minute I walked up, all that humor disappeared. Her face grew hard and her eyes narrowed. She'd even stopped using my name and had started calling me boss like all the other hands. Only, the few times she said it, I could have sworn it almost sounded snide. I fucking *hated* when she called me boss. I much preferred to hear the sound of my name coming from her lips.

The moment I walked away, she reverted to the light, breezy, smiling woman she'd been before my arrival, and if I were being honest with myself—something I was struggling with a lot lately—the lack of attention I was getting from her was pushing my buttons in a way I had never experienced before.

I wanted her to look at *me*. To smile at *me*. I wanted her to laugh at whatever lame joke *I* told her. But she wasn't giving me any of that, causing me to lash out at my guys as jealousy twisted in my gut like a rusty nail drilling down deeper with each turn.

The sun was dipping by the time I got back to the ranch, hauling the new baler behind me. Twilight had turned the clouds from white to peach, the color against the green trees that lined the mountains creating a stunning sky. It was my favorite time of day. Whenever I had the chance, I liked to sit on my back deck with a cold beer, or a bourbon in the colder months, and watch the sunset. It always managed to calm me down.

I pulled up to the barn and parked, climbing out of the truck and heading inside in hopes of finding someone to help me unload the machinery. This time of day things should have been winding down. Dinner was less than an hour away, and most of the crew would have headed back to the bunkhouse to wash up beforehand. But as soon as I stepped foot inside the barn, I heard the sound of voices coming from the other side. More voice than I'd been expecting.

I followed them through the length of the barn and out the other side where the corrals were, finding a decent sized group hanging along the rungs.

Spotting Hal among the crowd, I headed in his direction and stopped alongside him. "What's goin' on?"

"Oh, hey, Boss," he greeted jovially enough. "Get everything taken care of with the baler?"

"Yeah. It's all sorted. Why's everyone standin' arou —" The question died on my tongue the moment I spotted Rae sitting on Sassy's back in the middle of the corral. "What the fuck is she doing?" I barked, panic reaching in and wringing the air from my lungs before grasping me by the throat and squeezing.

"Relax. Everything's goin' just fine."

"Have you lost your goddamn mind?" I bellowed, a

sense of rage and fear unlike anything I'd ever experienced before crashing into me like a tidal wave, making my skin turn cold at the same time my vision turned red. "What the fuck, Hal? You let her up there? She's gonna get herself killed!"

I grabbed hold of the top rung of the corral, ready to vault over, only to have my foreman put a staying hand on my shoulder. Never in all the years I'd known the man had I wanted to cause him physical pain, but in that moment I wanted to punch him in the face. Lay him the fuck out for endangering Rae. Then I wanted to fire his ass for good measure.

"Boss, just take a breath. She's got this. See?" He pointed back to Rae, and I followed his gaze as my heart threatened to burst right out of my chest. Despite the panic, I couldn't help but notice how steady she looked. She didn't appear to be nervous or jittery like she'd been the first time I put her on the back of Roam. There was a confidence in her frame as she leaned over in the saddle, stroking a soothing hand down Sassy's mane. I could see her lips move, most likely soft and soothing, offering words of encouragement, using that same tone I'd heard her take with the horse before.

My heart lodged in my throat as she gave the reins a gentle tug to turn Sassy to the left, and to my surprise, the horse obeyed the command without an inkling of attitude. Where she'd thrown off every hand who'd tried to ride her before, she let Rae guide her back toward the fence where everyone was gathered. Rae didn't take her beyond a slow, steady walk, but I could see in the way she held herself there was an ease I hadn't seen during the one and only lesson I'd given her.

Something cold and bitter tied my insides into knots. "How long has she been doin' this?"

Hal shrugged, oblivious to the storm brewing inside of me. "A little over a week, I suppose."

A week and a half. I reached up to rub at the ache that had suddenly formed in the center of my chest.

"We've been workin' on Sassy every day after quittin' time, mainly ground work to get her used to Rae. Then gettin' Rae comfortable on a horse. I've been puttin' her on Huckleberry. He's got the right temperament for her, and she's pickin' it up really fast."

That was a good call. The gelding had a gentle nature similar to Roam's. I would have picked him for her myself, but I'd liked the idea of seeing her up on *my* horse. Not that it mattered now. Because she clearly wanted nothing to do with me. *I* was the one who was supposed to teach her to ride. *I* was the one who was supposed to help her work on Sassy. But instead, she'd gone to Hal, cutting me out completely.

A fire started to burn inside my gut. Anger at myself

for screwing up lit the embers, but it was jealousy that acted as gasoline, spreading the flames. Jealous of Hal for being the one she went to. Jealous of my crew for getting to work beside her day after day, getting those goddamn smiles and laughs. Hell, I was even jealous of Sassy for getting her affection.

Christ, I was a fucking mess.

"Didn't realize I was payin' everyone to stand around doin' nothin'," I barked, finally getting the attention of the rest of the ranch hands. "If you're on the clock, get back to work. If you're not, stop distracting everyone else and get your asses outta here."

I could feel Hal's bewildered stare drilling into the side of my face, but I didn't bother looking at him. I kept my focus trained on Rae, taking in the way her cheeks and ears flushed the moment she spotted me before ripping her gaze away. *Damn it.*

Everyone cleared off, leaving Rae and me alone for the first time in a week and a half. I stood at the fence, silently watching as she dismounted and began guiding Sassy toward the opened gate without a single glance in my direction.

"I don't recall givin' you permission to get up on that horse." I hadn't meant for my tone to come out as hard as it did, but I was having trouble keeping my emotions in check. This woman had me twisted up like a goddamn pretzel, and I didn't know how on earth to act when it came to her.

Her back shot straight, her shoulders squared, but she didn't stop or turn to face me as she said, "Hal said it would be okay."

I followed after her and that damn horse as she led her into the barn. I was like a damn puppy starved for attention. "I seem to recall tellin' you that *I* would help you work Sassy."

She stopped Sassy and got to work removing the saddle. I might as well have been a ghost for all the attention she was paying me. "Yeah, well, you're a busy guy. I didn't think it mattered who helped me."

"Goddamn it," I clipped, my harsh voice bouncing off the walls like the crack of a whip. "Will you just fuckin' look at me already?"

Her nostrils flared on a harsh exhale as she finally stopped and turned to face me. She slammed her hands down on her waist and cocked a hip. Those sweet caramel eyes of hers flashed with an anger I'd only seen from her once before. That first day when she thought I'd been shaming her. I'd found that fire attractive then, but now . . . Jesus, I might as well have been a teenager for all the control I had over my dick going hard. It sure as hell wasn't a good time for the damn thing to try and bust its way through my zipper.

"What can I do for you, Boss?"

Oh, she was throwing attitude. It pissed me off as much as it turned me on. My mind fell straight into the gutter, wondering what she'd do if I were to punish her by putting her over my knee and spanking her ripe peach of an ass bright red.

"You can start by losing the attitude."

She looked like she was seconds away from breathing fire, and I had to admit, it was a hell of a lot better than the cold shoulder I'd been getting the past week and a half. At this point *anything* would have been better than her silence, but I loved seeing that fire in her. Most days she seemed so unsure of herself. I saw how she worked her fingers to the bone, never once complaining. It was almost as if she was scared to mess up or make it known she was tired or in pain.

My jaw ticked, my back molars grinding together. I hated that she thought she couldn't speak up for herself, so if it took me pushing her buttons to breathe that life back into her, I'd damn well do it.

I arched a brow, almost in a challenge. "I thought you were a grownup. My mistake."

Her chest expanded on a massive inhale. I knew the signs of a woman about to explode. I'd seen them enough with Rory and Lennix, and a breath that big meant danger ahead. "*Excuse* me?"

"You heard me." I braced my hands on my hips, opening myself up to the tidal wave of emotions that had been consuming me the past several days, allowing myself to feel the anger and frustration at having the woman I hadn't been able to think about since that goddamn kiss act like I didn't exist. I knew I was the one who said it couldn't happen again, but I hadn't been able to stop thinking about it. It was the first thing on my mind in the morning when I woke up, the memory of her lush mouth making my cock ache until I had no other choice but to wrap my fist around it and beat off until I came on my stomach. It was the very last thing I thought about at night when I tried to sleep. *Every . . . damn . . . day* I thought about that fucking kiss, wishing things were different so I could kiss her again. I'd jerked my own dick more than I had since I was a teenage boy, for Christ's sake. And there was Rae, going about her business like nothing ever happened. Ignoring me like I was inconsequential.

A man's pride could only take so many hits.

"You've clearly got a chip on your shoulder about something, but instead of acting like an adult and talking to me about it, you've decided to ignore me." I kept jabbing at those buttons of hers, in desperate need of a reaction. Now that she was finally looking at me, I knew

I wouldn't be able to stand it if she stopped again. I needed to draw that fire out, damn it.

Her mouth fell open. "Are you *kidding me*?" She dragged those four words out slowly, voice rising several octaves with each one, until she finished on a screech that had Sassy twitching and the other horses whinnying in their stalls. "Are you seriously accusing *me* of not being an adult?" She shook her head in disgust. "Wow, you really have a lot of nerve. I'm not the one who kissed you then bailed out the very next morning."

"You know why I left," I defended harshly.

"Oh yeah, you made it perfectly clear when you ran out the door like I was an embarrassing little secret you couldn't get away from fast enough." She let out a bitter, caustic laugh. "Shame and regret." She spit the words out like they were poison. "I know those feelings very well."

I rocked back on a foot, the impact of what she said slamming into me like a punch to the chest, knocking the wind right out of my lungs.

"You . . . you think I'm ashamed?" I croaked.

She crossed her arms over her chest, hugging herself protectively. "It's not what I think. It's what you said," she spit back. "You regret what happened. You said it yourself."

"Rae, I—"

"Just go." She turned away from me, but not before I saw the sadness in her eyes. "I have work to finish up and I'm on dinner duty tonight. I don't have time for this."

She turned her back on me, making it crystal clear she was finished with the conversation, whether I was or not. I hated the idea of walking away from her, especially now that I knew what she'd been feeling since I walked out her door a week and a half ago. I felt like the biggest piece of shit in the whole world.

I had to make this right, but something in my gut told me this wasn't the time. I needed to give her some space. Just for a little while. Then I was going to fix this, because the very last thing I felt for her was shame and regret.

Chapter Nineteen

Rae

I tried my best to calm my racing heart as I brushed Sassy down, focusing on slowly counting to ten on each inhale. The anger I felt toward Zach was still at a boil, setting me on edge. I couldn't believe that asshole's nerve, accusing me of not behaving like an adult.

"Why are some people such jerks?" I asked Sassy, knowing full well she didn't understand a single word I was saying. "I mean, can you believe he said that? Talk about being a hypocrite."

I held on to the rage he'd ignited with both hands, refusing to let it go. Anger was so much easier to deal with. If I clung to that anger, I could forget he'd hurt my feelings. I could forget, despite the humiliation I felt when he ran out on me, I was still harboring a crush that couldn't seem to go away. Anger was safe. Sadness was something a person could get sucked into and drown. That was a risk I couldn't take, so anger it was.

As if sensing my mood, Sassy kept hooking her chin over my shoulder and pulling me in like she was trying to give me a hug. Each time she did it, I laughed, feeling my mood lighten bit by bit. She really was the most perfect horse in the whole world.

"All right," I giggled when she nuzzled at my pockets, looking for peppermints. "I've got you covered, sweet girl, don't you worry your pretty head about it."

I pulled a mint from my pocket and held it in the flat of my palm for her. She deserved it, for sure. With Hal's guidance, I'd started my training with her, doing what he called ground work. A few days ago we'd moved to saddling her so she could get familiar with the equipment, but today was the first time I'd actually gotten on her back. I would have been lying if I said I wasn't nervous. I'd seen her toss a couple of the guys off her with the ease of swatting at a fly when I first got here. I didn't think I'd bounce back from that kind of fall as easily as they did, but just like she'd been from the start, she was different with me. There had been a moment when I climbed on that she'd tensed up, but she relaxed quickly enough after some soothing words and a few strokes of her mane.

We'd taken it slow, just like Hal had told me to do, keeping her at a slow, steady pace until we were comfortable with each other. She'd followed every one of my commands without throwing any of her signature attitude around. It was like she knew when I was on her back, it wasn't safe for her to mess around, so she saved that for after.

She trusted me and I trusted her, and as I'd guided her around the enclosure, pride had swelled in my chest. That kind of thing wasn't something you could demand, loyalty and trust like that had to be won. I'd earned that from this magnificent animal by being a safe place for her, as she'd been for me all these weeks I'd been at Safe Haven Ranch.

"None of these guys around here know what they're talking about," I said softly, wrapping my arms around her neck and giving her a hug. I breathed in deeply, pulling in a lungful of distinct barn smells, surprised that I actually *liked* it. The smell, just like the cabin, was becoming a comfort to me. "You're just the sweetest thing, aren't you?"

"You're really good with her."

I whipped around with a surprised yelp at the unexpected voice. "Oh my God." I pressed my hand to my chest, resting it over my racing heart and blew out a gust of air. "You scared the crap out of me."

The man held his hands up in surrender as he continued in my direction. "Sorry about that. I thought you heard me," he said with an easy grin that dripped with charm. I'd seen that kind of grin a million times. It was a playboy's grin. The kind that could make a woman believe he was pure innocence before he lured her into his bed and showed her the side that was all sin.

I had no doubt this man was skilled when it came to the art of seduction. That smile, his easy swagger, and the confidence that bordered just on the right side of cocky were proof enough. But no matter how attractive he might have been, there was no flutter in my belly or heat building beneath my skin as he directed that charm at me. Not like there was every time Zach entered a room I was in.

I threw him a quick smile before turning back to Sassy. "It's fine," I said as I rubbed the curry comb along her side in a circular motion. One of my favorite parts of this whole experience had been learning to groom my girl. I found the steady rhythm of brushing her out with each different comb helped to clear my head, and I loved how much she enjoyed being pampered. My Sassy girl would have been content to stand there and let me groom her for hours. "You just caught me by surprise is all. You're Connor, right?"

He stopped a few feet away, resting his shoulder

against a wooden beam. His hands were shoved casually in the pockets of his jeans, one booted foot crossed over the other. "That's me. And you're Rae."

"Yep."

"Pretty name for a pretty girl."

I shot him a flat look. "Are you flirting with me right now?"

One corner of his mouth hooked up in a smirk. "Depends. Is it workin'?"

I had to give credit where credit was due. The man certainly wasn't lacking in confidence. Before I came here, I would have fallen for this guy's game in a matter of seconds. I was glad to see I'd managed to grow up in that aspect. "No. Not really."

He laughed, the sound far from unpleasant, and pushed off the post to come closer. Sassy let out a snort that didn't sound all that happy as she shifted to the side, pushing against me like she was trying to put her big body between me and Connor.

"Easy girl," I said with a laugh, giving her a pat. "He's harmless . . ." I cast him a narrow-eyed look, raising a single brow as I added, "mostly."

"Completely," he admitted with a chuckle, reaching out a single hand so Sassy could get a sniff. When she didn't go in for a bite, he slowly stroked her muzzle.

"Your owner's got nothin' to worry about from me, fierce girl."

"Oh, Sassy's not mine."

Connor grinned again, and this time the innocence was real. He'd made his move, got shot down, now he was perfectly content to move on to his next conquest. "Not so sure she agrees with that. I've been around my fair share of animals, and it's clear as day this horse has picked you."

My chest puffed out slightly, a smile tugging at my lips. "You think so?"

Just then, Sassy butted my hip with her nose, her way of communicating that she wasn't happy that I'd stopped brushing.

"Absolutely. Some horses like everyone, or at least tolerate them. Then there are some who can't be broken. Refuse to let a soul on their back. Then you have horses like this one right here. They pick their person, and that's it for them." He gave me a considering look. "Like some people. It's you and no one else."

My cheeks heated and the tips of my ears caught fire under his scrutinizing gaze. I ducked my head, pulling my gaze away from him and concentrating on making perfect, precise circles against Sassy's coat with the curry comb. "Yeah, well, I'm not so sure Zach would like me staking claim to one of his horses."

I caught another flash of Connor's grin from the corner of my eye. "Sweetheart, I'm almost certain he'd sign ownership over to you this very moment if you asked."

My head whipped around in his direction. "What do you mean?"

He shook his head good-naturedly, but also with an air about him, like he was holding onto a secret. "Not really for me to say. Guess that's something the two of you need to figure out."

That flutters that had been missing at Connor's attempt at flirting suddenly filled my belly at his implication, but as difficult as it was to ignore the tiny threads of excitement trying to sprout, I stomped them and reminded myself what Zach had said after our kiss. I knew better than to let myself get carried away in a fantasy. It never led anywhere good.

Quickly shifting the topic to something safer, I said, "You know a lot about horses. Are you a rancher too?"

"Nah. I'm here to catch up with an old buddy and kill some time. I'm a bull rider."

My eyes bugged out and my jaw dropped. "Like, you climb on the back of a big, scary pissed-off bull? You can do that for a *living*?"

He chuckled again, nodding his head. "Sure can. A pretty decent one if you're good at it."

That cockiness was back. Either this man was destined to be a bachelor for the rest of his life, or he was going to meet a woman one day who knocked him on his ass so hard he wouldn't know up from down.

"And I take it from that arrogant smirk on your face that you're good at it?"

The man actually preened, and I couldn't help but laugh. "Oh, sweetheart. I'm not just good. I'm the best. You'll have to come to a rodeo and see me in action."

If I felt like a fish out of water coming to this ranch, I imagined walking into a rodeo would be like stepping into a whole new world.

"I don't think so. I'm sure you're as good as you claim, but I don't think I'd be able to sit there and watch guys try not to get murdered by an animal that weighs almost as much as a Fiat."

"You'd be surprised. It's an adrenaline rush, not only for the man on the bull, but for the people in the crowd too."

Oh, I was sure it had to be. Connor struck me as the kind of man who thrived on adrenaline. Was that a good thing or a bad thing? I wasn't sure.

"So, if you're supposed to be some hotshot bull rider, what are you doing here? Shouldn't you be in an arena somewhere, trying not to get gored in the ass?"

His grin widened. "I'm here while I let my knee

heal, but I'll be back at it soon enough. I try to come for a visit every chance I get. It's always nice to see Zach, and there's just something about this place, you know?"

I let out a long, slow exhale as I looked past the open barn doors to the land beyond. "Yeah," I said quietly. "I do know. This place is kind of incredible."

His brows dipped in at the center, his head cocking to the side as he studied me. "You say that like you're surprised."

I bit down on my bottom lip. "I kind of am. I didn't really expect to like this place when I first got here. It's . . . not really what I'm used to. But it kind of grows on you. I actually like it better than the city. It'll be an adjustment when I have to go back." Realization dawned as soon as those words fell out of my mouth.

This was temporary. The cabin, Sassy, the jeans and boots, my new friendships . . . Zach. It was all temporary. This wasn't actually my home, even though it might feel like more of one than L.A. had.

Something slid across Connor's expression, dulling a bit of the shine on his charming, good-old-boy façade. "So you aren't plannin' on stayin'?"

My shoulders came up in a shrug, the knots that had suddenly formed in my stomach feeling like led weights. "I don't really have a plan for what comes after this."

That admission left a sour, unpleasant taste on my tongue. "My move here wasn't exactly permanent."

"Yeah, well, maybe not, but this place has a way of stickin' with you, whether you stay or not."

With that ominous statement, he pushed off the workbench, knocking his knuckles against the wood as he took a step back. "Well, I'll let you get back to it. You gonna be at dinner tonight?"

I nodded. "I'll be there shortly. It's my turn to cook."

He hit me with that signature smile of his once more as he continued to back out of the barn, pulling the ballcap from his head and slapping it against his thigh before tugging it back into place. "Then I'll see you there."

I watched as he walked out of the barn, staring at where he'd disappeared before Sassy eventually nudged me back into the present.

I let out a snort and shook my head as I re-focused my attention on her. "That guy's kind of weird, huh?"

I liked to think the snickering sound she made was her way of agreeing, so I gave her another peppermint for being such a good girl, then did my best to push the strange conversation out of my mind as I finished grooming my favorite animal on the planet.

Chapter Twenty

Rae

I closed my eyes and did my best to clear my mind as my body sank deeper into the clawfoot tub. I drew my knees up and slid down the warmed porcelain until my ears sank beneath the surface of the hot water, muting all sound.

I'd done it. I'd managed to cook my first dinner for the ranch and lodge staff, and it had been a glowing success. Well . . . that might have been giving myself a bit too much credit, but it hadn't sucked. As far as I was concerned, that was a win. The food was eaten without a single grimace, and I didn't catch anyone gagging or trying to sneak food into the trash or down the garbage disposal when they thought I wasn't looking.

My German pancakes had turned out exactly how they were supposed to. I hadn't accidentally mixed up

the salt and sugar or mistaken the cornstarch for flour—
something I'd done during my many practices—or
cooked them until they resembled circular charcoal
disks.

I couldn't go so far as to say they were the best
pancakes ever made, but I'd followed the recipe and
hadn't screwed up any of the steps. I was damn proud of
myself and already thinking about what I wanted to try
to make next time.

Everyone had been kind, telling me they'd enjoyed it
and thanking me for taking the time to cook for them,
and as I sat at the long wooden table, surrounded by all
the people I was getting to know better with each
passing day, I let the stress of my earlier confrontation
with Zach slide off my shoulders like water off a duck's
back.

Sure, I might have watched the door closer than I
should have, and I might have felt the smallest niggling
of disappointment when he didn't show up to eat with
everyone, but I managed to push it out of my mind and
concentrate the best I could on the million different
conversations that had been taking place around the
table.

Ivy and Lennix had come to eat with us—and to
provide me with moral support—so I enjoyed my time
with them, refusing to let thoughts of Zach filter into my

head. It became easier to stay in the moment when I caught Ivy's attention drifting down the table to where a certain cocky bull rider sat.

Lennix had spotted our friend's moony-eyed expression as well, and from the giddy way she'd smiled, I had a sneaking suspicion she was going to try and play matchmaker. I wasn't quite sure yet if Ivy and Connor would be a good fit. Ivy was sweet and bubbly and funny as hell. And Connor was . . . well, he was a playboy, no doubt about it. I was sure he'd left a string of broken hearts from town to town as he traveled, doing his rodeo thing. But given my shitty track record, I didn't feel it was my place to voice my concerns.

I breathed in deeply, filling my lungs with the scent of jasmine from the essential oils I'd put in the water to help loosen the knots in my back and neck after a hard day's work. There wasn't much I missed from my old life in L.A., but after hours spent in the sun, hauling heavy bales of hay and checking miles of fence line on an old ATV with shitty suspension, I missed the hell out of Olga, the masseuse I used to see once a week. Her hands had been instruments of magic, and she would have worked those knots out in no time.

A dull, muted thump pulled me from my fantasy of flying Olga all the way to Virginia, plopping me back to reality. My eyes popped open and I pushed myself up to sitting, the water sloshing around me in gentle waves as I listened for the sound again. Sure enough, there was a knock on the door of the cabin a few seconds later.

I let out a sigh of disappointment that my relaxing bath had been cut short as I climbed out of the tub and squeezed the excess water from my hair. "Just a second," I called out as I wrapped myself in my favorite silk robe. It was unusual to have a visitor after nine. Back in California, I would have only just started getting ready for a night out on the town, but things were a lot different here. Work usually started as the sun came up, so if you wanted to ensure a full night's sleep, most people were either already in bed or gearing up for it.

I padded to the door and lifted up on the tips of my toes to reach the tiny peephole. I'd forgotten to turn on the porch light when I got home earlier, so all I could make out was a large figure standing on the front porch. I squinted, trying to see better, but it was no use.

"I know you're there," the shadow figure said in a voice that sounded exactly like Zach. "You blocked out the light from the peephole when you looked through it."

I quickly crouched down, slapping a hand over my mouth to muffle my gasp.

"Now the light's back."

Damn it. Well, it looked like I wouldn't be adding stealthy to my list of special skills any time soon.

"Open the door, Hollywood. We need to talk."

I squeezed my eyes closed, desperately trying to calm my breathing. The peace I'd found in the bathtub only a handful of minutes ago disappeared with the sound of his voice. I wasn't sure I could handle another *talk* with him today.

"Please, sweetheart," he said, his voice much softer and lower this time. It was almost enough to make me soften to him. Almost.

Steeling my spine, I pulled in a fortifying breath and reached for the knob.

ZACH

FUCK ME.

All the air expelled from my lungs the moment she pulled the door open, and the carefully crafted speech I'd spent the past few hours rehearsing disappeared from my brain like a puff of smoke caught on a breeze.

All rational thought left me and the blood in my body traveled straight to my dick as my gaze slowly skated down her body. The glow from the lights inside the cabin created a backlight that looked almost like a halo, making her look ethereal. The robe she had cinched around her barely came to mid-thigh, the silky material clinging to her damp skin and putting all her curves on display.

Rae's hair hung down her shoulders, the water dripping from it and soaking the robe at her chest. The wet fabric formed perfectly to her breasts and accentuated her puckered nipples. Christ, all I could think about was leaning forward and pulling those stiff peaks into my mouth, sucking until I made her moan. I wondered what color they were. Were they a dusky pink like the blush on her cheeks, or would they be peachier? If I sucked them hard enough, would they turn the same rosy shade as her lips?

"Zach?"

Her voice pulled me from my lustful musings. I'd come here to apologize, now all I wanted to do was maul her, show her how I *really* felt about her. Put that need on display so she'd know what I felt was the furthest thing from shame.

"What are you doing here?"

"I'm not ashamed of you." I blurted the words out with a lot less finesse than I'd hoped for.

Her chin jerked back in surprise, the center of her brows dipping in a V as she frowned. "What?"

Determination coursed through me, heating my blood and making my heart pump harder. "In the barn you said I felt shame and regret. You were wrong."

"Zach, you don't—"

"I said I regretted the kiss because I was afraid you'd feel like I was taking advantage of you. That's the *only* reason I felt that way."

She blinked slowly, those big, beautiful doe eyes full of awe. "Really?"

"Absolutely. I feel like I've been walkin' around on eggshells since you got here, tryin' not to freak you out. I'd been trying to hide how I really felt from you, but I lost control that night. I hated the idea that I might have forced myself on you or put you in an uncomfortable position. I'm your boss and I'm a lot older than you—"

"Not that much older," she interrupted, her tongue peeking out to sweep across her plump bottom lip.

Her words caught me off guard. "What?"

"You aren't that much older than I am," she said in a quiet, throaty voice, her chest rising as her breaths came faster.

"Twelve years is a pretty big gap, sweetheart."

She pulled her bottom lip between her teeth and bit down, drawing all my focus to her mouth. Christ, I wanted my lips on hers again. "Not to me," she whispered. I could have sworn my heart stopped beating at her words.

My dick was doing its best to bust through my zipper. I couldn't remember a time in my life when I'd been this hard. It was *painful*, the way I wanted her. The kind of deep, throbbing ache that no amount of fucking my own fist would ever alleviate. The only thing that would take the pain away was sinking deep inside this woman, getting lost in her.

My throat worked on a swallow, the cords in my neck straining as the muscles in my entire body tensed. "You don't think so?"

She shook her head. "No. And I never once felt like you were taking advantage when you kissed me. I . . . I liked it," she admitted, her barely-there voice a whisp on the breeze that fluttered her silky robe around her smooth thighs. Hearing that made my dick pulse. "I *wanted* you to kiss me. I'd been wanting it for a while, actually, and I was excited when you finally did. Then you said it was a mistake." She blinked, casting her gaze down to her bare feet. Her toes were the prettiest shade of pink. "That hurt."

Oh, fuck me. Hearing that was a punch straight to the gut. I was desperate to take away the sadness I saw on her face.

I reached out, unable to keep from touching her

another second. I took her chin between my fingers and lifted her face, giving her no choice but to look at me. "You weren't a mistake. I wanted to kiss you too," I confessed, the truth of those words pulling from the deepest recesses of my chest and making my voice rough and craggy. "Fuck, I wanted to kiss you so bad. Still do. It's all I've been able to think about since that night."

"Zach." When she said my name in her beautiful voice it made me feel things I'd never felt before. She was the only woman who made me feel so out of control, and I was done fighting it. I was done trying to pretend I wasn't attracted to her, that there wasn't a single hour of the day where I didn't think of her.

"Tell me I can kiss you again, Rae. Because if I don't, I swear to Christ, I think I might die."

Her lashes fluttered, her cheeks blushing that gorgeous pink I loved so damn much. "I don't know if that's a good idea," she said quietly. "You're still my boss. That hasn't changed." She gave her head a tiny shake, her expression turning sad. "I've made so many mistakes in my life. When I came here I swore I'd be different. I swore I'd be smarter, and a hookup with my boss is the furthest thing from smart."

My grip on her chin tightened as I took a step closer, closing in on her. "That's not what this is," I gritted out. Her words stung, I was man enough to admit that.

Her lips parted on an exhale as she tipped her head back farther to look up at me. "I—I don't understand."

"This wouldn't *just* be a hookup. I can't tell you what this is, but it's *not that*."

"How can you be so sure?"

"Because I know myself. I know the moment I kiss you, I'll be wondering when I'll get to do it again. I know the moment I sink my cock deep inside your perfect body, I'll be planning ways to get back in there. I know one time with you isn't going to be enough, because I haven't been able to stop thinking about you. You consume my thoughts. It's been that way since you first got here. Every time you smile or laugh at one of the other men, I want to knock their goddamn teeth down their throats. I've never been a jealous man, but I want those smiles to only be for me. And I know deep down that once I have you, there isn't anything I won't do to make you mine."

She let out a stuttered breath, her gaze growing hazy as the seconds ticked by. Finally, she spoke.

"Zach?"

"Yeah, baby?"

"You can kiss me again."

Chapter Twenty-One

Rae

He moved faster than I expected. *Much* faster.

I stumbled back with a yelp as he charged forward, but he was on me before I had a chance to fall on my butt, his lips sealing on mine and swallowing down the noise. The instant Zach fused his lips with mine, time stopped. The world around us disappeared. There was only him and me and *the kiss*.

His hands slid over me, making me feel dizzy as his tongue coaxed my lips open. I'd kissed my fair share of men, mostly after having a little too much to drink at whatever nightclub we were all at, but none of them had ever felt like this. Zach wasn't just a good kisser. He was a master. He could teach classes on how to properly kiss a woman.

My knees turned to mush, refusing to hold me up any longer, but before I could fall, Zach wrapped one of his thick, strong arms around me, molding my body to his. I felt so small and soft against all of his . . . large and incredibly hard.

I placed my hands on his stomach, gasping at the feel of all the ridges and indents beneath the soft cotton of his shirt. Now that I was finally touching him, I couldn't seem to stop. I slid my palms up, over his defined pecs and broad shoulders. I rose up on my tiptoes to get closer, looping my arms around his thick neck and holding on tightly. My fingernails scraped against the nape of his neck as his tongue swept against mine, causing a needy whimper to claw up my throat.

"God, I've been dreamin' about this." His voice was thick and raspy, sending a delicious shiver down my spine. "Could kiss you for hours, baby."

A thrill shot through me like a bolt of lightning at hearing that, but while I was enjoying kissing him too—more than I could possibly put into words—there was this persistent buzzing beneath my skin that was only getting worse as the seconds ticked by. With every brush of his hands over the dip of my waist and the flare of my hips, a need for . . . more ignited deep in my core, sparking to life like a small campfire before growing into a raging forest fire.

Kissing him wasn't enough. I needed more. I *wanted* more. Only, I didn't have the first clue what I wanted or how to ask for it. I might have kissed plenty of nameless, faceless guys over the past few years, but I'd only taken two of them to bed, and neither experience had been much to write home about.

The first one had been when I was twenty. I'd been in L.A. for a year by then and all my friends were hooking up. I'd done it mainly because I was tired of being a virgin and wanted to get it over with. It had been painful at first, then . . . underwhelming. I hadn't orgasmed, hadn't even come close, but I'd faked it because I thought I had to, to spare his pride. I might have been willing to give him another shot if he hadn't run and told all his friends about it, bragging like he was some kind of sex god.

The second guy was someone I'd been seeing for a couple months. I thought there was potential with him. I thought he was the kind of guy I could see myself being with for a while, if not the long haul. We dated for a little less than a year, and the sex was pretty hit or miss. Sometimes I'd climax, but that was only if I was on top and really focused. And if he didn't get off first.

Our relationship ended because I thought we could be adults and talk about how to make things better in the bedroom. He'd taken it as a personal attack and broke up with me. I felt sorry for whoever came next, because they were in for a boring, mediocre love life, for damn sure.

Neither of them had made me feel even a fraction of what Zach did. It felt like there was an inferno inside me, building and building. Part of me was afraid I might combust while the other part of me welcomed the explosion.

"Zach," I whimpered, that one word coming out a plea.

"I'm right here, Rae. I've got you."

I threaded my fingers through the short strands of his hair, trying to hold on, to get closer, to fuse with him. "I need . . ." I rocked my pelvis forward, sucking in a sharp breath at the feel of the steel rod prodding me in the belly. He was so hard and *so big*.

"What do you need, baby? Tell me and I'll give it to you."

I let out a little whine as I desperately searched my brain for the right words. God, I knew I should have watched more porn. At least then I would know which way my tastes leaned and how to vocalize those cravings.

"I—I don't . . . I'm not sure."

Zach pulled his head back, blinking his eyes into focus. His pupils were so big his irises were solid black. "I think I know what you need." He reached up and tucked a strand of hair behind my ear, the pads of his fingers brushing against my temple and down my jaw. "You trust me?"

I nodded. In that very moment, there was no one I trusted more. If he didn't do something about this ache deep inside me, I wasn't sure I'd survive. "I trust you," I said on a rush of breath.

He reached behind his neck to grab my wrists where they were linked and pulled my hands down, bringing them to my sides as he slowly started walking forward, forcing me back step by step. "Good, because you have to know I'd never do anything to hurt you. I'll make you scream, hell, I'll do my best to make you cry tonight, but none of that will be in pain."

His words were like a bolt of lightning shooting straight to my clit. My center throbbed, the emptiness excruciating. I pulled in a gasp when my back collided with the wall, and at the sound, Zach gave me a smile I'd never seen before. It was wolfish and dark and full of the most tantalizing, forbidden promises.

"You're so fuckin' pretty," he said, his tone reverent as he slipped his fingers beneath the sash holding my robe closed at my waist and sliding them to the knot at the front. The touch felt sinful and worshipful at the same time.

Nerves jittered in my belly. A million doubts

suddenly flooded my head. What if *I* was the problem? What if the reason I'd never had the kind of sex I read about in romance novels was because I wasn't any good at it? What if he decided I wasn't worth it after tonight and took off again?

"Hey." He took me by the chin and forced me from those dark thoughts by lowering his face to mine. "Whatever you're thinking, stop it right now. Get out of your head, baby. You're supposed to be here with me."

I gave a wobbly nod and licked my lips. "I'm here."

"Good." His gaze traveled down to where his fingers were toying with the knot in my robe's belt. I'd seen those same fingers tie a rope more times than I could count, and I suddenly understood why I'd always found watching him do that so damn fascinating. "Because I need your focus on me. I need you to pay attention to every single thing I do to you." He tilted my chin up with his free hand. "You following me, Rae?"

"I follow," I answered without hesitation.

His gaze penetrated mine, making it impossible to look away. "And if there's anything I do that you don't like, I want you to say so right away and I'll stop."

He went silent for a beat, as though he was waiting for me to tell him to stop. That wasn't going to happen. Not when I felt like I was holding on to a fallen power-line and he was the only thing capable of grounding me.

He smiled with approval when I returned his silence and gripped the sash with both hands, making quick work of undoing the knot and sliding the two ends free of each other.

His molten gaze slowly traveled downward as he toyed with the silky lapels between his fingers before finally letting them go so they could fall open.

The sound he made was like something you'd expect to hear in the wild, sending a pulse straight to my center. I clenched my thighs together, spreading the wetness that was dripping from me across my upper thighs. I'd never been so drenched in my life. I wasn't sure if it was normal or if I should be embarrassed. The air conditioning played across my exposed skin as he pushed the robe open farther, exposing everything. My nipples tightened painfully as goosebumps spread across every inch of my body.

"Damn it, baby. I knew you'd be perfect, and just look at you." The need to cover myself that I'd felt only a moment ago disappeared as his heated gaze dragged over me like I was the most beautiful thing he'd ever laid eyes on. "You're even better than I imagined. And I've imagined *a lot.*"

My lips parted on a shaky exhale when he reached out to drag the backs of his fingers over my skin from my belly button up toward my breasts. I hissed when he dragged a knuckle over an aching nipple, pulling my lips between my teeth on a whimper as my back arched off the wall.

Zach hummed appreciatively. "Look how responsive you are." He did the same to the other nipple, garnering a similar reaction. Each brush of my nipples shot straight to my clit like there was an invisible thread tied to both, connecting them. Everything he did to my breasts, I felt in my core. I could feel myself clenching around nothing, trying to get relief, but it seemed Zach was intent on torturing me.

"The moment you opened the door, I wondered what color your nipples were. I tried to guess if you kept your pussy bare or trimmed." He trailed his fingers back down, making my lower belly quiver as he passed it on his way farther south. He didn't stop until he cupped my mound in his large hand, letting out a groan while I cried out at his intimate touch. "Love this patch of pretty curls," he breathed against my lips, using his body to pin me in place against the wall as he slid his fingers through my slit. Back and forth, back and forth. "Love seeing them glisten with your wetness." He leaned in, nuzzling the crook of my neck before dragging the tip of his nose upward and whispering against my ear. "Tell me I can come inside, Rae. Tell me I can push my fingers inside this tight, drenched heat. That I can drop down to my knees and worship you with my mouth until you come on my tongue over and over, so much you have to beg me to stop. Tell me you'll let me make you feel like a goddess, Rae. Say yes, baby. Please."

Oh my God. He had a way with words; that was for certain. I wanted everything he said and so much more.

My breaths were coming at a rapid pace. I felt like something inside me was only moments from detonation. He pulled back, meeting my eyes, and I gave him what we both wanted so badly.

"Yes," I rasped. That one word carried off on a loud cry when Zach leaned in, pulling one of my nipples into his mouth and sucking deeply as he speared two fingers inside me.

The sharp sting of pain quickly faded into a pleasure I'd never experienced before. As Zach's mouth tormented my nipples in the best possible way, his fingers thrust into me, those long, thick digits sliding against a spot deep inside that no man had ever touched.

My whole body started to quake, pressure building from somewhere deep. The intensity of everything my body was experiencing was almost too much. I'd had orgasms before, but none of them compared to what was brewing.

My eyes fell closed, my head dropping back against the wall on a low moan as I felt Zach's mouth move to the valley between my breasts before traveling down. His tongue licked a scorching path, circling my belly button and traveling lower, lower, lower.

"Open your eyes, beautiful," he ground out, his words like sin and honey and the finest wine. I blinked my eyes open, forcing my heavy lids to half-mast to find Zach on his knees in front of me. It was the most intoxicating sight I'd ever seen, this big, strong, rough cowboy on his knees for me, all for my pleasure. "There she is." His lips curved upward when my hazy gaze collided with his. "I want you to watch as I devour you. I want you to see exactly who's making you feel so good."

On that order, he buried his face between my thighs, his magical tongue joining his fingers in raising me to heights I hadn't thought I was capable of reaching.

"Oh God, *yes*," I called out, my hands slapping against the wall behind me as Zach sucked my clit between his lips, the tip of his tongue flicking over the swollen bundle of nerves while his fingers continued to drive inside me, rubbing against that place that made stars burst in front of my eyes. "Zach," I panted, my voice sharp. My hips began to rock forward, chasing every sweep of his tongue as he continued to play with me. He grabbed one of my legs and threw it over his shoulder, opening me wider for him and groaned loudly against my folds as he lapped up my arousal.

"You taste like heaven and hell in one perfect package." Those brown eyes of his were like velvet when he looked up from between my legs. "I could die a happy man with your taste on my lips, baby."

"Don't stop," I pleaded as that screw deep inside me twisted tighter and tighter. "Please, Zach," I begged, his name coming out in a sob as my voice cracked. "I'm so close. I need to come."

He growled against my bare skin, turning his head just enough to sink his teeth into my inner thigh. "You can always count on me to give you what you need."

He dove back in, burying his face in a way he couldn't possibly be able to breathe, but he seemed perfectly fine with that.

His mouth and fingers worked in tandem, building me up to the point the sounds I was making became incomprehensible.

I felt my release closing in, the pressure mounting so much it almost scared me. Unable to hold myself up, I bent forward, bracing one hand on his head and the other on his shoulder, my nails digging in as my orgasm blazed through me, the raging inferno burning me alive.

I did exactly as he'd insisted, screaming his name, first as a benediction, then, as he continued to coax my release on and on, dragging it out, as a sob. I couldn't possibly take any more. I hadn't understood until that moment what people meant when they said you could have too much of a good thing. I didn't know if it was a million smaller orgasms all lined up or one cosmic one, but by the time Zach lowered my leg from his shoulder and stood in front of me, I felt destroyed. He'd wrecked me completely, and I didn't think I would ever be the same.

His mouth came back down on mine in a hard, demanding crash, the taste of my release still on his lips. His breaths were sawing in and out of his lungs, each one jagged and harsh when he pulled back and rested his forehead against mine. "I need to feel you, baby. I need that heat of yours wrapped around my cock."

I needed that too. More than anything.

Looping my arms over his shoulders, I gently brushed my lips against his, once, twice. "Then take me to bed."

And that was all the permission he needed.

Chapter Twenty-Two

Zach

I knew with the first swipe of my tongue in her sweet, honey-drenched pussy I'd been right. I wanted more. I would *always* want more.

Just that one taste and I was addicted. The sound of her whimper, the way she moaned my name, and the way her heat clenched around my fingers as she came on my mouth solidified it. I was done for. I hadn't even fucked her yet, but I already knew that was an absolute certainty.

The way her legs wrapped around my waist, how her ass fit perfectly in the palms of my hands as I lifted her off the ground and started down the hall to the bedroom, told me she was made for me; she fit against me perfectly.

I kicked the door to her bedroom open with my boot,

and carried her over to the bed, laying her out on the mattress and pushing the robe open completely so I could see every bit of her. She was even more beautiful than what I'd dreamed up. Her nipples were a rosy pink, just like her lips, the color complementing her smooth peaches-and-cream skin.

Her pussy had tasted like heaven, and I knew from how tightly it had clutched my fingers that it was going to squeeze my dick like a goddamn vise, and I couldn't fucking wait.

"Do you have any clue how much I want you?"

Her chest shook on choppy exhales as she pushed up on her elbows and drew her knees up, pressing them together timidly and looking at me through the fan of her sooty, thick lashes.

"Uh-uh. You don't get to hide from me, baby. Not when I finally have you. You're so fucking perfect, Rae. Let me see you."

She pulled that bottom lip between her teeth and bit down again, stirring my insides into a frenzy. Never in my life had I wanted a woman the way I wanted her. All rationality flew right out the window. She was the last piece of chocolate cake, the final lick of an ice cream cone on a hot summer day. She was a cold glass of water after a miserable trip through the desert.

She slowly spread her legs wide open, opening

herself up to me again, and it felt like the best gift I'd ever received.

She blushed from her cheeks all the way up to the tips of her ears as she wet her lips. "I . . . I want to see you too."

I raised a brow, a grin tugging at my lips. "Is that right?"

"Yes," she said more confidently, jutting her chin up for added measure. "Lose the shirt."

I let out a low chuckle as my dick twitched beneath my fly. "I'm here to serve." Reaching one arm behind my neck, I fisted the collar of my shirt and yanked it off, tossing it onto the floor. The way her eyelids drooped and her whole body flushed as she took me in with a hungry gaze made my chest swell. She liked what she saw, that much was clear from the expression on her face, and I had to admit, it was a relief. It wasn't me being arrogant when I said I knew I was attractive, but it wasn't like I had the time to hit a gym regularly. The muscles I had were the ones I'd earned from working the ranch.

Despite her claim of not being bothered by the twelve-year gap between us, until this very moment, it had left me feeling a little wary. I was in great shape, but I wasn't in my early twenties anymore. Not like the guys she was probably used to. I was thirty-five, and hard work guaranteed that I felt every one of those years in a sore back or creaky knees. There wasn't a chance in hell I would have been able to keep up with those California model types she used to run with.

One night, when sleep had been hard to come by, I had let my curiosity get the better of me and ended up googling the woman who had plagued most of my thoughts. I clicked through more pictures than I was willing to admit to so I knew I was the polar opposite of every one of the men she'd been photographed with before coming to Safe Haven.

"God, Zach," she sighed my name as her eyes darkened. "I want you."

That was enough to ease any insecurities I might have felt, and I didn't waste another second. I made quick work of grabbing the condom I had stashed in my wallet before yanking my fly open and shoving my jeans and boxer briefs down my legs. I kicked off my boots and shucked the rest of my clothes, leaving them in a pile as I stalked the two feet between me and the bed.

I didn't miss the way Rae's eyes flared as she stared at my straining cock while I ripped the condom wrapper open with my teeth and slid the latex over my length.

"Zach," she said, her throat working on a swallow. "I —I don't think . . . I don't think you'll fit."

Christ, this woman was good for my ego. Placing a

knee in the mattress, I climbed over her and took her mouth in a heated kiss.

I kissed her until she went boneless, sinking into the mattress, until my cock practically wept to thrust inside of her. "Remember what I said about not causing you any pain?" She nodded, her hair fanning out around her. "I meant it. I'll make this good for you, baby. I swear it."

She brought one hand up to caress my cheek, and I couldn't help but lean into her touch. She was pure warmth and light, and I couldn't get enough. "I believe you."

She was undoing me. Each sweet, soft word unraveled me in the very best way. I reached between us, fisting my aching cock in my hand and lining it up with her. The moment the head notched into place, my lungs froze. Even through the condom, I could feel how hot she was, how wet, and I would have given anything to feel her with nothing between us, because I knew there would be no better feeling on the planet.

But that was for another time. And there *would* be another time, because this wasn't going to be nearly enough.

My jaw clenched and my molars ground together as I slid inside her slowly, one agonizing inch at a time. It took everything in me not to rut into her like a goddamn animal. She felt so fucking good. She was so tight; I knew she needed a chance to adjust or this wouldn't be as good for her as it already was for me, and that wasn't acceptable.

Her eyes widened and her lips parted on a surprised O as I continued to slowly work myself deeper. "Oh my God! Zach, you're so big . . ." Her breath hitched. "I'm so full."

As my body screamed at me to keep going, I stopped, needing to check on her more than I needed to get off. "Tell me if I'm hurting you and we'll stop."

Her head thrashed against the pillows. "No, please, Zach. Oh God. No, don't stop. If you stop, I'll die."

Thank Christ. I would have stopped if she wanted me to. I would have pulled out and put an end to this here and now, but it would have killed me. You couldn't get a small taste of heaven and be expected not to want more, and that was exactly what having her cunt wrapped around me like a glove was. *Heaven.*

A sweat had broken out across my forehead and down my spine. My arms were starting to shake as every other muscle in my body twisted tight. "I'm almost there, baby. Just a little bit more."

Her mouth dropped open. "You—you aren't all the way in yet?"

I couldn't help but laugh. "Fuck, you're perfect."

Finally, I slid home, buried as deep as I could get, and I could have sworn I'd just experienced nirvana.

I lowered my head, resting my forehead against hers as I pulled out a couple inches and steadily pushed back in. "You have no idea how good you feel."

"Do that again."

That was an order I couldn't possibly ignore. I pulled out and thrust in again, a little harder this time, testing to see how much she could take. Her lips parted on a silent gasp as her neck and back arched. I felt her clutch on me give slightly, her body accepting me and allowing me more room to move.

Each forward snap of my hips was a little faster, a little rougher, as the grip on my control started to slip, until finally, I was fucking her the way I'd been fantasizing for weeks. Her pelvis tilted with every powerful drive of my cock into her, her body rocking in time with mine, meeting me thrust for thrust.

Her hands grabbed at my biceps and shoulders, her nails sinking in and leaving crescent shapes behind as she did her best to hold on to me. The sounds she made drove me insane, the unintelligible words spilling past her lips spurring me on.

"I can feel you. You're right there." Her walls clamped down on me like a fist, squeezing almost to the point of pain. "Give it to me, Rae."

Her hands went to my head, her fingers tangling in my short hair and fisting it tightly as her entire body locked up beneath mine. She came on a crashing wave, my name echoing off the walls as her pussy did it's best to milk my cum from my balls, but I refused to let go until her release finished completely. I wanted to watch every single second of her coming. It was the most beautiful thing I'd ever seen.

Finally, her body sagged against the bed, and I lost all control. Wrapping my arms around her tightly, I gave her my weight, burying my face in the crook of her neck as I plunged in and out. The tingle at the base of my spine grew, my balls drawing up tight against my body, and seconds later, I came harder than I ever had, spilling myself into the condom as I groaned and growled against her neck, my hips rolling against hers until there was nothing left. I slowed before finally coming to a stop and releasing a gust of air that made her hair flutter.

It took a few more seconds for me to get my bearings and for the strength to return to my limbs, but I was finally able to push up so I could look at her face. My heart raced at what I saw, the brilliant smile that stretched across her beautiful face.

I reached up with one hand, brushing a strand of hair off her forehead. "Did I hurt you?"

Her cheeks heated as she shook her head and bit

down on her bottom lip again. "No," she whispered. "Not at all."

The tension left my shoulders on a relieved sigh as I shifted us on the bed, taking us both to our sides, face to face, while making sure I stayed inside her. I knew I'd have to get up and dispose of the condom eventually, especially if there was going to be a round two, but I wasn't ready to break our connection. There was something about this first time with her that felt different. It was more profound than any other sexual encounter I'd had. Even when I lost my virginity. Keeping us locked together like this kept me grounded. She was the only thing preventing me from floating off.

"You're breathtaking when you come," I told her as I trailed my fingers up and down her hip, needing to touch as much of her as I could reach.

Her smile was shy and slightly giddy. "You aren't so bad yourself."

I chuckled, wrapping my arm around her waist and pulling her even tighter against me. "Just so you know, I'm sleeping here tonight."

I felt her smile form against my chest. "Okay," she said on a quiet giggle.

"And we're going to do that at least one more time before I let you get any sleep."

"Okay," she repeated, this time pressing a kiss right above my heart, and I knew I was a goner.

Chapter Twenty-Three

Rae

I pulled the sheets off the mattress and tossed them into the laundry bin on my cart as a huge yawn cracked my jaw.

I might have woken up with a spring in my step after spending the night with Zach, but that had quickly worn off once I started my shift at the lodge. I was functioning on three hours of sleep. I couldn't complain, however. Especially after the number of orgasms he'd given me well into the early hours of the morning.

Despite being exhausted, I couldn't seem to wipe the smile off my face. I might have been tired, but my mood was exceptionally bright. I'd gladly live the rest of my life sleep deprived if it meant I got more of what he'd given me the night before.

Once we both finally passed out from exhaustion, I

slept sounder than I had in a very long time. I wouldn't have pegged Zach for a cuddler, but he held me all night long. Even when I moved, he'd follow after me, that arm coming back around my waist to hold me against him. Being in his arms like that, safe and secure after he'd worked my body to the point of collapse, had been the best sleep of my life. Not even the mattresses at one of the swanky five-star hotels I'd stayed in during my lifetime had compared to cuddling with Zach Paulson.

"What's that smile about?"

I whipped around at the sound of Ivy's voice, bringing a hand to my chest. "You scared me." I shook my head at her. "I need to put a freaking cat bell on you or something. I didn't hear you coming."

Her brows rose high on her forehead. "It's not my fault. I made plenty of noise. I even knocked," she defended, pointing to the opened door of the room I'd been cleaning. "You didn't hear me because you were too busy daydreaming."

I fought the grin that pulled at my lips, forcing my expression into a scowl. "Was not." I really was.

"Oh, you absolutely were." She smiled giddily and pointed at me. "Your cheeks and ears are turning red and you have this glow about you—" Her words stopped abruptly and she pulled in a gasp that sucked all the air from the guest room. "Oh my God! You had sex!"

"Shhh!" I hissed, flapping a hand wildly and looking around like someone might have been lurking around, ready to pop out at any moment. "No, I didn't. And even if I had, you don't need to go around yelling stuff like that."

She checked in the hallway behind her before rushing into the room. When she continued her voice was a whisper, but no less enthusiastic. "Yes, you did, you dirty little liar. You have to tell me. Who was it?" She pulled in a sharp breath. "Was it Raylan? I've known him since we were kids, but there's no denying that man turned out *fine as hell*. Or was it one of the other ranch hands?" She clasped her hands in front of her and bounced in place as she begged. "*Please*, you have to tell me."

"There was no one." I continued with the lie, feeling shitty for it, but, even though I'd had the best night of my life with Zach, I wasn't sure it would be wise to broadcast that around the ranch. He was still my boss, after all, and I was here to prove that I was a grownup capable of making healthy decisions. My feelings for Zach were very real and very raw, and while a part of me wanted to climb to the highest point of the lodge's roof and shout it at the top of my lungs, there was still another part that was worried the people I'd come to know, and come to respect and care for, might look at me differently if they found out. "There's nothing to tell, Ivy. I just had a good night's sleep." *Lie.* "And that put me in a good mood." *Truth.*

Her smile fell, her bottom lip sticking out in a pout. "Whatever. You're no fun."

I smiled, shaking my head at her ridiculousness. She stuck around and helped me finish the room so we could head to lunch together.

"Hey girls," Becky Hightower called from the front desk as we descended the stairs to the lobby. I'd gotten to know Zach's grandmother pretty well from working at the lodge, and I had to say, I adored the woman. She was fierce and funny and said what was on her mind, whether it was appropriate or not. She reminded me of Betty White whenever she cussed or told sex jokes. She'd quickly become one of my favorite people.

"Hi Becky." I smiled brightly, heading her direction. I stopped in front of her desk and rested my elbows on the ledge. "How's your day going?"

"Can't complain. No guests testing my nerves so far and making me want to smother them in their sleep, so that's a win."

My laugh morphed into another huge yawn. "Sorry about that."

"No worries, dear. Looks like someone needs to get a good night's sleep tonight."

"Hmm. Interesting." I felt Ivy's scrutinizing look drilling into the side of my face. "She said she had a great night's sleep," she said accusingly.

Becky's confused gaze bounced between us, waiting for my response, but before I could formulate one, the door to the lodge opened, and the air turned electric, brushing against my skin like static and causing the tiny hairs on my arms to lift.

I felt Zach's presence the moment he entered the same room and looked in his direction a few seconds before Becky and Ivy spotted him.

"Oh, hey, sweetie." Becky smiled brightly as her grandson drew closer. "This is a pleasant surprise. What brings you by?"

My heart started to beat harder when I noticed his gaze remained fixed on me as he closed the distance, a look of fierce determination on his gorgeous face. I kept expecting him to acknowledge the other two people with me, but when he didn't, a tiny bolt of panic shot through me. He got closer, homing in on me like a heat-seeking missile. I took a step back, but there was nowhere for me to go without calling attention to myself.

He caught my tiny retreat and smiled wickedly, looking at me like I was a tiny, helpless bunny and he was a wolf about to strike. And that was exactly what he did. The instant he was close enough, his arm shot out and banded around my waist, yanking me into the solid wall of his chest.

My hands came up in an attempt to push him back as my eyes bugged out. "What are you doing?" I hissed under my breath, not that it mattered. Becky and Ivy were gaping at us already.

"What's it look like I'm doin'?" His voice came out in a delicious rumble. The smell of leather and sunshine and clean cotton wafted off him and filled my lungs, the scent like an aphrodisiac. "I'm sayin' hello to my girl." I leaned back as he leaned in, my eyes darting between Ivy and Becky worriedly. His brows sank into a frown when I dodged his kiss. "Why are you avoiding my kiss?"

"Uh . . ." I wet my lips nervously. "Your grand-mother and Ivy are *right* there."

His head reared back in confusion. "So?"

I applied a little more pressure to his chest, but it was like trying to move a brick wall. He wasn't budging and I wasn't going anywhere. That much was clear. "What do you mean so? We haven't discussed going public like this," I continued to whisper. "You're my boss, Zach. I don't want people to think—"

"Fuck what people think," he growled, his arm around my waist growing impossibly tighter. "I don't give a shit what anyone thinks. I'm not your boss, I'm your man, and I'm damn well gonna kiss you when I want to. I don't give a shit who's around to see it."

"But—"

He proved his point by closing the rest of the distance and sealing his lips with mine. The kiss wasn't soft or slow. It was hard and possessive. He was proving a point, not only to me but to whoever was around to see it. I would have been lying if I said it didn't turn me on.

My legs had gone wobbly by the time he finished, and I had to lean deeper into him to stay upright. The frown he'd been wearing a second ago was replaced with a smile that lit me up from the inside. I would have given anything for a lifetime of smiles like the one he was wearing right then.

"Let's try this again," he said, giving me an affectionate squeeze. "Hey, baby."

I blushed on my own grin, feeling downright giddy as I whispered, "Hi."

"I *knew it!*"

Ivy's loud declaration shattered the moment, reminding me that we weren't alone. Instead of letting me go, Zach shifted me to his side, making sure to keep that arm around me like he was afraid I'd run. My entire face felt like it was on fire as Ivy gawked and Becky smiled like she'd just won the lottery.

"Ivy," Zach greeted amiably, his tone softening as he

shifted his attention to his grandmother. "Grandma. Lookin' beautiful as always."

"Ooh, I like this. I like this a whole lot. My boy gets himself a good woman and he goes from a miserable grump to a smooth talker with the flip of a switch."

I looked up at him in confusion. "You've been a miserable grump?"

Affection shone clear as day in his eyes as he traced my jawline with the tips of his fingers. "For the past week and a half," he admitted, making my heart skip a few beats before it righted itself. "But that's all been straightened out now."

It sure had.

"How long has this been going on?" Ivy asked, that excitement from earlier having returned.

"Just since yesterday," I answered at the same time Zach said, "Since the day Rae arrived."

My head whipped back around, my jaw falling open as my belly swooped. "Really?"

He let out a raspy chuckle and shook his head good-naturedly. "Christ, you're pretty."

I didn't think I'd ever get tired of hearing him say that. I also wasn't sure I'd ever get used to it. If my flush got any deeper my face would look like a stop sign.

"Seems you two have a little more communicating to

do and a little less bed shaking, if you know what I mean," Becky said with a waggle of her eyebrows.

I barked out a bewildered laugh as Zach let out a pained groan. "Christ, Grandma. Can you not?"

She held her hands up innocently as Ivy cackled with delight. "I'm just saying. Seems like you two aren't quite on the same page yet. It's important in every relationship for that to happen quickly."

Was that what we were in, I wondered to myself. A relationship?

As if reading my mind, Zach looked back down at me, that strong resolve of his returning. "I plan on taking care of that right now." he said, shifting back to Becky and Ivy. "It was good to see you both, but if you'll excuse us, I'm gonna steal Rae away for lunch."

"Oh, but I don't think I have time—"

"See you when you get back," Ivy butted in, her face saying it all. She was thrilled for me and wanted me to enjoy my time with my new *man*.

"See you soon," I returned, smiling goofily as Zach began to lead me away.

"Oh, sweetie," Becky called, bringing us to a stop. "You know I'll be telling your mama and daddy all about this the first chance I get. So we'll all be expecting you to bring her to the party tomorrow night."

He let out a groan and dropped his head back. "I tell you guys every year, we don't need to have a party."

"Is it your birthday?" I asked, my mind reeling as I tried to think of how I could get a gift on such short notice. Gift giving was kind of a love language of mine, and I needed at least three weeks to guarantee I find the perfect present.

"It's his adoption day party," Becky answered.

I was turned partially away from her, so she couldn't see the look of pure shock on my face, but Zach didn't miss it. His eyes communicated everything he was thinking. *I'll tell you all about it.*

I silently responded. *You damn well better.*

"She'll be there, Gram. We'll see you guys in a bit."

He picked up the pace, hustling me out of the lodge before anyone could drop any other bombs.

Chapter Twenty-Four

Rae

I couldn't pull my gaze from Zach's profile as we bumped along the gravel lane in his truck, the lodge growing smaller in the rearview mirror. We reached the T in the lane that would take us off the ranch if we made a right or toward the barn if we went left. Zach cranked the wheel to the left.

"Where are we going?" I asked as a country ballad played at a low volume through the truck's speakers.

"I'm taking you to my place. Thought I might make lunch for you there."

My brows winged up toward my hairline. "You cook?"

He grinned and nodded his head without taking his eyes off the road. "Sure do. Grandma was an incredible cook and taught my mom everything she knew, and in return, Mom taught me."

I felt a tiny smile pull at my lips. "Is that your roundabout way of saying you're a pretty good cook?"

He glanced in my direction, his smirk wolfish. "No, baby. That's my roundabout way of telling you I'm a fuckin' awesome cook."

My head fell back on a laugh. I liked that he wasn't humble about it, that he didn't hesitate to brag about his skills. It wasn't narcissism or false bravado. He knew what he was good at and he owned it. There was something insanely attractive about that.

He pulled his truck up beside his house, ordering me to stay put as he hopped out and jogged around the hood to my side to open my door and help me out. I looked at his place, taking in the outside and noticing that it was kind of a cross between a grownup version of the cabin I was staying in and the large ranch house his grandparents used to live in, the beautiful one near the barn that sat empty.

I'd been curious about Zach's place since I first spotted it tucked into the grove of trees. I wondered how a man like him would decorate, which way his tastes leaned. Was he a messy bachelor, or did he like things tidy? What did he do in his downtime? Did he like videogames or did he prefer to relax in front of the television? There was so much about Zach I wanted to know, and now that we were . . . whatever we were, I could finally put some of those curiosities to rest. Starting with how he kept house.

A few pairs of boots, all dusty and well used, were beside the front door for easy access, but the living room was spotless. There was a large television mounted above the fireplace, facing a buttery leather couch the color of tobacco, but there were no gaming consoles in sight. Instead, I noticed rows of paperbacks on the built-in shelves on either side of the fireplace. Thrillers mostly, with some murder mysteries thrown in.

"You've got quite the collection here," I said as I moved in the direction of the shelves while he headed for the kitchen at the back of the living room. The open concept of his house made it easy for us to carry on a conversation. I dragged my fingers along the spines. "Have you read all of these?"

"About half, maybe. Some more than once."

"Is that what you like to do when you're trying to relax? Read?"

"Mostly. I also like to watch the sunset from my back deck with a beer or a glass of bourbon. Much better quality than that shit I was drinking in the barn. Or there's a place I have on the ranch where I like to go to clear my head."

I spotted a couple picture frames and bent forward to get a better look. One of the pictures was of Zach and a group of guys. Some I recognized like Connor and Raylan, but the others weren't familiar. Then there were the obligatory family photos, high school graduations, a couple family Christmas photos. But the one that caught my eye was of a much younger Zach. He couldn't have been more than twelve years old in the photo. He was all arms and legs in the picture, at that awkward age where the growth spurts start, but the weight hasn't quite caught up yet. He was lanky, his hair overly long and falling across his forehead and into his eyes in a style I assumed was popular at that time. The photo was taken in front of a small, red brick courthouse. On either side of Zach stood Rory and Cord Paulson, his parents.

The three of them stood on the wide cement steps, all of them beaming brilliantly at the camera. In Zach's hands was a very official looking piece of paper. I squinted and leaned in to get a better look, reading the words *Certificate of Adoption* across the top.

The picture warmed my heart at the same time a pang of sadness worked its way through me. If that was a picture from the day he was officially adopted by Rory and Cord, how long had he been in the foster system?

My curiosity got the best of me, and I moved away from the bookshelves and into the kitchen where Zach was in the middle of preparing some kind of pasta salad. I sat on one of the stools across the island from him and rested my chin in my hand as I watched him work.

"How old were you when you were adopted?" I finally asked.

"Twelve." He answered the question easily, like it was nothing at all. "I was raised in foster care my whole life up until that point." He offered the information like he knew how badly I wanted to know, but was too nervous to ask.

When I remained quiet, he lifted his gaze from the tomatoes and cucumbers he was slicing and looked at me. "I don't mind talkin' about it, baby, so if you have questions, just ask."

I started with the one that had been bouncing around in my head since Becky dropped the bomb about the adoption day celebration.

"How in the world did I not know you were adopted until now?"

He lifted one large shoulder in a casual shrug. "I don't mind talkin' about it, but that doesn't mean I advertise it. I don't introduce myself by sayin', 'Hey, I'm Zach. I'm 35, a Sagittarius, and I was adopted when I was twelve.' If it comes up organically, I'm an open book."

My lips curled in a slow smile. "You're a Sagittarius?" I asked teasingly.

He chuckled at my question. "Hell if I know. I've never really paid any attention to that shit. That was just the first one that came to mind."

"Well, if you're interested in knowing, I'm a Libra. We're compatible with Aquarius, Gemini, Taurus, and . . ." I paused for dramatic effect, "Sagittarius." I shot him a saucy wink, earning a full-blown laugh that made the apex of my thighs tingle.

"Good to know." He pushed the vegetables to the side and began chopping a bunch of fresh herbs I wouldn't have been able to name if my life depended on it. "Honestly, I'm surprised you didn't realize it until now. I mean, I am the only blond-haired, brown-eyed person in my family."

I shrugged, reaching out and grabbing a tiny piece of cucumber and tossing it into my mouth. "I figured there were relatives farther down the line that you took after, but it makes sense now."

"Yeah, well, whether or not I look like any of them, they're my real family. Cord and Rory took me in, they made me their son when I thought I was going to end up staying in the system until I aged out. I couldn't have asked for better parents if I'd picked them myself."

"I'm really glad you all found each other. How did you guys meet?"

He smiled down at the cutting board as he scooped

up the herbs and tossed them into a tiny blender, squeezing in some lime juice by hand and added a couple other liquids to the mixture. He pulsed it for a few seconds until it was all combined before answering.

"I threw a rock through the window of Rory's bar." He looked up at me through his lashes. "I was a bit of a troublemaker. Anyway, I threw the rock and Cord chased me down. He'd been a foster kid too, so he knew one when he saw one. It kind of snowballed from there."

"I love that," I said with a soft smile. "And they brought you here? To the ranch?"

"Yep. This has been home since that night, and I couldn't imagine ever wanting to be anywhere else."

I was starting to understand that feeling. I looked down, tracing the veins of gray in the white marble countertop with my finger. "I get that. The longer I'm here, the more at home I start to feel. I never felt like that in L.A."

"I'm glad to hear that. It would make keeping you kind of difficult if you kept trying to run off to California when I wasn't looking."

My belly swooped as I met his gaze, but I forced out a laugh, trying desperately to play it off. "You say that like you're in this for the long haul." I tried to keep my tone even, injecting lightness into the conversation.

"That's because I am."

I choked on air, sputtering at the seriousness in his tone. "Zach," I croaked once I was able to breathe. "We've been together for like, five minutes. You can't possibly know me well enough to make a call like that. We haven't even had the talk where we decide if we're dating or if we're putting some kind of label on this."

He pointed the spoon he'd been using to stir the boiling pasta on the stove at my face. "First, it's been a hell of a lot longer than five minutes. I wasn't lying when I told my grandma and Ivy that this has been goin' on since the day you got to the ranch. That's when it started for me. And I know you better than you think. I stood at that window your first night here and watched as you screamed at a bird for five minutes before crying like your heart was being shattered into pieces."

My jaw dropped open as I rocked back on the stool. "You—you saw that?" I squeaked, humiliation burning the tips of my ears.

"I did. First I thought it was cute as hell, then the sound of you crying gutted me. It still cuts me open every time I think about it. I think that might have been the moment I knew you were supposed to be mine, because all I wanted to do was go to you and hold you. Then I wanted to fix everything so you'd never cry again." He stole the breath right from my lungs with that confession. My mouth hung open, but I couldn't find the words.

"As for a label, I don't really care. If you want to call me your boyfriend, go for it. All I know is that I'm yours and you're mine. Nothing else really matters."

I closed my eyes and lifted my hands, my emotions swirling around too fast for me to control. "This is all happening so fast." I tried to steady my breathing and calm my racing heart. "I don't know what to say. I'm kind of overwhelmed right now."

I hadn't realized he'd moved, rounding the counter to reach me until I felt his fingers pressing beneath my chin, startling my eyes open as he lifted my face to his. "There's no set rule saying how fast or slow a relationship is supposed to go. I'm moving at the speed that feels right. But if you need me to slow down so you can catch your breath, all you have to do is say the word, baby. This is real for me. I'm in this, all the way, and I'm willing to wait for you to catch up."

"God," I breathed out. "You've got to stop being so perfect. I can't take it."

His lips curved upward in a beautiful smile before he pressed them to mine in a gentle kiss. "I'm just bein' me, Rae. And you can handle so much more than you give yourself credit for." He kissed me again, this one harder, more urgent.

"Zach," I whispered. "You can't turn me on like this right now. We're supposed to have lunch then get back to work."

He groaned against my mouth and grabbed me by my hips, twisting me around on the stool so he could push my knees open and fit his hips between my legs. He moved in close enough that I could feel his steely erection against my belly as he feasted on my mouth.

"Fuck work. I'm your boss and I'm ordering my girlfriend to take an extra-long lunch break so I can fuck her until this ache she causes beneath my skin goes away."

Who was I to argue with the boss?

Chapter Twenty-Five

Rae

The hunger in Zach's gaze lit an inferno inside me. That look alone was enough to make me wet, but when he kissed me like his very life depended on it, my entire body turned into a live wire. Every cell, every nerve ending, was sparking white hot.

He hefted me off the stool like I weighed nothing, giving me no choice but to lock my legs around his waist as he carried me over to the long dining room table placed in front of a wall of windows that overlooked the trees surrounding the property. I would have loved to take in the view any other time, but just then, he was the only thing I could see. The only thing that existed for me.

He trailed biting kisses along my neck as he sat me down on the table, and I knew what was about to happen. The idea of seeing him on his knees for me again was enough to make me melt, but there was something else I wanted to do this time, something I'd been fantasizing about for longer than I'd been willing to admit until just recently.

Before he could lower himself to the floor, I pushed off the table, placing my hands on his shoulders and switching our positions around.

"Baby, what—?" I silenced him by going up on my toes and kissing the words away.

"You got your taste last night," I informed him. "Now it's my turn."

His groan sounded downright painful as I lowered myself onto my knees in front of him. I looked up at him through the fan of my lashes as I worked his belt loose and popped the button of his jeans open.

My nipples tightened and my clit pulsed in time with my frantic heart and the steady whoosh of blood in my ears. I'd never been much of a fan of blow jobs in the past, but Zach was different. I couldn't wait to get my mouth around him. Just the thought of it had my body primed and ready for him.

"Fuck, Rae," he hissed, his teeth clenched as I pulled his jeans and boxer briefs down enough to free his erection. My tongue shot out instantly, swiping at the bead of pre-cum that had formed on the tip. "*Ah, shit!*" he barked loud enough to make me jump. My gaze shot up to his face, worry that I'd somehow hurt him coursing through me, but I saw that wasn't it in the way his eyes had grown black, in the way his knuckles had turned white as he gripped the edge of the table so hard it was a wonder he hadn't ripped a chunk of the wood clean off. He wasn't hurting, he was delirious with want. And *I* was the one who made him that way.

"Please, baby," he begged, his chest rising and falling with each rapid breath. "God, please put your mouth on me. I'm fuckin' dying here."

How could I deny a plea like that? Opening my mouth, I leaned forward and took him as far as I could, only stopping when the head of his cock bumped the back of my throat and made me gag.

"Oh, fuck me," he grunted, his words spurring me on. "Fuck, your mouth. It's so goddamn perfect."

I fisted the base of his shaft, working my hand and mouth in tandem as I began to bob up and down his length. His dick twitched in my mouth as I picked up the pace, flattening my tongue against the underside of his cock on an upward glide before flicking the slit at the crown with the tip of my tongue.

The sounds Zach was making were driving me out of my mind. I had to clench my thighs against the steady thrum in my core as I continued to suck him off, hollowing out my cheeks and giving this blow job my all. He was losing control, and I wanted to push him over the edge. I *needed* it. I needed to feel the power that came with driving a man like Zach Paulson to insanity.

"Baby. Baby, stop," he panted, his hands coming up and fisting in my hair, but I was too far gone. "I'm gonna come if you keep doing that."

Good, I thought to myself, tightening my fist around him. I wanted him to come in my mouth, down my throat. I wanted to taste him, to swallow his release down, knowing I was the one who had gotten him there.

I let out a moan at the thought of his hot release filling my mouth. I was prepared for it, but just as my eyelids started to sink lower, Zach reached down, grabbed me under my arms, and hauled me up.

I yelped as he spun me around and placed a hand in the center of my back. He pushed me forward until I was bent at the waist sprawled across his table, "I'm not comin' down your throat," he snarled as he ripped my leggings and panties down my thighs and placed a sharp, stinging smack against my ass cheek. I squeaked, the pain lasting only a second before it bloomed into pleasure. It was on the tip of my tongue to beg for another, but before I could get the words out, I felt the blunt head of his cock notch into place, and in the next breath, he buried himself completely on one powerful thrust.

We both shouted out and froze in place. "Zach," I pleaded as the seconds ticked by and he didn't move.

"Fuck, *fuck*," he hissed, his entire body locked so rigid I thought for a moment he might shatter into a million pieces.

"What's wrong?" I braced my palms on the table and tried to push up, but his hand on my back held me in place.

"Don't move," he grunted. "Just . . . gimme a second."

I twisted my neck, looking back at him over my shoulder. "What's going on?"

His nostrils flared on a ragged inhale and his eyes had gone hazy. "Forgot the condom," he said, continuing with his grunting speech like he'd reverted back to his earliest caveman. "And your mouth drove me to the edge. I need a minute to calm down."

Oh God. That's why this felt so good, I thought to myself. It was because there was nothing between us.

"I—I'm on the pill." My voice wobbled ever so slightly. "And I'm clean. I mean . . . if you want to."

He moaned, long and low, his eyes threatening to roll back in his head. "You'd let me come inside you, baby?"

"If that's what you want to do."

"Christ, I'm dyin' to see my cum drip out of you. And I'm clean too, I swear it. I'd never put you at risk."

I already knew that. I trusted this man with every single cell in my body. The only people who'd ever gotten that from me were my parents, and now Zach. He was the only other person on the face of the planet who made me feel safe, protected. The way he ran a hand along my spine beneath my shirt was reverent. He made me feel cherished. A woman could get used to this kind of treatment, that was for damn sure.

"I know. Now, please, Zach. I need you to move."

"Can't be soft with you this time. I'm too far gone."

"Do it," I said on a moan. "Be rough with me, Zach. I won't break."

That last word had barely passed my lips when he pulled nearly all the way out and drove in so hard the legs of the table scraped across the floor. "*Yes!*" I cried out, my voice echoing through the open space, bouncing off the walls and traveling back to us.

"You're so perfect for me. You know that, Rae?"

"Don't stop." My voice was rough and throaty. My nails dug into the wooden surface of the table as Zach fucked me like a man possessed, each thrust so hard and deep I knew I'd feel him for days.

"Can't get enough of you, baby. I'll *never* get enough of you. I can't stop wanting you."

"I want you too," I said on a broken sob as the pressure in my core built and built. I felt like the boiler in the Stanley Hotel, reaching critical levels, about to explode and burn everything in my path.

"Say you're mine." Those words came out as a plea, not a command. "Tell me you're mine, Rae, that you're feeling this too. Tell me I'm not the only one."

"I feel it," I whimpered, my inner walls clutching at Zach as my release grew closer. "It's not just you."

He grabbed my hair, wrapping the length around his fist and yanking, bringing my head up as he leaned down over me, his chest against my back. Every inch of my upper body was pinned to the table. I couldn't have moved if I wanted to, but I'd never felt safer in my life. "Tell me what I want to hear, baby," he growled, and this time it *was* a command. "Tell me you're mine."

"I am, Zach," I assured him, my voice rising on every word. "I'm yours. You have me."

"That's right," he rasped against my ear, his tongue coming out and sweeping along the column of my throat. "I have you. And you have me. Completely, Rae."

"Oh God."

"I feel you," he grunted. "Your pussy is squeezin' me like a silky vise. Give it to me, baby. Come all over me and milk me dry."

His words were all it took to send me soaring over

the edge. My release hit with surprising strength, the rush like the biggest, fastest drop on a roller coaster. Stars exploded behind my eyelids as I screamed his name until I went hoarse.

Before I finished, he let go on a roar of my name. Those first hot jets of his cum were enough to drag my release out, making it last even longer. By the time we were done, we were both boneless and out of breath.

The condensation from my breath created a cloud over the glossy surface of the table. "It's never been like this for me," I admitted. "Is this what sex is always supposed to be like?"

My eyes fell closed on a contented sigh when I felt the pads of his fingers brush gently across my temple, tucking a strand of hair behind my ear. "I don't know, sweetheart. This is a first for me too. But . . ."

I managed to peel my eyes open and twisted my head just enough to see him over my shoulder. "But what?"

"But I think it might be because it's you. At least for me. And I think it's the way it is for you because you're with me. I don't think anyone else could make us feel the way we make each other feel."

That thought was as exhilarating as it was terrifying, because what if this didn't work out?

I swallowed, pushing that thought away. This wasn't

another of my mistakes. This was different. *He* was different. This was something special, I knew that down to my soul, and I wasn't going to let fear dictate my actions any longer.

"I think you're right."

Just then, my stomach grumbled loud enough there was no way Zach missed it. He grinned and chuckled as my cheeks heated. "Come on, baby. Let me get you fed before we have to go back to work. It's the least I owe you after what you just gave me."

He stood tall, letting his half-hard erection slip free before taking my hand and easing me off the table. He righted my pants before going to work on his.

"Pretty sure I'm the one who had the most orgasms this time around," I said teasingly as he pulled me into an embrace.

His face was warm and full of affection. "I'm not talking about the sex, baby," he said tenderly before leaning in for another kiss. Then he let me go and moved back to the kitchen to finish lunch like he hadn't just sent my world into a tailspin.

Chapter Twenty-Six

Rae

I was a nervous wreck.

I woke up anxious as hell, and it had only gotten worse as the morning progressed. I couldn't stop thinking about the party tonight and the fact that this was the first time a man was taking me to his parents' house.

Sure, I knew his family, and I saw them multiple times a week, but this was different. Before I was only another Safe Haven Ranch or Second Hope Lodge employee. Tonight I'd be seeing them as Zach's girl-friend—or his label-less woman or whatever I finally settled on. My reputation wasn't exactly sterling, and they all knew the reason I'd ended up on this ranch in the first place.

I couldn't stop worrying that they wouldn't approve

of their son dating me. They would want to protect him from the drama that was my life before I came here—most of that drama I had either caused or willingly participated in.

This really was a crappy day to have off from work, because after Zach left earlier this morning, I'd had way too much time to pace my cabin and think of the million and one ways tonight could be an epic failure.

I tried to keep my mind off it and busy myself by cleaning the cabin, but as it turned out, it barely took an hour to clean a space that was less than eight hundred square feet if you didn't have to scrub cobwebs and a years' worth of un-lived-in grime off things.

I puttered around the tiny kitchen, experimenting with other recipes before I snapped. I couldn't stand my own company any longer. I had to get out of there, and only one person I could think of had the power to talk me off the ledge I was currently teetering on.

I headed out the front door and booked it to the barn in search of Zach. Anticipation at seeing him fizzed in my belly like a bottle of champagne that had been shaken up. I'd seen him a handful of hours ago, yet I already missed him. I wasn't sure whether or not that was healthy, but I decided to follow his lead and go with how I felt.

Sassy was out at pasture with the other horses, so I

moved past the stalls, checking the tack room and other areas of the barn, and out the other side, keeping an eye out for Zach. Gretel was standing at the fence of her pen, watching me intently while the other goats played. I shot the animal a glare and pointed my finger in her direction. "I know you're thinking up ways to cause trouble. Whatever you're concocting in that head of yours, knock it off."

I was officially losing it. I was talking to animals like I was Dr. Doolittle or something. That couldn't have been a good sign.

"Rae?"

I spun around at the sound of Zach's voice and let out a heavy sigh of relief. Being in his presence was enough to calm the turmoil that had been swirling inside me all day.

"Hey. I was looking for you, but I thought maybe you were out in the east pasture today."

He hooked his thumb over his shoulder as he started in my direction in that trademark swagger that was natural to him. I took him in, every inch, from the backward baseball cap on his head, to the tee that stretched over his defined chest and biceps and the jeans I knew first-hand hugged his ass to perfection, to the dusty boots on his feet. He was walking, talking cowboy porn, in the flesh. "I was in the back office trying not to die of boredom as I went over some paperwork." His hand shot out as soon as he was close enough, his finger catching in the beltloop of my jeans and tugging me into him. "But things are lookin' up now that you're here."

My interest piqued, I rolled up on the balls of my feet and glanced over his shoulder. "There's an office in here? I didn't know that."

"Sure is. My least favorite place on the whole ranch." He grabbed my hand and pulled me along with him. "Come on, I'll show you. Maybe you'll let me talk you into making out there and I won't dread havin' to work there so much."

I let out a little giggle as I skip-walked to keep up with his longer strides. He took a left just past the tack room and moved farther down a hall I'd never been down. There was an open door at the very end, and as soon as we stepped through, I understood why he disliked it so much. It was pretty bleak. The furniture looked like it hadn't been replaced since the mid-seventies. And not in the cool vintage way that was coming back into style. The desk was littered with so much paperwork you could barely see the surface. Zach was the kind of man who needed fresh air, sunshine, and wide-open spaces, but the only sunlight filtering into the room was through a tiny, dingy window that had about twenty years' worth of grime coating it.

"What do you do in here?" I asked as I let go of his hand, curiosity tugging me toward the desk. I flipped through different charts and ledgers.

He groaned as he collapsed in the old, creaky executive chair behind the desk. I let out a yelp when he grabbed me by my hips and tugged me into his lap. "I have to work in here a few days a month to get caught up on mind-numbing clerical work. Bookkeeping, inventory, calendars, that sort of shit. My least favorite part of the job, but an unfortunate necessity. Without all this shit, the ranch would fail."

He shifted sideways so I could see him and I looped my arms around his neck as his fingers toyed with the loose strands of my hair, twirling them around his fingers absentmindedly. "If you hate it so much, why don't you hire someone else to do it so you can spend your time out there?" I jerked my chin toward the door.

"I want to, believe me, but it's hard to find the time when every hour of every day is crammed full."

I looked back at everything strewn across the desk. I don't consider myself a whiz at this kind of thing, but I had a knack for numbers. Back in school, I'd always been the top student in all my computer classes, and I was surprisingly good with spreadsheets and schedules. "Well . . . if you really need the help, I could do it," I offered, the thought of doing something instrumental in keeping this place afloat making me feel light inside.

"Baby, I can't ask you to do that."

I sifted my fingers through his short-clipped hair, enjoying the way the spikey ends rubbed against my palms. "You didn't ask. I offered."

"Yeah, but you'd be bored out of your mind in no time."

I shook my head. "I wouldn't, actually. I'm pretty good at this kind of thing. You show me the ropes and I'll have the hang of it in no time, trust me. I'm much better at this kind of work than I am out there."

He took my chin between his fingers and tilted my face down so he could nip my bottom lip with his teeth before soothing the sting with a tender kiss. "Don't sell yourself short, Rae. You've been an excellent hand since you got here."

I smiled at the praise, and at the easy way he touched me. "I appreciate you saying that, but I'm serious, Zach. I could be a much bigger asset to you in here than I am out there. Let me help. Please?"

He let out an exhale as his eyes danced across my face. "Okay, I'll show you the ropes. If you make it so the only reason I ever need to come in here is to see you, and maybe feel you up a little, I'll name our first-born child after you."

The laugh that bubbled up from my chest slowly tapered off when I realized he wasn't laughing with me.

"Speaking of kids, do you want them?" I choked on my own spit.

"Jeez, Zach, talk about zero to sixty in a minute."

His arms tightened around me. "Told you, baby, there's no rule saying how fast or slow we can go. I'm not sayin' I want to knock you up right now, but I'd be lyin' if I said I didn't like the idea of seein' you pregnant with my baby one day. So I have to know, do you see kids in your future?"

"I don't know. Maybe. Someday," I sputtered. "Honestly, I haven't given it a lot of thought, but I can see myself as a mom one day." I quickly shook my head to clear it of the image that suddenly popped up. "But I don't want to talk about that right now. I'm freaked out enough as it is. Talking about pregnancy and kids is going to make me spiral."

He leaned back in the chair, taking me with him despite the ominous groan it let out. I made a mental note to replace that chair first thing. "What are you freaking out about?"

I let out a huff and chewed on my bottom lip nervously. "I'm scared about the party tonight."

Zach's brow furrowed. "What? Why? I told you, it's

not a big deal. They call it a party, but it's really just the family and a few close family friends."

"I know!" I cried. "That's why I'm freaking out. I've —I've never had a guy take me home to meet his family before," I admitted quietly.

"But, baby, you've met my entire family already. Many times."

I smacked him on his rock-hard chest and shot him a glare. "You know what I mean. Yeah, I know them . . . as Rae Blackwell, ranch hand and housekeeper. When I show up there tonight, I'll be there as Rae Blackwell, their only son's girlfriend. What if . . . what if they don't like the idea of us being together?"

He studied me for several seconds before dropping his head back on a long, deep belly laugh. I struggled in his lap, trying to get free, but he wouldn't let go. "Baby," he sputtered once he got ahold of himself. "You have nothing to worry about."

"You can't know that," I said with a pout.

His grin was light and mischievous. "I can, actually. Grandma spilled the beans yesterday about two seconds after we walked out of the lodge, and I've already been fielding calls and texts from my mom and sister. Lennix is beside herself, and Mom keeps goin' on about how happy she is that her son is dating the daughter of one of her best friends. Apparently it's been a dream of hers for twenty-three years."

My eyes widened, my lips parting. "Really?"

He chuckled, leaning in to nuzzle the crook of my neck. God, I loved it when he did that. "Really, Rae. My family only wants me to be happy, that's all. And if you make me happy, they're gonna love you."

I let my eyes fall, watching my fingers as I anxiously toyed with the collar of his shirt. "You make it sound so easy."

"That's because it is." Zach's fingers pressed beneath my chin, tipping my face back up to his. "This place comes by its name honestly, Rae. It's a safe haven for every person who sets foot on it. This place is big on second chances, and the minute you crossed under that wooden arch, your past was wiped clean. You won't find any judgement here. As long as its where you want to be, you'll belong. I want you to belong here, Rae. I want you to belong with me."

My heart did summersaults in my chest. "I want that too."

He pulled me in, bringing me close enough that he could brush his lips against mine. "Then that's all that matters. Put everything else out of your head."

It was easier said than done, but for him, I'd try my hardest.

Chapter Twenty-Seven

Rae

The mirror above the bathroom sink wasn't big enough for me to see much of myself in the reflection so I had to trust that everything worked. I'd resurrected one of the outfits from my old life, hoping to impress. I grabbed my lipstick and dabbed a bit more on the center of my puckered lips as a knock sounded on my front door.

Butterflies took flight in my belly as I looked toward the front of the cabin and pulled in a steadying breath before heading in that direction. Zach stood on the other side of the door, dressed in a navy button-down and a pair of jeans that were substantially less faded than his usual ones. His boots were fancier than the ones he wore for work and buffed to a shine instead of covered in dust.

His clean-cotton scent was still there, but it was

combined with a hint of spice and amber from his cologne that made me all tingly and warm.

"Wow," I said on a gust of air. "You look . . ." I didn't have the proper words to finish that sentence.

"Goddamn, baby. Right back at you." The air around us sparked with electricity as his lids lowered like they had weights tied to them. His gaze went molten, lighting me up from the inside. "That dress should be illegal." His nostrils flared, reminding me of a bull only seconds away from charging.

His arm shot out, banding around me and yanking me forward. My squeak turned into a giggle as I fell into him. Bracing my hands on his broad chest, I lifted up on the toes of my high-heeled sandals and pressed my lips against his.

"Hey, baby," he rasped once I lowered back down, smiling at me with an affection that warmed my heart. I would never get tired of him looking at me like that. Like I was everything.

"Hi," I returned, smiling giddily.

"Screw the party, I want to fuck you in that dress. Then I want to strip you out of it and do it all over again."

I laughed, feeling lighter than air. It was the effect Zach had on me. When he was around, I was just . . . *happy*. "We can't skip it. It's for you!"

He let out a groan, pulling my hips to his so I could feel the evidence of his arousal prodding my belly. "You feel what you do to me? I'm gonna walk around like this all damn night because of you."

Man, he was good for my ego, that was for damn sure. Knowing I could drive this man as crazy as he drove me made me feel incredibly powerful. "I'll make it worth your while, I promise."

"Fine," he said on a displeased grunt. He nipped my bottom lip. "You ready to do this?"

"Yeah. Give me a second." I turned and jogged back into the kitchen, grabbing the bottle of wine I'd bought in town earlier after borrowing Ivy's car. I *really* needed to learn how to drive a stick shift, for crying out loud.

"Ready."

He took the bottle from me and grabbed hold of my hand, lacing our fingers together. I pulled the cabin door open and let him lead me to his truck. I could have met him at his parents' house or his place after he got off work, but he'd insisted on picking me up. "You didn't have to bring anything."

I shot him a look as I climbed into the passenger seat when he held the door open for me. "Our moms are friends, so I know yours taught you not to show up at someone's house empty-handed just like mine did."

He chuckled and passed the bottle back to me.

"Valid point." He closed my door for me as I buckled up then rounded the hood, climbing in behind the wheel. "This is going to be great," he assured me as he started the engine. "You'll see."

LENNIX RUSHED out the front door of her parents' house, bounding down the steps, lunging forward, and wrapping me in a crushing embrace the second my feet hit the ground.

"I can't believe you're dating my brother!" she squealed loud enough to burst my eardrum. I pulled back with a wince, hoping she hadn't rendered me partially deaf. "This is the best news *ever!*"

"Jesus, Len. Give her some space, will you?" He yanked me from his sister's embrace and tucked me into his side, giving Lennix a frown. "You're either gonna crack all her ribs or scare her off."

She clasped her hands together beneath her chin and did a little dance-y hop. "Oh my God, you're so stinking cute, all protective over her and stuff. I love it! You two are so cute together."

I curled my lips between my teeth to hide my smile.

Zach rolled his eyes, but I could see the way the

corners of his mouth twitched with a suppressed smile. "Are you about done losing your mind so we can go inside?"

Lennix shot her big brother a vicious glare and crossed her arms over her chest. "You know, she might be your girlfriend, but she was *my* friend first. Uteruses before dude-eruses, jerk face."

Zach tilted his face down to me like he was looking for some sort of confirmation. I lifted my shoulders in a shrug. "It's true. It's scientifically proven."

"Christ," he grunted, but I knew it was all in good fun. "The two of you teaming up together will be my nightmare, won't it?"

"Probably," Lennix chirped sunnily as she reached forward and grabbed me by the arm. She pulled me out of Zach's hold and looped our arms together, leading me toward the porch steps. "Consider this payback for the way you threatened every boy I ever brought home." She cast me a look and said, "He scared my prom date so bad the guy was afraid to lay a finger on me. I spent the entire night dancing by myself because he thought even that would be too intimate."

My head fell back on a deep laugh. Maybe Zach was right. Maybe this night wouldn't be so bad after all.

"This is ridiculous," Zach grumbled for the millionth time since we arrived at the party a little over an hour ago. "I can't believe you guys did this."

I'd laughed so much since Lennix pulled me through the door into her parents' house that the muscles in my stomach ached. This really had been the best night so far.

The cake in the center of the table had to have been the biggest sheet cake I'd ever seen. There was no way this group of roughly ten people was going to make a dent in it. The words piped across the center in swirly, feminine pink icing read *Happy Adoption Day*, and there were twenty-three bright sparkler-style candles lit up like flares.

The Paulson family went *all out* for Zach's adoption day party. There were mylar superhero balloons and streamers and printed out photographs of Zach through the years, only it appeared that they'd picked the worst, most unflattering ones to put on display.

Apparently, as soon as Becky called to inform them of Zach's and my relationship status, they'd gotten the brilliant idea to throw the most embarrassing party their imaginations could concoct, and they'd done a fantastic job. They'd even reworked the words to Happy Birthday to make it about adoption. Each terrible picture had a hilarious story behind it, and I hadn't been able to get enough.

As soon as the last strains of the song came to an end, Zach shot a scowl through the entire group and grumbled, "Tomorrow I'm findin' a lawyer and filing whatever is the equivalent of divorcing your family."

Rory came up to him, looking unfazed as she leaned up to press a kiss to his cheek. "Oh please. It's our right as your family to embarrass you in front of your girlfriend, and since this is the first one you brought to a family function, we're finally exercising that right."

I gaped at Zach. That was the first I'd heard of him never bringing another girl home, and I was beyond honored to be the first.

I lifted the glass of wine to my lips and took a sip, trying not to show how happy I was to have heard that.

Zach had been right when he said his parents wouldn't care that we were seeing each other. The moment I walked through the door, the Paulsons had treated me like one of the family. Rory had pulled me into the living room with her, Lennix, and Becky so they could share embarrassing stories. They made me feel like I belonged and gave me no reason to believe they were anything but happy to have me as their son's girlfriend.

Becky cut into the cake once the sparkler candles had been extinguished, plating massive pieces of cake and handing them out as people broke off into groups to chat.

Zach pulled me closer to him and leaned down to speak softly in my ear as I forked off a corner of my cake slice and took a bite. It was delicious. "You having fun, baby?"

I smiled up at him, my heart fuller than it had ever been. "I'm having the best time."

He grinned as he said, "I'm glad. I won't take offence that most of it is at my expense."

I giggled, rising up for a quick peck. I couldn't seem to stop kissing him. "Only a little bit was at your expense," I clarified. "But seriously, I love watching you with your family. You all love each other so much." I reached up and caressed his cheek, loving the way the short whiskers coating his jaw abraded my palm. "I'm so happy you all found each other."

He took my wrist, holding my hand in place and leaned deeper into my touch. "I am too. Only thing I'm happier about is the fact that I managed to find you too."

God, this man could undo me with only his words. Every time I thought my feelings for him couldn't possibly grow any bigger, he did or said something that proved me wrong. I was falling for him, spinning head over heels at lightning speed.

"You are the best man I've ever met, Zach Paulson," I whispered, my voice raw with emotion.

He came in for another kiss, this one bordering barely on the right side of appropriate. Seconds later, he was pulled away by some family friend who wanted to talk cattle. I took another bite of my cake and let my gaze scan over the room, taking everyone in. When my eyes landed on Rory, she was already staring at me. Her eyes were a little glassy and her expression was warm, her lips tilted upward ever so slightly as she placed a hand on her chest resting it right above her heart.

She'd witnessed that intimate moment between her son and me, and whatever she saw between us made her happy.

Chapter Twenty-Eight

Zach

"**Z**ach, I'm not so sure this is a good idea," Rae called out from behind me. "I really do have a ton of work to do. I don't have time for a midday ride."

I walked past her, ignoring her complaints as I guided Sassy and Roam out of the barn by their reins. It had been three weeks since my adoption party, and a lot had happened in that time. I'd resumed Rae's horseback lessons, taking them back from Hal now that my girl and I were in a good place. A *great* place, actually. She was comfortable enough in the saddle to ride on her own, and after weeks of working with Sassy, the girl was finally ready for more than a few loops around the corral. Today was as good a day as any. The sun was shining, the sky was blue, and there wasn't a cloud in sight.

Rae had officially taken over the administrative work for the ranch right after the party, and as she claimed, she'd excelled at it. The filing was in order, all the invoices were going out on time, and she'd scheduled everything out almost a year in advance. She was a whiz at the payroll system, and she'd even managed to fly through the old ledgers, digitizing the old files from back in my grandpa's heyday a hell of a lot faster than I would have. I was beyond grateful to hand all those tasks over. I could die a happy man knowing I never had to sit behind that desk again. But the thing that mattered to me the most was Rae seemed to love what she was doing.

However, she was also working insane hours. Most nights I had to track her down, and nine times out of ten, she was still in that office. It was hers now, and I'd given her free rein to make it her own, something she hadn't hesitated to do. She'd replaced the shitty old executive chair and the ratty old sofa that had been resting against the back wall. She bought two new chairs to go in front of her desk for visitors, something she seemed to have regularly now that she wasn't doing ranch work or taking shifts at the lodge. The people there and my crew here had really come to love her, and now that they didn't get the chance to see her regularly, they'd come in to catch up whenever they could. She had a ton of friends here. She was slowly building a foundation, and I wanted desperately to take those roots and sink them deep into the soil of this place.

The office was now cleared of clutter, everything placed in pretty, feminine file folders she ordered online. She kept the desk, claiming it was an antique, but had spent an entire day stripping, sanding, then re-staining it to return it to its former glory. The new furniture fit the esthetic of the new office. A style Rae referred to as barn-chic. Whatever the fuck that meant.

She'd made the place cozy and comfortable for herself and dove headfirst into her new job. She'd taken every job she'd done since arriving on the ranch seriously, but this was different. I could see the actual passion in her eyes for what she was doing when I went in to visit her or force her to shut down for the night. She loved this work, but more, she told me she loved being a crucial part of the ranch's structure and took keeping this place functioning to its full potential very seriously.

I wished she didn't push herself so hard. She still woke up with the sun, just like me, and most days, she was still at it long after it had set. She would overdo it if she wasn't careful. Burn herself out. That was why I decided I was going to force her away from that desk and out of her office today even if I had to drag her kicking and screaming.

"Get on the horse, Hollywood."

She shot me a scowl, planting her hands on her hips and staring me down for several seconds. When it became obvious I wasn't going to back down, she let out a dramatic huff and let her arms flop down at her sides as she stomped toward me and the horses I'd already saddled. "Fine. But if something happens while we're gone, I'm holding you responsible."

"I can live with that. Now climb on up."

She put her foot in the stirrup and hoisted herself onto Sassy's back, gathering the reins in her hands like she'd been doing it for years. It was hot as fuck seeing her so controlled and confident on the back of the animal when she used to be so nervous. My woman had a spine of steel. She was so much stronger than she gave herself credit for. I hoped that one day she'd see herself the way I saw her.

I was convinced there wasn't a woman on the planet more perfect for me than her. My family adored her, she was smart and funny and absolutely beautiful. And she loved this ranch almost as much as I did. This place meant something to her. I'd always hoped I'd find a woman who understood my love for this place, and Rae did.

I kept expecting her to ask where we were going as she guided Sassy along the side of Roam, but instead, she was too caught up taking everything in. She'd seen a good bit of the ranch so far, but this was all new to her, and I could tell by the wonder on her pretty face that she found it as beautiful as I did.

I noticed the way her back straightened as soon as we got close enough to hear the sound of rushing water, and the minute we cleared the tree line, the river that stretched through the property coming into view, she pulled in a gasp.

I climbed down from Roam and moved to Sassy, leading both horses to a tree and tying off their reins before reaching up, taking Rae by the waist, and pulling her down. "What is this place?" she asked as she moved toward the water.

"This is my special spot. I told you I'd bring you here one day. Well, today's that day."

"Oh, Zach," she breathed, taking everything in. "This is so beautiful." The sunlight bounced off the water as it rushed past us over the rocks and tree limbs that had fallen with time. It created a white noise that I'd fallen asleep to more times than I could count.

"This is where I come when I need peace. When I need to silence my mind and find my center. I come here." I guided her to the tree I always sat under and lowered myself to the ground, pulling at her hands until she was settled in my lap. She sank back against me, her head tucking beneath my chin as I wrapped my arms around her and held her against me.

"No wonder you love this place so much," she said after a few minutes of relaxing silence. "It's so tranquil. You can sit here, listening to the water, and almost forget the rest of the world exists."

She was it for me. I knew it right then and there, the realization slamming into me with the force of a runaway train. There would never be anyone else.

"I knew you would understand. That's why I wanted to be here the first time you saw this place."

She twisted her neck, looking back at me and smiling so beautifully I couldn't stop myself from closing the distance and sealing my lips with hers. She opened for me, her immediate acceptance making my cock stir to life. No amount of touching or kissing calmed the fire inside me that burned just for her. The need for her never eased, it only grew. The kiss went from slow and sweet to hungry in less than a second. I couldn't help myself. I swept my tongue against hers, swallowing her needy moan as I lifted her up and spun her around so she was straddling me.

"I need you," I groaned into her mouth as she tilted her pelvis, settling herself over the throbbing erection behind my jeans. Her lips parted on a stuttered breath as she rocked against me, causing stars to burst in front of my eyes. "God, I always need you."

"I'm yours," she whispered against my lips.

My control snapped. I had us both stripped naked in a matter of seconds and spread Rae out on the lush green grass, leveling my body over hers and settling my hips between her thighs as she wrapped her long, lithe legs around me.

Our kiss went from hungry to frantic as I reached between us and lined my cock up with her entrance. The moment the head notched into place, I pushed in to the hilt, sheathing myself in that silky wet heat. Her body stretched to accommodate my girth. She cried out my name as her back arched off the ground and her head pressed farther back, exposing the long, delicate expanse of her neck. I dragged my teeth over the column of her throat, my body igniting with the sounds she made as I thrust in and out.

"Zach," she whimpered, her nails digging into the back of my neck as she held on tightly. "I need more. I need you deeper."

I hooked an arm behind her right knee, pushing it up toward her chest so I could drive into her even farther. "Yes!" she shouted up at the bright blue sky. "God, yes! Just like that, baby. Don't stop."

"Never," I growled, pumping in and out of her,

beads of sweat building and trailing down my spine as her pussy clutched me like a fist. "You're close already. I can feel it."

"You feel so good. It's always so good."

"Rae, I—" I had to force myself to stop, those three little words right there on the tip of my tongue, desperate to escape. *I love you.* It had been beating around in my head and in my chest for days . . . weeks. I knew beyond a shadow of a doubt that it was true. That what I felt for her was real, but I didn't want to scare her away. I knew what she felt for me was as strong, but I needed to let her go at the pace that felt right for her. "I'll never get enough of you." She blinked those warm caramel eyes up at me. "You are so beautiful."

"Zach, I'm—" She exploded around me, her cunt clamping down around me like a vise. She screamed my name up at the sky as her body forced mine to follow her over the edge into the abyss. I let out a roar as the first hot ropes of cum let loose, coating her walls. Her pussy milked me dry, pulsating and quivering around me until every drop had been drained from my balls, until I could no longer hold myself up.

I collapsed on the ground, shifting us both to our sides so I didn't crush her beneath my weight.

"I think I love this spot even more now," I panted as my dick started to soften inside of her.

She let out a giggle that filled me with joy. "Glad to be of service."

As much as I would have loved to stay with her like that forever, we still had other things to do. I gave myself five more minutes to cuddle before forcing us both up. "Come on. We need to get dressed."

She blinked sex-drunk eyes. "What? Why?"

I grinned wickedly as I pulled my jeans back on. "Because there's one other place I want to take you today, and as much as I'd love to experience having you naked all day long, it requires clothing."

She twisted her arms in the strangest ways as she settled her bra back into place and managed to hook it from behind without seeing. "Fine," she said, giving a little hop as she hiked her jeans over her luscious ass and hips. "But once we're home for the night, I think we should revisit this whole naked thing."

She would be getting no argument from me.

Chapter Twenty-Nine

Rae

As it turned out, the other place Zach wanted to take me was the local coffee shop in town. He remembered me saying I hadn't yet tried the coffee and had taken it upon himself to remedy that. We stood on the sidewalk outside the coffee shop called Muffin Top, each of us holding a large coffee and a small pastry bag.

When I first got to town, I remember thinking the name was ridiculous and the coffee was probably mediocre. Now Zach stood in front of me, his expression eager as he waited for me to bring the white paper cup to my lips and take a sip.

The moment the sugary, caffeinated beverage hit my tongue, I knew I'd been wrong. There was nothing mediocre about the coffee at all. It was . . . sublime. There was no other word to describe it. If the coffee was this good, I couldn't wait to try the almond croissant I'd ordered as well. But I liked the idea of making him sweat a little before giving him my reaction.

Doing my best to keep my eyes from rolling back in my head as I took another delectable sip, I made a show of holding it in my mouth like a sip of wine I was tasting for the first time before slowly swallowing it.

"Well?" he finally prodded when he had enough of my silence. "What do you think?"

Living in L.A. for so long had made me a good enough actress that he bought it when I lifted my shoulder in a shrug and mumbled, "Meh, it's okay, I guess. I've had better."

He looked downright crestfallen, and it took everything in me not to burst into laughter. "Are you kidding me?" he asked loud enough to draw the attention of people strolling along the sidewalk around us. "This is the best coffee in the entire state, and you think it's just *meh*?" He raked a hand through his hair. "Oh my God. My girlfriend has terrible taste."

Man, he was cute when he was flustered and distraught. I couldn't keep up the charade any longer. My lips curled upward.

He narrowed his eyes at me. "Are you messin' with me?"

I nodded on a tiny laugh. "I am. Sorry. I couldn't help myself. It was just too tempting."

"You little jerk," he said, but there wasn't an ounce of venom in his voice as he pulled me to his side and slammed his lips against mine in a quick, demanding kiss. "I thought you were serious. What do you really think?"

I took another sip, unable to stop myself. If it wasn't so hot I probably would have chugged it down by now. "It's so good," I admitted on a groan. "Like, seriously, Zach. I think this is the best cup of coffee I've ever had. I want to find the creator of this liquid gold and pledge my life to them. I'm talking bend the knee and promise to give my life for theirs."

He chuckled, shaking his head at my ridiculousness. "Christ, you're cute." He went in for another kiss, but before his mouth fused with mine a shrill voice full of rage and hatred shot through the air. "*Heathen*! You're gonna burn in hell, sinner!"

Zach's entire body locked up. He was frozen solid like he'd been encased in a block of ice. Worry replaced the happiness that had been filling me when I noticed all the color had drained from his face.

"Zach?" His eyes got this strange, far off look as he focused on something over my shoulder. It was like he hadn't heard me. "Zach," I repeated, sharper this time, causing him to blink out of it. "Who is that?"

The muscle in his jaw ticked as he ordered, "Get in the truck, Rae."

"God's gonna strike you down! You're wicked, you hear me? *Wicked!*"

I started to turn my head to look over my shoulder at who was suddenly causing a scene, but Zach's arm fell from my waist and he grabbed hold of my arm tightly, almost to the point of pain. "Truck, Rae," he barked, using a voice I'd never heard him use before. "Get in the goddamn truck now."

I caught sight of a woman screaming the vile epithets as Zach hauled me to the truck he'd parked along the sidewalk outside the coffee shop. She was raging against the man trying to hold her back. Her stringy brown hair flew every which way, partially blocking her face, but I could see how red she'd gotten; I could see the hate filling her eyes as she fought against the man's hold. Her arms and legs flailed, reminding me of a crazed, feral animal, and it looked like she was trying to break free to get to Zach.

He picked me up and stuffed me into the passenger

seat unceremoniously before slamming the door so hard the truck wobbled on its frame. I could still hear the woman's screams as Zach booked it around the hood of the car to the driver's side. He was breathing like he just ran a marathon as he threw himself behind the wheel and cranked the engine.

"Zach, talk to me," I pleaded, panic gripping my chest as he wrenched the wheel around and hit the gas pedal so hard the tires squealed and the whole cab lurched forward. I braced one hand on the dashboard to keep from slamming into it and used the other to yank my seatbelt around me and snap it into place. "Please, baby. You're scaring me."

I looked over at his profile and barely recognized the man sitting beside me. He was pale and sweaty, every muscle pulled so taught it looked like a small breeze might make him shatter into a million pieces. "What's going on? Who was that woman?"

He remained silent, the muscle in his jaw fluttering so wildly I worried he might crack all of his molars. I wanted to keep pushing, but I knew I wasn't going to get anywhere. I sank down in my seat and the anxiety in my belly churned.

It wasn't until he turned onto the lane leading to the ranch that he slowed the truck to a reasonable speed. He pulled up in front of my cabin a few minutes later, throwing the truck into park and staring out the windshield almost in a daze as he choked the steering wheel in a white knuckled grip.

I unbuckled the seatbelt and slowly reached for the handle. "Are—are you coming in?" We needed to talk. I'd only ever seen him like this once before. The day at the grocery store. And he'd shut down on me afterward. I couldn't stand the thought of that happening again, of him closing himself off and shutting me out. I wasn't sure I'd survive it.

"Got somewhere to be." He never once looked in my direction, his tone devoid of all emotion. He sounded like a robot. This was déjà vu all over again.

"I think you should come inside," I said. "I don't think you should be alone right now."

"I'll see you tomorrow." To drive home the point that he wouldn't be joining me, he threw the truck into gear and kept his foot pressed down on the brake as he waited for me to get out. My heart dropped to my feet as I pushed the door open and climbed out. Tears burned the backs of my eyes as I turned to look back into the cab of the truck. It felt like someone had reached into my chest and was tearing my heart into tiny pieces. Zach was hurting, the agony and pain was rolling off him in waves. But he didn't want my help.

The instant I shut the door, he took off, sending dust

and gravel spitting up from his tires, leaving me despaired and worried sick.

I DIDN'T KNOW where Zach had gone after he dropped me off at my cabin, but it hadn't been back to his house. After a few hours of frantic pacing, helplessness weighing heavily on my shoulders, I walked over to the barn to see if he was there, but there was no sign of his truck. It wasn't at the lodge either.

I called and texted, but each call went straight to voicemail and all my messages showed they were delivered but not read. I thought about heading to his special spot to see if that was where he was, but I wasn't familiar enough with the route we'd taken earlier that day to get there on my own.

The sun had long since dipped behind the mountains surrounding the town when I finally had enough. I couldn't stand it any longer. The secrets, the silence, the closed off zombie he'd become. Pulling my phone out, I scrolled through my contacts and tapped the screen when I got to the one I needed.

"We need to talk," I said as soon as the line connected.

Lennix's sigh carried heavily through the line and I could feel the weight of it from all the way over here. "I know."

"Your place or mine?"

Sadness dripped from her words as she answered. "I'll be there in ten."

When she showed up at my door ten minutes later, I was already half a wine glass in. I opened the door for her, thrusting the second glass into her hand before she'd even had a chance to enter. I had a feeling we were both going to need it.

She took two deep gulps while still standing on the front porch before finally moving inside. She sat on one side of the tiny sofa while I took the other cushion.

"I assume you've already heard about what happened in town earlier today?"

She nodded. "Small towns. My parents and I started getting phone calls almost as soon as it happened."

I wasn't surprised. The sidewalks had been busy when the whole thing went down, and it seemed like everyone in this town knew the Paulsons.

"Who was she?" I might have worded it like a question, but there was no mistaking I was demanding to know.

Lennix's chest deflated as she heaved out a breath. She finished off the glass of wine in seconds, then collapsed against the back of the sofa, drawing her knees up and wrapping her arms around them, curling in on herself.

"Obviously, you know my brother was adopted. Before my mom and dad found him, he was living with another foster family. Have you heard the name Caswells?"

I shook my head, my stomach sinking with each word she spoke. I didn't know where she was going with this, but I knew it wasn't going to be good.

"Doreen and Charles Caswell were his foster parents at the time. He and a few other kids were living in that house. I didn't see it, but my dad did, and I've heard stories. That house was a nightmare, Rae. If hell on earth existed, it was that house."

Tears welled in my eyes, fat and hot. I did nothing to try and stop them from breaking free and slipping down my cheeks as I sniffled. "Tell me."

"They forced those kids to live in their own filth. I mean that literally and in every way you could possibly imagine. Zach was one of the oldest, so he got it the worst. They beat them, starved them, locked them in a dark room with no food or water or bathroom. They were tortured, basically. That was how my parents came to find him."

My brows pulled together in confusion. "He told me

it was because he threw a rock through the window of the bar."

"That's true. But he threw that rock because he'd been digging through the dumpster in the alley every night, looking for food. Mom thought it was racoons or something so she locked it up. The night he found it locked, he panicked. He threw the rock out of anger."

My hands slapped over my mouth, trapping in my sharp gasp as more tears spilled free. "Oh my God."

Lennix's eyes grew red and wet as she continued to recount the nightmare Zach had lived through. "My mom lost it when she found out what was happening to him. She and my dad weren't even together at the time. He was in the middle of trying to win her over, but they became a team after they found my brother. My mom was fierce. She demanded that CPS let her take him that very night. The next day my dad went with the police to the house and found all the other kids. Turns out, the woman, Doreen Caswell, was the cousin of Zach's case-worker. She'd been falsifying her reports to make it seem like they were a healthy, stable couple and they'd split the money they got for each of the kids they listed on the reports.

"They ended up going to prison where they all belonged." She sniffed and batted the tears off her cheeks as she shifted her body to face me. "There's a special place in hell for people like them. The case-worker is still locked up, but unfortunately, the Caswells were released shortly before you got here."

It was a strange thing to feel such a deep, gnawing sadness at the same time my entire body was lit from within with fury so strong it was a wonder smoke wasn't pouring from my ears. I'd never met these people, but I hated them. *Hated* . . . them. I wanted them to hurt. To feel the same kind of pain they'd caused Zach.

"It was her, wasn't it? Doreen Caswell."

Lennix nodded. "That was her. She's sick. Sick and twisted. She never should have gotten out."

That was the understatement of the century. "Have you talked to him?" I asked once my tears had run dry. "Have any of you?"

She shook her head, her shoulders sinking forward with sadness. "We've tried, but I think he turned his phone off. He gets like this sometimes. We try to let him work it out on his own, but if my folks think it's taking too long, they intervene. They didn't want to wait this time, but we don't know where he is."

I nodded, understanding that we were all in the same boat, all feeling a level of helplessness that was nearly debilitating.

Lennix stayed a while longer, both of us using the others' presence to fill the gaping hole in our chests. But none of it would get any better until Zach came back. I walked her to the door, standing on the front porch and looking out toward Zach's house. His truck was still gone and the whole house was dark.

"Don't give up on him," Lennix called out, something in her tone slamming into me. It almost sounded like desperation. "I know it's hard when he shuts you out over things like this, but other than finding my parents, you're the best thing that's ever happened to him. So just . . . don't give up, okay?"

"I won't," I assured her.

She drove off and I closed myself back inside the cabin. I carried our wine glasses to the sink and shut off the lights on my way to the bedroom.

I wasn't going to give up on him. No matter what. But I also wasn't going to sit by and watch him suffer while I did nothing.

Curling up in a ball on my bed, I thumbed through my contacts until I got to my father and hit call. He answered, a ring and a half later.

"Hey, princess. How's it going?"

"Not too good," I admitted. "Dad, I need your help. Are you still friends with that PI who helped you track Mom down all those years ago?"

A beat of silence filled the line before he said, "I

think maybe you should tell me what's going on before I answer that."

So I did. I told him everything, and he listened as I gave him everything, beautiful and ugly alike. Then, once I was finished, my cheeks tight from the salty tears, my father proved that he was one of the best men on the face of the earth by saying, "Grab a pen, sweetheart, and I'll give you his number."

Chapter Thirty

Rae

"**R**ae, are you sure you want to do this? That's a lot of money." My annoyance grew as the man on the other end of the line asked the same question for what felt like the hundredth time.

"I've already told you, Tony. I'm doing this, whether you agree with it or not." I'd never been more determined in all my life.

His sigh carried through the line as I looked out the driver side window of Lennix's little red car to the ratty, dilapidated singlewide trailer I was parked in front of. "Fine, if you're going to do this, I'm not going to stop you, but I feel like I should remind you that the contract I drafted won't hold up in court if it were to ever reach that point."

I wasn't worried about whether or not it was enforce-able. Something told me these people would take one look at the document my father's attorney had worked up for me in the middle of the night last night and wouldn't have the smarts to question it.

"So you've said."

"Jesus. You're just as big a headache as your father, you know that?"

I couldn't help but smile. "I'll take that as a compli-ment, Tony. I have to go. Talk soon."

"I hope not," he grumbled through the line before I disconnected the call and shoved the phone into my purse.

I turned off the car and pushed the door open, climbing out and brushing the wrinkles from the front of my pencil skirt. I'd decided to pull out more clothes from my old life for this, dressing in a skirt, a designer blouse, and expensive heels. I'd even slicked my hair back into a bun, taming all flyaways to project a look of importance and authority.

I hooked my purse over my shoulder and tucked the folder with the documents inside under my arm. It also contained the check Tony wasn't happy about. Fortu-nately, when I told my mom and dad my plan, they'd been fully supportive, and as long as they had my back, I didn't care what anyone else thought.

I puffed out a breath and steeled my spine before starting up the cracked walkway to the trailer. I probably should have been scared—or hell, even nervous—given I knew what these people were capable of, but I was too angry to feel anything else. It also helped that I'd noticed the truck parked at the corner of the four-way stop a few yards away and spotted Zach's father, Cord, sitting inside. I had a feeling Lincoln had filled him in on my plan, and the man was there to make sure nothing bad happened.

It had been three days since the scene outside of Muffin Top, and no one had seen or heard from Zach. I was beyond worried about him, and the more worried I got, the more my anger at these horrible people grew.

It was time to put an end to all of this. I stomped up the rickety front steps and lifted my hand to knock, banging my knuckles right over the top of the eviction notice taped to the door. I could hear sounds coming from inside. Something that sounded like a game show playing on the TV inside.

I waited a few seconds, but when no one answered, I knocked again, this time putting my fist *and* my foot into it.

"Jesus Christ!" the man inside barked. "Hold your damn horses, will ya? I'm comin'."

The door flew open a second later and the man I'd

seen holding Doreen Caswell back as she screamed horrible, nasty things at Zach stood in the doorway, one forearm braced on the frame. "Charles Caswell?"

He looked me up and down, a sneer curling at his lips. "Who's askin'?"

"My name's Rae Blackwell."

He squinted, looking closely. "You're the woman my wife and I saw with that piece of shit the other day," he growled. He was going for intimidating, but his words had the opposite effect. I wanted to reach down and rip off my shoe so I could use the heel to stab him right in the eye.

"I'm the woman you saw with *Zach Paulson* while your vile bitch of a wife verbally assaulted him," I corrected on a hiss.

He narrowed his eyes in a glare. "Got nothin' to say to you." He started to close the door, but I slammed my hand against it.

"That's where you're wrong." I looked to the eviction notice and back to him, cocking a brow. "You're going to want to hear what I have to say."

"Oh yeah, little girl? What makes you think that?"

I reached into the folder and pulled out the rectangular slip of paper. "Because this is a check for fifty thousand dollars, and it's yours if you do exactly what I say."

Just like that, I had him. He crossed his arms over his dingy T-shirt that probably started out white but was now a nasty grayish brown.

I flipped the folder open and pulled out the stapled stack of papers. "This is a contract that states the fifty thousand dollars is yours, free and clear, as long as you and your wife move out of the state of Virginia."

He reared back, his eyes flaring. "Why the fuck would we do that?"

The smile I gave him was downright vicious. "Because out of everyone in this town, you two are the most hated. Unlike Zach Paulson, who is admired and loved by everyone, you have no friends here, no family, and there isn't a single person in or around Hope Valley who would be willing to give a job to either one of you. Your checking account is overdrawn, your car has been repossessed, and you're being evicted." It had to be said, Lincoln Sheppard was good at his job. When I gave him the go ahead to dig, he dug deep.

"There's nothing for you here. No one wants you here. The longer you stay, the more likely it'll be that you end up living on the streets." I held up the check and flipped it over so he could see it was already filled out. I'd pulled the money from my trust fund, and I couldn't imagine spending my money on a more worthy cause.

"You think fifty grand will last us now-a-days? That money'll be gone in no time."

I shrugged. "I don't give a shit how long it will last you. You'll be lucky to see this amount of money before you die. I'm not trying to give you a comfortable life. Neither of you deserve it, and if I thought for a second that it wouldn't affect the person I care about, I'd be more than happy to let you stay here and rot. God knows there are a ton of people living in this town who agree with me. I'm giving you enough to get the hell out of here. This is the best offer you're ever going to get. The *only* offer."

His nostrils flared. He wanted to argue. He wanted to turn down the money. But he knew I was right. And he hated it. Part of me wished I had the forethought to record this whole thing so I could show it to Zach, so he could see how dire things were for these miserable people.

"Sign the papers, Mr. Caswell, and the money's yours."

A growl worked through his chest. Finally, he relented. "Gimme a fuckin' pen."

I slapped the documents against his chest and fished in my purse for a pen. "Just so you know," I started before passing the pen over, "there are a few stipulations. First, you'll have exactly one week from the time of signing to leave the state. If you aren't out of Virginia by that time, you forfeit your right to the money and will be made to pay it back. Second, if you *ever* set foot in this state again, you have to pay back every dime of that fifty thousand dollars." And to put the fear of God into him, I added a little fib. "My lawyers are chomping at the bit to rake you and your wife over the coals in court should you violate any terms of this contract." I extended the pen to him, biting the inside of my cheek to keep from smiling, because I knew I had him. I'd won, it was only a matter of time before he finally conceded.

I could see the hate in his eyes, but it didn't faze me one bit. In fact, it spurred me on.

He flipped to the last page with the signature lines and slapped the contract against the siding of the trailer. A second later, he scrawled his name along the line that would guarantee Zach would never have to see the Caswells again. His nightmare was officially over.

"There. There's your contract," he hissed venomously. "Now gimme my money." I passed him the check with one last warning that I would have people watching to make sure he didn't violate our terms. Then I turned on my heel and sauntered back to Lennix's car, feeling a level of pride in myself I had never experienced before.

I hadn't backed down. I hadn't depended on

someone else to handle this. I fought for a man who meant the world to me, and I won. For him.

At some point, Cord had gotten out of his truck and started across the street, reaching Lennix's little coupe at the same time I did.

"I take it Lincoln tattled?"

He smiled, nodding in the affirmative. "Used to work for him at Alpha Omega before the wife wanted us both to retire. He called me as soon as you walked out of his office. Told me your plan."

I inhaled, lifting my chin and squaring my shoulders. "Thank you for not trying to stop me."

He surprised me by reaching out and pulling me into a tight embrace, and when he spoke, his voice cracked a little. "Thank you for loving my boy as much as you do."

Oh, man. I was going to cry. That would really ruin the badass image I'd been striving for. I didn't bother denying it. My feelings for him were obvious. I loved Zach. I loved him more than anything, and there wasn't anything I wouldn't do to make him happy.

Cord pulled back, his deep green eyes shining with appreciation. "Now get the hell out of here. You're too good to be in a place like this."

He didn't have to tell me twice. Grabbing the

handle, I opened the door to climb in, but paused, twisting back in his direction. "Cord?"

"Yeah, sweetheart?"

"Will you do me a favor? Will you find him and bring him home?"

He dipped his chin. "Consider it done."

Chapter Thirty-One

Zach

I knew the second I heard the knock on my motel room door who I'd find on the other side.

Sure enough, Cord stood across the threshold from me as soon as I pulled it open. "Son," he greeted before shoving his way inside the room I'd been holed up in for the past three days. After the confrontation on the sidewalk with Doreen Caswell, I'd taken off with no destination in sight. I drove until I couldn't any longer, pulling off at the first roadside motel I came across.

I turned my phone off and hadn't left these four walls for the past three days as I tried to loosen the vise grip that panic had on my heart. I handled everything poorly, I knew that, but I hadn't known what else to do. Going home hadn't been an option, neither was staying anywhere in Hope Valley, not while the Caswells were there. If I'd stayed, the panic attacks would have crippled me. I needed time. Even if my father hadn't shown up when he did, I would have climbed back in my truck and gone home today. I couldn't cut the world out forever, after all. I had a lot of explaining to do, and even more apologizing. I'd shirked my responsibilities, pawning everything off on Hal and the other hands. I'd probably worried my family sick. And I knew I hurt Rae when I shut her out.

There was so much I needed to fix. I hoped I hadn't screwed up so epically that it wasn't possible.

Cord moved to the small desk that was bolted into the wall and sat in the chair as I moved to the foot of the bed and sat down across from him. "How'd you find me?"

He lifted a single brow. "You forget what I used to do?"

A humorless chuckle rattled up my throat. I hadn't forgotten. Before I came along, my dad had been a Navy Seal. He retired from service before I knew him and had taken a job at a private security and investigation firm called Alpha Omega. That place had its own lore in our town. No one really knew exactly what they did there. All we knew for certain was that the place was run by and employed serious badasses. They were all ex-special forces from different branches of the military. Some of the men who had worked there with my father were retired like him, but they'd been replaced with other badasses, and the man who built it all, Lincoln Sheppard, was still running the show.

"If your plan was to come here and drag me home, you should know, I was already plannin' on leaving today."

He shrugged like he already knew that. "Figured you'd have gotten yourself back to rights by now, but I made a promise to your girl I'd bring you home, and I keep my promises."

My throat tightened at the mention of Rae, my heart rate spiking. God, I missed her. I could only hope she didn't hate me.

I swallowed past the lump in my throat, staring down at my feet as I asked, "You talked to Rae?"

He nodded. "This morning."

I heaved out a sigh and asked the question I had been dreading the answer to. "How mad is she? On a scale from *I've lost her* to *I still have a chance*?"

"She wasn't mad. At least from what I could see. She was concerned. And sad."

"Fuck," I hissed, dropping my head and rubbing a hand over the back of my neck. "I really screwed up."

"Not gonna lie to you, bud. You did. I get what you're goin' through, but a man can't take off every time something gets hard. You have to stand your ground and handle it. And if you're not equipped to handle it in the moment, you need to lean on those around you to lighten the burden. But you can't keep running. Especially when you have your family to think about and a good woman waiting for you."

"I know. I'm sorry. I know I can't keep handling this issue the way I have been. I—" My mouth went dry. "I called Dr. Henson yesterday," I confessed. "I have an appointment with her later this week."

Dr. Henson had been my therapist since I was a teenager. She'd helped guide me through all the upheaval in my life from leaving an abusive home to adjusting to my new normal with Rory and Cord. She really helped me back then, and I trusted her to help me with this. I shouldn't have waited so long.

"I'm proud of you, son. That's a big first step. I'm glad you made it."

I exhaled loudly. "Yeah, well, I'm gonna have to get my shit together. I can't put my whole life on pause every time I run into those people."

"I agree that you need help finding a better way to cope, but I don't think those people are gonna be a problem for you anymore."

My head came up, my brow furrowed. "What? Why?"

"Your girl took care of it."

I shot to my feet as my heart rattled against my ribcage. "What? How? What did she do? Is she okay?"

"Calm down, Zach." He held his hands out in a placating gesture. "Relax and have a seat. She's fine. I was there to make sure of it."

That didn't make me feel any better. "You were *where?*"

His expression remained calm as he answered, "At the Caswells."

"Goddamn it!" I began to pace the room, raking my fingers through my hair. "I didn't want her anywhere near those people, Dad. They're toxic. Poison. She's not safe around them."

He stood, stopping me mid-pace with his hands on my shoulders. "She was perfectly safe. But she was also determined. Even if I'd tried to talk her out of what she had planned, it wouldn't have done any good. She saw you get hurt and did what she could to protect you. That's what you do for the people you love, and that girl loves you, son. I knew it when I saw you together at your party and what she did today only solidified that knowledge. You're it for her."

"What—what did she do?"

"She got her lawyers to draw up a contract that she'd pay them fifty K if they agreed to move out of Virginia and never come back. I stood there and watched as she ripped that fucker Caswell a new asshole so beautifully I wanted to applaud her. She might have walked away fifty grand poorer, but she got him to sign, and I hung around long enough to watch them throw all their possessions in the back of a rundown station wagon and take off."

I had to have heard him wrong. I blamed the blood that was rushing in my ears. He couldn't have said what I thought he said.

"She—she really did that?"

He nodded solemnly. "You hurt her when you ran away. There's no doubt about that. She had every right to be mad. Hell, she had the right to be done with you completely, but she did *that*. Because she couldn't stand to see you in pain and she wanted to make sure it could never touch you again. A man is lucky if a woman like that comes around once in his lifetime, Zach. Some men never get that. You lucked out." He let go of my shoulders and took a step back. "Now get your ass out of this miserable room and go make things right, yeah?"

"Okay, Dad. And . . . I know I don't say it all the time, but I know how lucky I am that you and Mom found me."

"We found each other, Zach. Because we were meant to be a family. Now get out of here."

I made it back to the ranch in record time, thanks to breaking almost every law of the road, but I would have gladly paid the cost of any ticket if it meant getting back to her. My truck skidded to a stop outside the barn, spitting up gravel and dust. I barely got the gear shift into park before I launched myself out of the cab and started toward the open doors.

"You're back," Connor said as I blew past him on the way to Rae's office. I wasn't even sure if she'd be in there, but I wouldn't stop until I found her.

"I'm back," I replied, turning to walk backward as I addressed him without breaking stride.

He grinned like he knew exactly who I was on the hunt for. "You get your shit sorted?"

I jerked my chin up in the affirmative. "It's all taken care of."

"Good. Then go get your girl. Last I heard, she was rippin' someone a new asshole over the phone. Think it was a feed supplier. I'll catch up with you later." He turned and disappeared out of the barn, and I whipped back around, jogging the rest of the way to my girl. Sure enough, she was sitting behind her desk, her elbows braced on the top and her head cradled in her hands. Her fingers slowly massaged circles over her temples like she was trying to relieve a headache, and I had no doubt I was the cause of it.

"I've been in love with you from the moment I saw you blow out of that cabin with a frying pan held over your head as a weapon." The words poured out of their own accord. I hadn't planned what I was going to say other than begging for forgiveness, but the moment I saw her, I knew she needed to know the truth.

Her head shot up, her eyes going wide. "You're back," she whispered in shock.

"I'm back." I moved deeper into the office, needing to be closer to her. "And I swear to Christ, I'll never leave you again."

Her eyes welled up, the shimmer of tears ripping into my gut like a rusty hunting knife. "Oh, baby. Don't cry. Please. It'll kill me." I pulled her up from the chair and into me, wrapping my arms around her and holding her close to my heart, right where she was meant to be. I'm so sorry. I fucked up. I should have come in like you asked. I should have talked to you, but you have my word, I'll never make that mistake again."

She sniffled, and I felt her lift her hands and brush the tears from her face. She wriggled out of my hold and took a step back, her back rigid and her shoulders square. That fierceness was in her eyes, that fire I loved so goddamn much, and seeing it filled every single empty space in my heart that had been left after Rory, Cord, Len, and my grandparents filled the spaces meant for them. Thanks to her, I was finally whole.

"I'm mad at you," she said. "You shouldn't have taken off like that. And you shouldn't have gone radio silent. You pissed me off. But . . . lucky for you, I love you, so I'm willing to forgive you this time." Her finger came up and jabbed at my face. "But so help me, if you do it again—"

I grabbed her wrist and jerked her forward so she'd crash into me and took her mouth in a hungry kiss. "I won't." It was a vow. One of many I planned to make to this woman over the course of the rest of our lives. "I know what you did."

She lifted her chin haughtily. "I won't apologize. It was just money, and I have plenty of it. I'd do it again if it meant they'd go away. I would give them every single dime I have, and there is nothing you can say to change my mind," she issued with a sniff. "You helped me find myself, helped me discover what I'm capable of, so when I saw a chance to return the favor, I took it, and I don't feel even a little bad about it."

I smiled, reaching up to brush her hair back from her cheek and take her chin in my fingers. "I'd never expect you to apologize for doing what you did. When you love someone, you protect them. Thank you for protecting me, for loving me. But so you know, I plan to spend the rest of my life protecting you right back, because you're it for me, Rae. I want to build a life with you, right here. On our ranch."

She pulled in a shaky breath. "I'd love that," she whispered. "Zach, nowhere ever felt like home to me until I came here. Until I met you. You're all I want, and I want you forever."

"Good, baby." I leaned in, my lips brushing against hers as I said, "Because forever starts right now."

Epilogue

Zach

Six months later

I STOOD at the edge of the river, watching the water rush by as nerves twisted my gut into sailors' knots. I'd been preparing for this moment for months; everything was in place. I'd double and triple checked every little detail. Nothing was going to go wrong, but I was still freaking out.

I rested my hand against the front of my pocket, feeling for the ring inside to make sure it was still there. Roam chittered from where I had his reins tied to a branch, alerting me that someone else was approaching.

She was right on time.

I wiped the sweat beaded on my forehead and made sure my expression appeared neutral as I turned to watch Rae ride up on Sassy. She was a natural on horseback now. In fact, she was a natural at everything that had to do with the ranch. If I didn't know better, I would have thought it was in her blood. She smiled brilliantly when she saw me, and everything inside me calmed. That was the magic of Rae. It wasn't one big thing that made me fall in love with her. It was a million little things. It was the way she laughed. The way she smiled. It was the fire inside her whenever she got mad. It was the way she loved this ranch and wanted to help me make it better. It was the way she fit into my family so seamlessly, like she was meant to be part of it. And with every day that passed, those little things kept adding up.

I'd done a lot of work with Dr. Henson over the past several months, but it was Rae who kept me grounded. I still loved this spot, and now it was special for all new reasons, but this woman was my calm, my center.

"Hi, baby."

She pulled Sassy to a stop beside Roam and dismounted, heading in my direction. "I got your text to meet you out here." She stopped, placing her hands on my chest and rising up on her boots to kiss me. "Is everything okay?"

Everything was perfect. Or at least it would be.

"I don't know. It depends on your answer to a question I have for you."

"What quest—" The furrow in her brow smoothed out and her eyes shot wide on a gasp as I pulled the ring from my pocket and lowered myself down on one knee. "Oh my God, Zach." She clapped her hands over her mouth.

"Hollywood." I grinned up at her, using the nickname she hated when she arrived all those months ago. "I lucked out the day I met my parents. I thought the day my adoption went through was destined to be the best day of my life. I didn't think it was possible for a man to experience that kind of luck more than once. Then I met you, and every day since has been better than the one before. Will you make me the happiest man in the world and be my wife, baby? Will you have my babies and move into that big house that's been sitting empty, waiting for our family? Will you spend the rest of your life letting me love you?"

She dropped down on her knees in front of me and took my face in her hands. "Of course I will," she rasped as tears slid down her cheeks. "I'm yours and you are mine. It's been that way since the very beginning, and it will be that way until our last breath."

I slid the ring down her finger and pulled her with

me as I stood up, circling my arms around her waist and lifting her feet off the ground as I kissed her hungrily.

She let out a needy moan and arched into me, her body begging for more. Any other time I would have gladly given her exactly what she wanted. But . . .

I set her down, taking her by the shoulders and pushing her back. "Wha—" she asked dazedly.

"I'm sorry, baby, but that has to wait. We have somewhere we need to be."

Her jaw dropped open. "You just proposed," she squeaked. "Where could we possibly need to be right now?"

I grinned wickedly, taking her hand and tugging her back to the horses. "At the engagement party your mom and my mom are currently putting together."

She sucked in an excited gasp and gave a little hop. "My mom's here?"

"Both your parents. We've been planning this for months. All of us. You're literally the only one on the ranch who didn't know."

She narrowed her eyes in a glare that didn't hold an ounce of anger. "You sneaky little jerk. You're lucky I love you so damn much."

"Believe me, I know exactly how lucky I am. Now get a move on. The faster the party starts, the faster it ends. I've got very naked plans for you later tonight."

She giggled and lifted herself up into her saddle. "I can't wait. Race you back to the barn!" she shouted, then took off in a flash.

My beautiful, sweet, fierce woman.

I would never get enough of her.

The End.

Thank you so much for reading! I hope you enjoyed returning to Hope Valley.
Keep reading for a sneak peek of Cord and Rory's story,
STAY WITH ME*.*

Sneak Peek of Stay With Me

Want to know where Zach got his start? Check out Cord and Rory's story, **STAY WITH ME**, now.

Prologue

Rory

My body ached from spending hours upon hours curled up in that uncomfortable chair, either sleeping or watching the steady rise and fall of Cord's chest the whole time. The arid hospital room had dried out my sinuses, making it difficult to breathe, but still I refused to budge. Not until he woke up and I could see for myself that he was going to be okay.

As I sat in that cold, sterile room, memories of the past bombarded me.

I could still remember the exact moment I first met Cord Paulson with perfect clarity.

I could recall exactly what he was wearing the first time he walked into The Tap Room as if it were just yesterday. The jeans, the faded black tee with a picture of a Harley Fat Boy on the front, the unbuttoned flannel he wore over it. There was nothing special about *what* he wore, but *how* he was wearing it made my belly heat and my skin grow tight and tingly.

I remembered how I'd watched with rapt fascination as he moved through the thick crowd with the kind of confidence that couldn't be learned or faked. He walked with a self-assuredness that had to be ingrained in a person from birth. I hadn't met many people with that brand of confidence, but this man had it in spades.

The first words he'd spoken to me were still stuck in my head. "Dig the shirt, dollface," he'd teased, eyeing my cherry-red T-shirt with the words "Tap It Real Good" stretched along the front in big white bubble letters.

That endearment hit my belly and took bloom like a field of wildflowers. "What can I say, stud?" I grinned playfully. "It's excellent marketing."

He'd turned to take in the bar. It was only a Wednesday evening, but we were still hopping. "Don't doubt that for a second."

I even remembered the very first beer he ordered and how his gaze felt like a physical touch as he watched me pour his Guinness.

But the most potent memory I carried with me, the one I went back to every night when I curled up in bed alone, was the very first thought I had when he stepped into my life.

Dear Lord, I want this one. Please, please *let me have him.*

He was *it*.

I didn't know how or why I knew that.

I just did.

My life changed in that moment. It was the start of something unexplainable, something that felt important and all-consuming, and I knew I'd never be the same.

I didn't have a single doubt that I'd just met the man

of my dreams, the one meant just for me, the guy I'd been waiting on for most of my life.

Those were the memories that had plagued me for the past three days as I waited for him to wake up, fear clutching my heart in a vise grip the entire time.

All the bad had been drowned out when I received the call days ago telling me he'd been shot while trying to save my friend Eden from some very bad men.

"We're not sure he's gonna make it, sweetheart," Lincoln had said through the line. I wanted to collapse to the floor, but if he was truly dying, there wasn't time. I had to get to him.

It was amazing how the mind worked. In times of tragedy or stress, it was only the good we held on to. I didn't care that he'd broken my heart. I didn't care that he'd been my best friend until the day he cast me aside. None of that mattered. The only thing that mattered was that he pulled through this, because I needed him to come back. I could live in a world where he wasn't a part of my life as long as he was happy and healthy. But a world where he didn't exist at all was unimaginable.

"You should go home, get some real sleep," my friend Nona said, rounding Cord's hospital bed and resting her hand on my shoulder. "You look wrecked, doll."

"I..." My gaze slid back to the bed and my throat grew uncomfortably tight. Cord's naturally olive-toned skin was frighteningly pale. The man who'd once been so imposing looked frail. I hadn't thought it possible for a man with his size and personality to look so weak. It was terrifying. "I can't," I managed to whisper. "I just... I don't want him to wake up and be all alone."

"She should be here," Nona bit out, her voice as hard and jagged as stone.

My fear gave way to anger, just as it had every time I thought about *her*. Laurie Dutton. The woman who held Cord's heart and the reason he'd thrown everything we were to each other away. In the three days I'd been sitting vigil, she hadn't shown her face once.

"Don't bring her up," I clipped. "Not here. Not now when he's..."

Her voice softened immediately. "All right, honey. I'm sorry." She gave me a moment to pull in a calming breath before speaking again. "I'm not gonna be able to convince you to take a break, am I?"

I didn't bother replying to a question she already knew the answer to.

When I didn't say anything she let out a heavy sigh and squeezed my shoulder. "Okay, Ror. But if you need me you just call, okay? Any time. I'm here. All your friends are."

She left a minute later, and I resumed my task of counting each of Cord's inhales. Bone-deep exhaustion from constant worry and lack of sleep tugged at my senses and weighed my eyelids down. My vision began to blur and that weariness started to seep deep into me and pull me under when a sudden noise gave me a jolt.

My gaze shot up to Cord's face just as his eyes fluttered and his lips parted on a craggy, pained groan.

Uncurling my legs, I shot to the very edge of the chair and leaned over to gently take his hand. "Cord?"

His eyelids continued to flutter for a second more before they finally opened all the way. Those dark forest green eyes were glassy from the medication, but that didn't make them any less beautiful. The sense of relief I felt when his gaze landed on mine was so strong it brought tears to my eyes.

"Hey sweetie," I whispered, smiling so big my cheeks ached. "Welcome back."

"You're here."

"Of course I'm here, Cord. I've been waiting for you." A watery laugh slid up my throat as my tears broke free. "You scared the life out of me."

"You're here," he repeated, pulling his hand from mine and lifting it to caress my cheek, brushing the wetness away with his thumb.

Leaning into his touch, I wrapped my fingers around his wrist and pulled in a shaky breath, silently thanking

God for bringing him back to me. "I'm so glad you're okay," I whispered. "So, so glad."

Cord's hand traveled up and into my hair, coming to stop at the base of my neck. His fingers put pressure on the back of my head, forcing me to bend lower as he lifted off his pillow.

His lips pressed against mine, and time suddenly stopped. The world stopped turning as the air froze in my lungs. When my lips parted on a surprised gasp, Cord's tongue slid inside, and I was lost. Completely and happily lost in all that was him.

With that one kiss, all the dreams I'd started having the moment Cord Paulson came into my life, all the dreams I'd locked inside a box and tucked into the back of my mind for the past year and a half, came spilling out.

As gentle and slow as it was, that kiss was the best kiss of my life. Melting into him, I caressed his cheek as I took it deeper, brushing my tongue against his.

His fingers in my hair tightened as he pulled me even closer. A ragged moan rumbled from his chest, and I swallowed it down greedily, desperate for more.

It felt like an eternity passed before we broke apart, both panting and desperate for oxygen.

I rested my forehead against his, feeling his featherlight breaths whisper across my face as his eyes drifted shut again. His grip on my hair loosened as his arm went slack and his head dropped down onto the pillow in exhaustion.

Then he spoke. One word spoken with a reverence that shattered the illusions I'd let creep back in and give me hope.

On a heavy sigh, just before he slipped back into sleep, he whispered, "Laurie," effectively breaking my heart beyond repair.

CLICK HERE TO KEEP READING

Acknowledgments

To Josh. Your support is the only reason I'm still doing this. Thank you so much for believing in me and telling me I can do this, even on the days when I'm not so sure.

To Jacob. Being your mom is the best job I've ever had. Thank you for being proud enough of me to tell all your friends and teachers what your mother does. And for making me laugh.

To my family. You are the best support system a person could ask for.

To Adriana, Bella, and Dylan, my writing buddies. We might procrastinate like crazy, but I couldn't do this without you.

To the author friends I've made along the way. This can be an isolating career at times. Having you guys in my corner means everything.

To Karen and Jan, for taking my words and making them into something understandable, and for not firing me when I blow through EVERY SINGLE deadline.

To my ARC team and all my readers, I wouldn't be

here if it wasn't for you. Thank you so much for loving my words as much as I do and sticking with me all this time. Here's to more to come!

Jessica's Princesses

Come be a part of Jessica's Princesses Reader Group, where you'll get first looks at cover reveals, what's coming next, and so much more.

Jessica's Princesses

About Jessica

Born and raised around Houston, Jessica is a self proclaimed caffeine addict, connoisseur of inexpensive wine, and the worst driver in the state of Texas. In addition to being all of these things, she's first and foremost a wife and mom.

Growing up, she shared her mom and grandmother's

love of reading. But where they leaned toward murder mysteries, Jessica was obsessed with all things romance.

When she's not nose deep in her next manuscript, you can usually find her with her kindle in hand.

Connect with Jessica now
www.authorjessicaprince.com
Jessica's Princesses Reader Group
Newsletter
Instagram
Facebook
TikTok
authorjessicaprince@gmail.com